# UP
## All Night

# UP
## All Night
### Adventures in Lesbian Sex

Edited by Rachel Kramer Bussel and Stacy M. Bias

alyson books
los angeles

MANUFACTURED IN THE UNITED STATES OF AMERICA.

THIS TRADE PAPERBACK ORIGINAL IS PUBLISHED BY ALYSON PUBLICATIONS,
P.O. BOX 4371, LOS ANGELES, CALIFORNIA 90078-4371.
DISTRIBUTION IN THE UNITED KINGDOM BY TURNAROUND PUBLISHER SERVICES LTD.,
UNIT 3, OLYMPIA TRADING ESTATE, COBURG ROAD, WOOD GREEN,
LONDON N22 6TZ ENGLAND.

FIRST EDITION: JANUARY 2004

04 05 05 06 07 **a** 10 9 8 7 6 5 4 3 2 1

ISBN 1-55583-747-6

LIBRARY OF CONGRESS CATALOGING-IN-PUBLICATION DATA

UP ALL NIGHT : ADVENTURES IN LESBIAN SEX / EDITED BY RACHEL KRAMER BUSSEL AND
    STACY M. BIAS.—1ST ED.
    ISBN 1-55583-747-6
    1. LESBIANS—FICTION. 2. EROTIC STORIES, AMERICAN. 3. LESBIANS' WRITINGS,
    AMERICAN. I. BUSSEL, RACHEL KRAMER.. II. BIAS, STACY M.
PS648.L47U6 2004
813'.01083538'086643—DC22                     2003058376

CREDITS

· "ELECTRIC SHOCKS/LESBIAN COCKS" FIRST APPEARED IN *THE VILLAGE VOICE*, JUNE 27,
  2000, AND SUBSEQUENTLY APPEARED IN TRISTAN TAORMINO'S *TRUE LUST: ADVENTURES
  IN SEX, PORN, AND PERVERSION*, CLEIS PRESS, 2002.
· "KIM" WAS ORIGINALLY PUBLISHED ON THE WEB SITE KUMA: BLACK LESBIAN EROTICA
  (WWW.KUMA2.NET), MAY 2000.
· "MADE TO ORDER" WAS ORIGINALLY PUBLISHED IN *PHILOGYNY*, PRIDE 2001 ISSUE.
· "THE SEX TEST" WAS ORIGINALLY PUBLISHED IN *NAUGHTY STORIES FROM A TO Z*, PRETTY
  THINGS PRESS, 2001.
· COVER PHOTOGRAPHY BY STUART MCCLYMONT.
· COVER DESIGN BY LOUIS MANDRAPILIAS.

# Contents

# Acknowledgments

I would like to thank my amazing girlfriend, Amy, for her endless patience with my myriad projects. I would also like to thank Rachel Kramer Bussel for being strong where I am weak, and Angela Brown and the staff of Alyson Publications for the opportunity to be involved with this project! —Stacy M. Bias

Thank you so much to Stacy Bias for giving me the opportunity to work on this project, and the staff at Alyson Publications, especially Angela Brown, Dan Cullinane, and Tammy Stoner, for all their constant support and encouragement. Thank you to all of the contributors for your amazing stories and your fast turnaround on them, and for those who referred me to other writers. Thank you also to: Bess Abrahams, Kate Allen, Cheryl B., Adrienne Benedicks, Cara Bruce, Kat Daly, Robin Dann, Karen Dean, Bevin Hartnett, Dionne Herbert, Lesley Higgins, Elizabeth Kapstein, Jodie Kaufman, Lesbian Sex Mafia, Barry Mack, Claudia Miller, Natasha Morris, Lea Policoff, Lawrence Schimel, Heidi Schmid, Seth Shafer, Irena Solomon, Tristan Taormino, and my family for their support. —Rachel Kramer Bussel

# Introduction

*Up All Night* is a truly varied collection that captures some of the high points of modern dyke sex. These authors have gone above and beyond our call for submissions, offering deliciously tantalizing tales of sexual adventures that veer far beyond the average bedroom tumble and into dangerous, charged, and often public waters. These writers push their own personal boundaries, taking risks with their bodies and hearts, not knowing what will happen after they say "yes."

The women in these stories meet in all sorts of ways—at clubs, parties, jobs, or through friends—and some are already involved when we encounter them. We, the editors, were surprised—though perhaps we shouldn't have been—by the number of stories we received in which lovers meet over the Internet. In this thoroughly modern age, personal ad sites are connecting queers from across the country and the world in a way that couldn't have happened in previous eras. The Internet allows us to pick and choose from specific criteria, making finding the woman of our dreams often as simple as clicking a button, geography be damned. From Bree Coven's dyke porn star lover in "Coming Soon to a Theater Near Me" to Mary Dumars's eagerly awaited long-distance passion in "What Ifs" to the intriguingly titled "Insert Three Fingers Here" by Alison Dubois, lesbians are taking the power of the Internet into their own hands (as well as other places). These stories sizzle with the unknown, the uncertainty each narrator feels before meeting her new date.

Another theme running through many of these stories is kinky sex, or BDSM. In Stefka's "Caged" and Anne Grip's "The Girl on the Stairs," these scenes happen in public, with the audience playing a role in these new exhibitionists' scenes. Others happen in private, as women dominate and submit, taking their top's orders and loving every minute of it, as in Stephanie Taylor's "Kitten" or Rachel's own "Made to Order."

Sometimes the promise of long-term passion fizzles into a one-night stand, with the narrator left with a sense of confusion or loss, as in Rosalind Christine Lloyd's "Kim" and Charlotte Cooper's "This Is Lesbian Luv." Though passionate and titillating, these tales also reflect the heartache we experience when our expectations don't match those of our lovers and the thrill of orgasm is paired with the despair of loneliness.

And while lovers can turn into strangers, strangers and friends often turn into lovers. In the opening story, "The Sex Test," Alison Tyler gets a little surprise in the middle of reading a women's magazine as she discovers the lesbian leanings of her best friend, while Zonna takes her "Games" to their most arousing and tormenting levels.

These tales don't always take place in the bedroom, and these stories come to life vividly with their unique sexual settings. In the course of putting together this anthology, we got to hear many tales from friends and acquaintances about their most fond and unique sexual memories, and one of those intrigued us enough to coax "What I Remember," a gripping tale of sex on an Amtrak train, from the adventurous Heidi Cowgirl. Train tracks are also prominent in Grover's punk road trip story, "If SpongeBob Could Talk." Rosalind Christine Lloyd's "Kim" takes place against a wall on a dark

New York street, while "Times Square" by Micky Small is set in the bright bustling center of Manhattan, and Julie Levin Russo and her lover work a special kind of "Overtime." (Hint: It's not something they expect to get paid for.)

Also reflecting our modern dyke lives and realities are the themes of genderfuck and gender play running throughout many of these stories. Tristan Taormino's tale of "strutting her strap-on" for HBO, "Electric Shocks/Lesbian Cocks," explores playing with roles that are not what the public usually thinks of as "lesbian." And Khadijah Caturani's "Ungentlemanly Behavior" has such a delightful twist (without spoiling the surprise element, it features a butch, a femme, role play, a tux, and a prom dress), while also examining how relationships, feelings, and attractions morph over time, sometimes turning into entirely new entities.

When a couple turns up the heat in their own relationship, braving new sexual territory, it can be even more threatening than trying something new with a stranger. Couples risk exposing each other's secret stash of fantasies, toppling the normal course of events in their sexual relationship—but sometimes the risk is more than worth it. In "The Watcher," Amie M. Evans breaks the rules by spying on her lover as she masturbates, making sure not to get caught and face her partner's wrath, while in Stacy's story, "Dream a Little Dream," a dream is the catalyst for a rougher, more energetic form of sex play.

*Up All Night* has the added bonus of being 100% true; you won't have to wonder whether "it really happened." These writers bravely bare their bodily secrets for your reading pleasure, but they also have something more to say about what turns us on, gets us off, and pushes us into overdrive. Whether you're reading about being tied up, seducing a stranger, or entering into the unknown, these stories are sure to leave you ready to crawl into bed and stay up all night devouring them (or your girlfriend!). From first times to last times (sometimes both at once), these stories will make your heart beat just a little faster, make you look around you in different ways as you wonder just what naughty tales that girl sitting at the bar has in her own sexual memory. We hope you enjoy and relish these stories as much as we did, and we hope they remind you of (and inspire you to create) a sexual adventure of your very own.

—Rachel Kramer Bussel and Stacy M. Bias

# The Sex Test
## ALISON TYLER

My best friend, Roxanne, and I share everything, from secrets to lipstick to the occasional man. Years ago we had keys made to each other's apartments, for those times when I'm out of town and she really needs to borrow one of my leather jackets. Or the occasions when I want to lift one of her treasured Led Zeppelin LPs and she doesn't answer her page. We lend, give, and trade items all the time. So when she brought over a stack of fashion magazines she'd finished reading, I thought nothing of it.

Still, there *was* something odd about the way she handed over the magazines to me. A subtle rosy blush colored her normally pale, freckled skin. A strangely charged heat shone in her dark-green eyes, and she ducked her head rather than staring at me straight on when she offered them to me. There was a nervous, jittery quality to her behavior that I'd never seen before. I ignored the signs that something bizarre was going on because I simply didn't understand—at least not until much later that night.

"Don't worry about giving them back, Ali," she told me. "I'm finished."

I hefted the weighty stack of magazines, then fanned out the top few, looking them over. She had all the girly genres covered—a gossip sheet, a magazine devoted to cosmetics, a fancy foreign number featuring a partially nude model on the cover, and a famous magazine devoted to helping women transform themselves for men. I would never buy any of these for myself, and Roxy knew it.

"They're just fluff," she continued, sounding somewhat embarrassed. Then, as if she couldn't help herself, she added, "But maybe you'll learn something." She motioned with a casual nod of her head to my faded Levi's and standard long-sleeve white T-shirt. I'm no risk-taker when it comes to my wardrobe. I like the clean lines of jeans and a tank top, the soft caress of well-worn leather, or sharp-looking suits when I need to dress up.

Roxy's the opposite. We're both long and lean, but she tends to dress more exotically, choosing splashier colors and tighter fits. She's gone through all the phases—punk, femme, even the military look that was the rage again this year. On her, I have to say that all the different styles have worked. Her attitude takes her through, and sometimes I'm even tempted to join her on a fashion adventure. Nobody but Roxy could get me to wear high heels instead of my normal Doc Martens, but she's done it. No one but my best friend could cajole me into wearing a bright lipstick-red sarong at the beach—Roxy's done that, too.

"Have fun," she grinned, watching as I placed the magazines on my glass-topped coffee table. "I'll call you tomorrow."

After she left, I got comfortable on the white leather sofa in my living room, perusing the various magazines in the fading summer sunlight. Outside my open window, I could hear the sounds of happy voices overlapping, couples giggling together on the gold-flecked sands of Santa Monica Beach. On my own that Friday evening, I was thrilled to have such mindless reading matter to fill my time. It would keep my thoughts away from the fact that I was dateless.

The first magazine was a slim volume filled with pages of

flirty outfits and a whole slew of tips for keeping a man. I flipped through that magazine in no time. I know how to keep men, and as I said before, flirtatious clothes aren't really my thing. The second, a European fashion edition, took me longer. I daydreamed my way through the 400-plus pages, pictured myself in the different designer suits, tried to imagine which pieces would look better on me and which would be more flattering on Roxanne. Not difficult at all. She'd wear the beaded ball gowns; the fantastic, frilly confections made of fluttering lace. I'd accompany her in the sleek black suits, the wide-legged crepe de chine pants, the butter-soft black leather.

By the time I'd visualized both of us in all of the different outfits, it was getting late, and I decided to move to my bedroom. First I poured myself a glass of chilled white wine, then I stripped down to a white tank top and a pair of gray silk boxers. In my room I slid beneath the covers of my bed and reached for magazine number three. This was a famous one, known for articles filled with sexual ideas, innuendos, and reader confessions. I consider it the equivalent of eating some brightly colored candy. Not necessarily good for you, but oh, so sweet. It was also something I'd never read if Roxy hadn't given it to me.

I worked my way through the magazine slowly, as if reading about an alien culture. As I flipped the glossy pages, I learned about the proper way to wear sheer pink lip gloss (as if I'd ever wear pink) and read the amazing statement that "Navy blue is the new black"—I still don't get that—before finally coming to a quiz in the very center of the magazine. "How Much of a Risk-Taker Are You Beneath the Sheets?" the headline queried. Below was the subhead "What Your Secret Fantasies Reveal About You."

Well, I'm not a risk-taker at all. I didn't need a stupid

quiz to tell me that. I'm the type to weigh my options, dipping my toes in the shallow end to test the temperature first. It takes a while for me to make decisions, and once I do my mind is set. But before I could simply turn the page and move on, I noticed that Roxanne had already filled out the questionnaire. She'd used a fine red pen, circling the different letters of the multiple-choice answers. Even though we're very different, I thought I'd test myself by reading her answers. I wondered whether I'd be able to guess the way she would respond to each question. That was the *real* test.

I hesitated for a moment before starting. Would she want me to know her innermost fantasies? Were there any I didn't know already? I thought not. Roxanne and I told each other everything, didn't we? This would simply be a fun way for me to exercise my brainpower, trying to guess how she would fill in a silly sex test.

The first question jumped right into the subject matter: *Choose the fantasy that most describes your hidden desire. A) Taking the upper hand in a bedroom situation. B) Sharing the power with a partner. C) Letting your lover set the stage.*

C was circled twice.

Hmmm. That one took me by surprise. My instincts told me she'd have chosen A for sure. Roxanne has the type of firecracker personality that often accompanies bright-red hair and golden-freckled skin. I'd assumed she'd be the one on top in any situation—between the sheets or otherwise. With a bit more interest, I read on. Yes, I continued to feel a little guilty for snooping, but not guilty enough to stop.

The second question asked the test-taker to put the following fantasies in order, with the one that was the most arousing at the top.

*Role playing*
*Exhibitionism*
*Voyeurism*
*Food play*
*Bondage*

Roxanne hadn't bothered ranking them at all, as if the question didn't interest her in the slightest. Instead, underneath the different choices, she'd written in this indecipherable statement: *Being found out.*

Now what did that mean—and why would it be a turn-on?

I took another sip of wine, considered calling her and asking her about her answers, but decided to simply keep on reading. This was the most exciting stuff I'd found all night. The next part of the quiz was a true or false question.

*I have participated in the following activities:*
*• Played with sex toys*
*• Acted out role-playing fantasies*
*• Tried a ménage à trois*
*• Experimented with bondage*
*• Been with another woman*

Each statement had "true" next to it—again surprising me greatly—and the final one had an exclamation point written in by hand. From sharing stories in the past, I knew Roxanne was in no way a tentative lover. She'd told me about the time she'd taken her panties off in the window of a café on Main Street. Without thoughts of reprisals, she'd spread her slim legs so her date would be able to see her naked, pantyless pussy when he returned from feeding the meter. He'd paid the check immediately, hurrying her out behind the restaurant for a bit of public sex in the parking lot. He was so excited that he couldn't even wait until they got home. Which was exactly what Roxanne had been hoping for.

Then there was the lover who liked to dress her up. They'd often enjoyed decadent fantasies come to life in the guise of a headmistress and naughty pupil, or a kinky nurse and shy patient. She had thrown herself into the fun of make-believe, dragging me with her to thrift stores on Melrose in search of the perfect costumes.

"I need a cheerleader skirt," she'd confessed. "Something short and pleated."

We'd spent hours perusing the racks at all of our favorite haunts until she'd come up with the perfect red-and-white number. "Dan's going to flip when he sees this," she'd said, pleased, before correcting herself. "Well, I'm going to flip, and he's going to come."

Roxanne never seemed to feel awkward talking about sex with me. She'd even called me late one night, needing to immediately share an encounter she'd had with two of her coworkers. After a late, stressful meeting at the ad agency, the threesome had gone out drinking to one of Roxanne's favorite high-end bars. From the top floor of a hotel, they had watched Malibu burning. It was that season when brushfires plagued this most wealthy of communities. Something about watching the destruction of all that valuable real estate had given Roxy the nerve to come on to both of her handsome coworkers. They'd gotten a room in the hotel downstairs, and these lucky men had spent several hours making her sexual-sandwich fantasy come true, with Roxy as the filling.

But somehow, even knowing all of these stories from her past, I'd never have guessed that she'd been with a girl. Or that she'd tried any sort of bondage. I couldn't envision her wild, untamed spirit reined in. Where had I been? Had she tried to tell me but felt I wasn't receptive?

I was anxious to find out what else I'd missed hearing about. Yet for another moment, a stab of guilt about reading the quiz stopped me. How would I feel if Roxy had stumbled on my own filled-out questionnaire? That was an easy question to answer: I'd never take an idiotic test like this, wouldn't think to waste my time on one. If I had, though, I wouldn't mind Roxy reading my answers. There was nothing about me that she didn't already already. So, taking another sip of wine, I quickly got over my moral issues and plunged ahead.

Question 4 was about dirty movies. Next to the titles were brief write-ups, in case the quiz-taker hadn't seen the flick. I'd seen them all. Apparently, Roxanne had as well.

*Which erotic movie would you most easily see yourself starring in:*

- *Basic Instinct (dominant woman)*
- *9 1/2 Weeks (submissive woman)*
- *Bound (lesbian relationship)*

The second and the third titles were underlined, letting me know that she wanted to try a submissive role in a girl-girl relationship. And suddenly instead of simply acting like a private detective, peeking into my friend's hidden fantasy life, I found myself getting aroused.

*Oh, Roxanne,* I thought. *You naughty, naughty girl.*

Suddenly the way she'd acted earlier in the evening made sense. She'd been revealing herself in an unexpected manner. Carefully, cautiously. And that wasn't like my Roxanne at all. A born risk-taker, she was used to spelling things out clearly from the start. With any other potential lover, she'd have been bold and outspoken. Not with me. The lengths she'd gone to get into my mind were both surprising and flattering. How she'd bookended the magazine between the others, using them as innocent props, knowing that I'd reach for this one later in the night, guessing easily my routine of climbing into bed to enjoy the fluffy volume.

*Oh, Roxanne,* I thought again. *You aced that quiz, didn't you? You're the number 1 risk-taker of all. Go to the front of the class, girl.*

But what did it all mean? She was coming on to me. That was for sure. Yet why hadn't we gone this route before? She knew full well that I like both men and women, and she also knew that I play the top role whenever I can. My personality may not be that of a standard risk-taker, since I'm very methodical. From my work to my social life, I enjoy order, calm, and the power of being in charge. It floods through me in a rush, from my very center outward to the edges of my body. Bringing someone else to that highest point of pleasure, being in charge of their fulfillment, that's what makes me cream. And if submitting is a turn-on for a lover, it works well with my need for dominance.

Sprawling back against the pillows, I slid a hand under my nightshirt, finding the waistband of my charcoal silk boxers, then stroking myself lazily through the material. My thoughts were entirely of Roxanne, of me and Roxanne, playing the way she obviously wanted to play.

In my fantasy, I saw Roxanne letting go. Tied, or cuffed, to my bed, her supple body trembling, her head turning back and forth on my pillow, that long glossy hair of hers spread in a fiery mane against my white sheets. And I saw myself, not undressed yet, still wearing a pair of my favorite faded jeans and a tight white tank top that perfectly fit my lean, hard-boned physique, and holding something in my hand. I closed my eyes tighter, as if that would make the image come clearer to me. Ah, yes, it was a crop, and I was tracing the tip of the beautiful weapon along her ribs, down the basin of her concave belly. A belly I've admired so many times in dressing rooms, or out at the beach, although never have I let my fantasies get away from me.

Now, I did, seeing it in my mind as I parted her pretty pussy lips and slid the braided edge of the crop up inside her, getting it nice and wet.

My hand pushed my boxers aside, needing direct finger-to-clit contact. Slowly but firmly, I made dreamy circles around and around. And I thought about Roxanne's tongue there, working me when I finally joined her on the bed. She'd still be tied. Bound to my silver metal bed frame. But her tongue would be free to act how it wanted to. I'd bring my hips in front of her, use my own fingers to part my nether lips, let her get a good look at me inside before allowing her to kiss my cunt.

When she was ready, and I was dripping, I would press myself against her face, would let her tongue-fuck me until I could hardly take the pleasure. Only then would I turn around, slide into a sixty-nine, rewarding her with the beauty of a well-earned orgasm. I'd eat her until her whole body trembled, slip my tongue up inside her, paint invisible pictures on the inner walls of her pussy—

Suddenly I stopped. Stopped touching myself. Stopped fantasizing. What if I was wrong? What if she had simply filled out the quiz for the hell of it, forgotten all about it, and given the magazine to me in perfect innocence. What if I was the one reading into this, making the wrong assumptions?

Yes, it looked as if we'd be prime mates in the bedroom, but maybe that wasn't what Roxanne had in mind at all. Hell, maybe she hadn't even been the one to take the quiz.

Feeling an unexpected sense of panic burst through me, I reached for the magazine again, skimming the remaining questions for signs that Roxanne was the test-taker and that she'd been answering the queries for my eyes only. It didn't take me long to find the proof I needed. There, as usual, at the end of the quiz, were the directions for tallying the results, followed by three different write-ups explaining the scores: cool-headed vixen, hot-blooded mama, and bungee-jumping bad-ass babe.

A heavily-handed X had been drawn fiercely through the three different write-ups, and Roxanne had inserted a new one in her careful handwriting. It said, "Frisky Femme Feline: loves her friends and loves to take risks, but sometimes doesn't have the guts to say what she wants. Which is this: you. I want you, Alison. Call me and let me know if you will play the way I like. Will you?"

Would I?

Now it was my turn to forget my careful, plodding manner, my style of weighing all facts and figures before making a decision. Roxanne's cell number is programmed into my phone, and I reached for the handset and pressed "1" on my speed-dial. Maybe she wouldn't be there—she'd said she had plans for the night—but I'd leave a message.

Turns out, I didn't have to. She answered on the very first ring, as if she'd been waiting for my call.

"It's me," I told her.

"Hey, Ali," she said, her voice ultracasual. She didn't know if I'd read the test. That was obvious from her tone.

"Where are you?" I asked her.

"Why?"

"How soon can you be here?"

Now I heard relief in the quickness and ferocity of her giggles, and then I heard another noise that made my heart race. The front bell. She was right outside. A risk-taker to the very end. Risking her heart. Putting herself out for potential embarrassment but probable pleasure.

Tossing the phone onto the bed, I hurried to the front door, just as she let herself in with her spare key. Through the open doorway, I saw from the scattering of cigarette butts that she'd been sitting outside on my front porch the whole time, waiting, hoping. The thought that she'd pictured me reading her fantasies turned me on even more than I already was. What would she have done if she'd known I was touching myself while fantasizing about her?

"Get inside," I said, motioning with my head toward the bedroom. But we didn't make it that far. We couldn't. Roxanne and I only had the patience to shut the door, stop in the center of my living room, and reach for each other. My hands worked quickly to undress her. Hers helped me as we got her T-shirt off, pulled down her faded cut-offs, revealed the wonder of her body as she kicked out of the navy lace thong she had beneath.

"Navy's the new black," I muttered to her as I pulled my own clothes off.

She gave me a quizzical look but didn't speak.

"That's one of the things I learned from your magazines."

As I spoke, I pushed her back against the leather sofa, making her knees bend as she sat and then kneeling on the floor in front of her. Unlike the cool quality of my fantasy, the steely way in which I held out her pleasure until the end, I needed my mouth on her pussy immediately, needed her taste on my tongue, her sweet, tangy juices spread over my skin. Slow and steady, as always, I worked her. She was divine, sublime, her creamy nectar like nothing I'd ever tasted. The way she moved, her hips sliding forward, her hands in my short hair. Every touch, every moan let me know how right we were together.

Now that we were really in sync, I started to relax. Roxy was almost desperate, yearning, wanting me to let her climax. I decided I would, if she could answer my questions. Lifting my lips away from her sex, I started off: "You want my mouth against your pussy…"

"Oh, yes."

"Let me finish," I admonished her, and when I looked up into her eyes I saw that she was paying me careful attention. "A) you want my mouth against your pussy; or B) you want to roll over on your stomach and let me play back there."

Roxy sighed hard, understanding what I was offering, and she answered by moving her body, rolling onto her stomach and pressing her face against the smooth surface of my leather sofa. Quickly, I parted her rear cheeks, touching her hole with my tongue. Just a touch, but I felt the electrifying shudder that slammed through her body. Roxy, my bad girl, loves to be explored like that. My fingers up in her snatch, my tongue probing and teasing. I ate her from behind for several minutes, and when I was ready to move on I leaned back and asked question number 2.

"You planted the test where I could find it…"

Again she interrupted me, sighing the word, "Yes," as if it were an entire sentence. "Yesssssss."

"Not finished, baby," I told her, and she shook her head, as if she knew she'd done something wrong. I could tell she was dazed by the proximity of her orgasm, and that was exactly why I wanted to keep teasing her. My main talent in bed is the ability to hold off. To force myself to wait for that final release, and to help my lovers wait for it as well. Anticipation is my favorite aphrodisiac.

"You planted the test where I could find it…" I said again, watching as Roxy bit her bottom lip to keep herself from responding too early. "Rather than simply telling me what you wanted because you thought that I might punish you for playing dirty."

"Oh, true," Roxanne purred. "True, Ali. True."

That was all I needed to hear. I brought one hand against her ripe, lovely bottom, spanking her hard on her right cheek, then giving her a matching blow on the left. Roxanne sucked in her breath but didn't move, didn't squirm or try to get away. How pretty my handprints looked against her pale skin. I wanted to further decorate her, but I couldn't keep myself from parting her cheeks again and kissing her between. Roxanne could hardly contain herself now. The spark of pain mixed with the pleasure confused and excited her, and she ground her hips against the edge of my sofa, wordlessly begging for something.

For more.

I gave her more. Alternating sharp, stinging spanks with sweet French kisses to both her ass and her pussy, sliding my mouth down along her most tender, private regions, pushing her further toward the limits of her pleasure.

Then, once again, I stopped all contact, sensing exactly the right moment to ask the final question on my own personal sex test. "You're about to come on my tongue," I said, my mouth a sliver away from her skin just before I brought her to climax.

"Oh, yes, Ali," Roxanne whispered as the pleasure rose

within her. "True…" She dragged out the word, as if it meant something else.

I brought her to the limits, and then was silent after that. There were no questions left to ask. Only answers, given silently by her body and by my own.

# Games
## ZONNA

We flipped a coin to see who'd go first. I called heads as she slapped the quarter down on the top of her hand, faceup.

"You win," she smiled, relieved.

"That just means I get to choose who I want to go first."

She shook her head. "Nice try. That's not what we agreed, though. It means you have to go—I mean, to come—first."

I tried to argue my way out of it, but fair was fair. So I gave in and carefully placed the blindfold over her eyes as she sat on the tan folding chair I'd set up earlier. "Can you see? And don't lie. Remember, it's your turn next."

"No, I can't see a thing," she said, smirking mischievously to keep me guessing.

I wondered if I should believe her. What if she could see perfectly? How would I know? What if she watched me? What if she reached out and touched me? Then we'd be breaking the rules, crossing the line. It would ruin everything. "Maybe I should tie you up, just to eliminate any temptation on your part."

"I'm not the one with the willpower problem," she reminded me. "Anyway, it's about trust."

"Right," I sighed. This had been my idea, after all. What had I been thinking?

We like to push the envelope. It's a running game with us, and one of the many things we have in common. We've only been friends for a few months, but we've grown exceptionally close. I've never developed such a strong bond in such a short time. It's sometimes confusing and hard to explain, but always interesting. The sexual tension between us leaves a sharp, smoky smell in the air whenever we're together, not unlike the forest when a tree's been struck by lightning. But life is much more complicated than just reaching out and taking what we want, and sex is not an option. As open and sharing as our relationship is, there's one rule, and it's carved in stone: No fucking. Neither of us wants to break that rule—or maybe we both do, but neither of us actually would. Our friendship is too important. Nothing is worth that risk—not even sex.

And so, we repeatedly search for ways to come as close to fucking each other as we can manage without actually ever doing it. It's fun and harmless, and it's almost like having sex.

This latest brainstorm had been mine. I'd suggested we take turns masturbating while the other sat in the room, blindfolded, unable to do anything but listen. No touching, no peeking, just audio erotica, with an up close and personal twist. For me it would be exciting times two—first, the idea of getting completely naked while she was in the room, even though she couldn't see me, and then touching myself while she listened... Now, that was scary. And then being right there while she did the same thing... What could be hotter? It had all the necessary elements for a good game—curiosity, sex, excitement, sex, fear, trust, tension, and release. And sex. Did I mention sex?

"Well, come on. Get undressed already." She sounded more eager than impatient.

"All right, all right. Give me a minute. I'm just getting situated."

"You're not scared, are you?" Her voice had a competitive but concerned edge to it. I was terrified. My hands were shaking. My knees were knocking. I was so turned on from the delicious fear of what I was about to do, my nipples were so hard they hurt. "Scared? In your dreams."

"Well, then…what's taking you so long?"

"OK, here goes." I took a deep breath and started unbuttoning my shirt. You'd think I'd never done that before from the amount of trouble I was having. Each button made my heart beat faster. I slipped my shirt off my shoulders and trailed it over her face for proof. She smiled and leaned forward in the chair.

"Don't try to peek," I accused her, feeling a thrill run through me from head to toe, making a few stops along the way.

"I'm not peeking, I promise. Keep going."

I undid the clasp on my bra, my fingers still clumsy and useless in their anxious state. When I finally managed to get it off, I threw it in her lap. She lifted it up and laughed. "Now we're getting somewhere."

I hesitated. Being topless was one thing, but my next step would make it all much more real. I unzipped my jeans slowly so she could hear every tooth. It was also an opportunity to stall for a few extra minutes. As I peeled them off I felt every nerve in my body tingle. Then I stepped out of my pants and dropped them in a heap at her feet.

"This is hot," she admitted. "Are you naked now?"

I considered lying, but I couldn't. Not to her. "Almost." The whole point of the game was to scare ourselves, so I might as well go all the way. I stood there in my underwear for a few seconds, working up my courage. I placed my thumbs under the elastic band and watched her face as I lowered my briefs. I felt the air on my cunt. I was already damp and the air felt cool. I was trembling. It was so exhilarating to stand there in front of her, naked and vulnerable. Could she see me? I didn't think so, but the possibility made me 10 times hotter. "OK."

"Really?" She looked skeptical. "Prove it."

I dangled my last article of clothing in front of her, letting her "see" for herself.

"What a turn-on…" She sat back. "Well, don't just stand there. Go for it."

I tried to swallow, but my throat was too dry. I thought again about faking it, but there was no point in that. I raised my hands and caressed my nipples, which were hard as cherries. I closed my eyes, getting into it. I spread my legs apart, feeling delightfully slutty as I did, and lowered one hand to my pussy. I started to touch myself. Each point of contact was like a little electric shock as I thought of her listening to my every move. I kept peeking to make sure she wasn't cheating. I imagined opening my eyes to find her sitting there with her blindfold off, watching me masturbate. If that happened, I'd die. Then I'd kill her.

"Does it feel good yet?"

Her voice startled me. "Yeah."

"Well, let me hear it then."

I squeezed my eyes shut again. I stopped holding back and let myself express what I was feeling. All of it. I'm not quiet. Even when I'm playing solitaire, I still play to a steady soundtrack. I knew it would excite her. That was the point, after all. I imagined her getting more and more aroused as my moans grew louder.

"You sound so hot," she whispered.

Her voice made me ultra-conscious of her presence, even with my eyes closed, and heat gathered in my cunt. I could hear how wet I was, and I knew she could, too. I rubbed harder and faster around my swollen clit, pushing myself right to the edge. I brought my other hand around and shoved two fingers inside as I rocked my hips. I opened my eyes and watched her listening as I came with a long, low, "Ohhhhhhh…"

Her hands twitched in her lap.

"Don't take that damn blindfold off till I tell you," I warned her.

She laughed.

I hurried back into my clothes. "OK. You can take it off now."

I knew my face was bright red when she looked at me.

"That was great," she smiled, and stood to give me a big hug. When we broke the embrace, she looked pretty nervous.

"It's your turn now," I announced, taking my place in the metal chair.

She secured the blindfold over my eyes, and the room instantly disappeared. She asked me three times if I was absolutely positive I couldn't see anything, and I reassured her, knowing exactly where she was coming from since I'd just been there myself.

"Quit stalling," I goaded, feeling a different kind of excitement build inside me at the thought of what I was about to witness: something totally private and secret. I was an explorer on the very brink of discovering a new land. Maybe even the Promised Land.

Suddenly I felt the soft material of her sweater brush across my cheek. Then I heard the snap of her bra. It was funny which sounds I recognized and which I couldn't. I was clueless when she slipped her shoes off, yet I knew exactly what she was doing when she slid out of her jeans.

At last she was naked. I could hear her heart pounding. Or was that mine? I imagined her standing there in front of me, close enough to touch. Aware that she was as much of a closet exhibitionist as I was, I knew she must have been as turned on as I'd been—her breasts aching to be touched, her cunt throbbing for attention. I wanted to rip the blindfold off and take her in my arms. I wanted to press my mouth to hers and kiss her till she melted into me. I wanted to run my hands over every inch of her body, bringing her the release I knew she craved. But I couldn't do any of that. I could only sit there and listen. It was maddening. It was torture. And it was the closest thing to fucking we could possibly do without crossing into that forbidden zone.

I heard the soft buzz of a vibrator as she flipped the switch. It hummed in my own cunt as I imagined her moving it in and out of hers.

"Are you fucking it or just rubbing it up against you?" I wanted more details than I could gather with only my auditory senses.

"That's for me to know and you to wonder," she joked, her voice not altogether steady.

And I did. I wondered if she was touching her nipples while she played with herself; if her eyes were opened or closed; what her face looked like when she made a particular sound. But these were things I could only guess at without confirmation, so I painted my own picture. It was bold and beautiful and suffused with energy, colored in all the brightest shades of lust. I opened up to feel that energy, to feel her hunger in the way the air moved around us, in the heat she gave off just a few inches away. And I listened as she brought herself pleasure, straining to hear every sigh, every whisper, every sacred sound. Her voice belied her passion as it rose and fell, singing a melody so sweet it made me want to cry.

"Don't you dare touch yourself!" she scolded.

"I'm not! I'm not!" I was. I stopped.

Her sultry voice lifted in a crescendo as she came, filling the room with her song of pleasure.

I sat there, mesmerized. If I moved a muscle I was sure I'd come again. Since that wasn't part of the game, I sat still, waiting to calm down.

She lifted the blindfold from my eyes.

I blinked as they adjusted to the sudden intrusion of light. "You're incredibly sexy," I said, as I gathered her up in my arms. I felt her warm breath in my ear as I hugged her close. It was soft and sweet, like the kiss I carefully placed on her cheek.

I look forward to our future games. Games where no one loses anything. Games with rules we don't dare break—staying just within the boundaries life has set for us, and those we've set for ourselves; sticking technically to the letter of our law, if not the spirit; and most important, not hurting or betraying anyone. Games where we play at giving each other only what we can, to find it's enough.

I like a game where everyone wins.

# This Is Lesbian Luv

CHARLOTTE COOPER

If I believed in God I would pray him to never, ever again let me get as crushed-out on someone as I did with this woman. I mean it.

I was obsessed, and I don't use this word mildly either. It was like a mental illness. It took me years to get over this woman, and I feel ashamed about that. I try not to think about her too much, even now. I can't even bring myself to say her name, like I don't want to infect my mouth with it, but I know I must; it was Lina.

I don't know how it started. I saw her around, I guess. We both went to this same nightclub, so it must have been there. I always thought she was out of my league, but then again I think all the women I like are out of my league. Yes, Oprah, you could say that I have self-esteem issues.

There were a lot of things I really liked about Lina. We shared cultural references, even though we were very different. This meant that we liked the same music, we were both in our 20s, we both liked modern art and films, we had similar politics, we both lived away from our birth countries, we both liked to get out of the house and do stuff. But you could have taken all that personality stuff away and I would still have been drooling like a starving dog because the thing I liked best about Lina was that she was totally fucking hot. It might surprise some readers, but it takes a lot to get my passion nodules throbbing. I'm not much of a horn dog in real life, but when it kicks in, it doesn't let go. Lina had an arse out of which I wanted to bite big fat chunks; it was hefty and wide, kind of at odds with the rest of her butchy bod. She had beautiful smooth skin, and she was dark, like something tasty roasted in oil. I salivated when I saw her. I wanted her.

My crush on Lina didn't start small and build up—it actually exploded. One minute I was happily dancing to the Breeders with my friends, the next I was dancing right behind her, willing her to notice me, trying to get in her face, being aware of her every movement, feeling drawn to her like iron filings to a magnet. Ladies, I did this week after week. Saturday nights at the club were my big thrill. Where other, more confident dykes would go for the jugular, I sashayed around, trying to look interesting, doing all I could to get an introduction to her, making sure I was seen. It worked—soon we were on nodding terms, and before long we were making small talk with each other. Whenever this happened I wondered if Lina could detect my simmering lust; I'm sure she could.

At the club's New Year's Eve party I kissed her. It was a kiss you'd have to pretend you didn't care about—that you'd kiss anyone, that you were drunk and it was meaningless. You'd have to pretend this because you're pretty sure it's what the other person is thinking. But it wasn't meaningless to me; at this point it was the highlight of my career as a newly sexually active dyke. We were sitting together, talking to different people. We turned around. I asked if I could have a kiss, and she leaned into me and put her mouth on mine. She was soft and mushy. I felt as though I were falling or screaming with happiness. I opened my eyes a little to sneak a peek at her face so close to mine, the skin of her cheek up against mine. I could have gone on for at least half an hour, or longer, but she pulled away and we continued with our separate conversations. I felt as though I had just kissed my favorite rock star. I danced all the way home because my life was so full of promise at last.

That week I wrote the following in my diary:

Here's how I know I'm obsessed:
1. I watched your favorite film.
2. I laugh at your jokes.
3. I think about you every spare moment.
4. ...and then some.
5. I smile and nod at everything you say.
6. I listen to records that remind me of you over and over again.
7. I try to think up new excuses to see you.
8. I allow my fantasies to keep me awake night after night.
9. I want to talk about you all the time.
10. I see men and women around the city who look like you.
11. I stuck your picture in my notebook.

Version number 2 looked like this:

1. She doesn't fancy me.
2. She thinks I'm weird.
3. She never thinks about me.
4. I bore her.
5. I'm too intense.
6. I'm full-on.
7. I irritate her.
8. She leads her own life and I am nothing to her.
9. She is repelled by me.
10. I will be hurt.
11. I will be hurt.

One night I stopped being afraid. I asked her out for a beer, and she said yes. We saw a movie and had a beer each at a bar afterward, then we both caught separate trains home. I was so nervous, I didn't know what she was thinking. Did she know it was more than platonic for me? Whatever—it was the most sex-free date in lesbian history.

I wrote her. I was so afraid of everything slipping away. I said, "I had a good time last night. I'm really into you, and I'd like us to get it on. I'm nervous about saying this and looking really stupid if I've read you wrong. Too bad for me if I have. Call/write, OK?" I planned two answers for when or if she replied. They went: "No? Oh, that's a shame. I understand. I'd still like us to be friends." And "Yes? So do you want to invite me over?" I was in such a state of hormone frenzy that I had to go through every possible outcome.

Lina replied with a polite little note explaining that she did like me and would call me. The note was so calm, a giant contrast to the turmoil I was feeling. I was just too new compared to her; she knew all the moves. I wonder how things might have been different had I not been so clumsy and awkward. I waited three days for her to call, and my heart thudded away in my throat every time the phone rang. When she finally called I was unprepared, just shaking, so excited.

We arranged another date, we drank more beer this time, and then, yes, she asked if I would like to go home with her. We took the bus this time, rode it through the dark London streets, then got off and walked in the cold night air. I loved walking to her house, I looked for familiar points along the route, hoping I would make the same walk again sometime, but I never did.

At Lina's house we both experienced that same awkwardness that has trailed me through everyone I've ever been with just before the fucking starts. It's wonderful and awful. This strange act where you're both denying what you know is going to happen, still being polite but giving out trails of fuck-me phosphorescence every time you move. I lay on her bed and stretched out; I felt her so close to me, her breath. I knew at last that she was interested. And then something happened that enabled us both to break through and get down to business.

We kissed, and it was good. She kissed me gently, and she bit me, too, which I encouraged by holding my neck out to her; I was so trusting. I licked and sucked her like a hungry beast, grabbing handfuls of flesh, pulling off her clothes. Lina's body was bigger and looser than I had expected. She was so lovely. She lay back and I crept down her belly and thighs as she watched me with large dark eyes. We were both silent; there was no talk of latex or safety. She opened up for me and I slid in my fingers.

Although fucking Lina was the pinnacle of my sexual career at the time, my memory of the event is actually sketchy. I was too self-conscious to let go, too busy taking mental snapshots of myself in action to really feel the pleasure of the experience. But let me tell you what I do know: Lina's pubic hair was perfect, thick, and straight, wet with cunt ooze. I remember her sighing and grinding on my hand as I pumped it into her. I made her sweat; I made wetness appear wherever I touched her, my fingers in her mouth, on her breasts, or my hand disappearing inside her tight snatch. I held her throat and kissed her hard, letting spit dribble into her. She bit my lips and I bit her back. Her whole body undulated as I fucked her. She grabbed my tits and sucked them, pawed them. Lina was on her back, her legs open to the world and between them I lay, working her clit, making her rush it all up for me, feeling her cunt contract around me. It took so little to get her off; I had no idea she was that ready. I knew that I had made her feel good, that I had done something real for her and that she knew it too.

There was no pause for breath. Lina crawled on top of me and ate me out. I rested my hands on her head as though I were blessing her. She pushed fingers one, two, three, then a hand curled up inside me. I felt my heart twist around and around inside my chest, like it was performing a duet with the fist in my cunt. I was made of electricity, buzzing with heat and desire. I saw her working at me and I wanted to sing with joy at the sight of her breasts shaking, the look of determination on her face, the smell of her, like pure sex.

I pushed down on my clit with my fingers, I couldn't give it up to her, I needed to get off, but I couldn't allow her to do it, so I jerked and circled and rubbed and pulled and got so close to coming, so fucking nearly there, like a dream it was, like something just beyond me. I worked at it while her fist twisted inside and her breath and my quiet groans grew hoarse with the effort. I tried every trick in my repertoire to get me there, fast, slow, pulling, grinding, filling my mind with images of dogs fucking, sleazy centerfolds holding it open for me, big guys jamming into me with their obscene cocks, and, of course, Lina, Lina, Lina.

I faked it. I couldn't go on. It was too much.

I asked Lina if she wanted me to go, because I thought that is what you did, and I could imagine nothing worse than wanting to be close to somebody who was alone. She laughed and said, "I want you here." Lina slept, she snored, but I lay awake all night. She had her arm around me, and occasionally she kissed my back, the tenderness of which surprised me. I was confused; if this was meant to be casual, why she was so loving?

In the morning Lina offered me fruit but I was too excited to eat. I just sat and talked to her flatmates and then made an excuse and left. We kissed goodbye and that was the last time. I jumped out of her house, and looking over my shoulder, I saw her laughing and waving at me as she closed the door.

She was late when I met her in a bar a couple days later. At first I didn't notice that everything had changed, but then I realized that she was embarrassed by me. I'd brought her a present with which she fiddled, then discarded. She was serious. She went to sit with her friends. She turned her back on me. I followed, uninvited. I said I'd had a lovely time with her and asked if I could see her again and she said, "I don't think so."

I went and fucked someone else that night. I acted as though what Lina said didn't matter to me, but it was devastating. *I don't think so.* I don't know what happened. How had I fucked up? *I don't think so.* It sent me into a tailspin.

I longed to see her. Places I knew she had been now seemed charged. To this day I look out for the apartment building where we fucked, though she has not lived there in years. I saw her in a bar one time and I hid, afraid that if I went in she'd turn her back on me once more. I pass that bar frequently and always remember her sitting on someone's knee and laughing with a group of friends.

Over time I developed a friendship with Lina that never went anywhere. I cherished the most minor communication from her, and I'd jump into action whenever she suggested anything. I would will her to call, though she often annoyed me. To my invitations she was noncommittal. She was not well-liked among my friends, and we rarely had anything real to say to each other. I maintained my awkwardness around her, but I never stopped wanting her. I tried to turn myself into someone she would want, and I knew it was pathetic of me to do so. And when we were in a room together I wanted her to notice me. I wanted us to pick up the lost connection and try again, but she was long gone.

I had therapy—a lot of crappy things have happened to me. It wasn't just about Lina, but she was definitely in the mix. I told my therapist about Lina, about how I really felt; she was the first and only person to whom I have ever told the truth about Lina. She asked me: "Are you in love?" I was shocked because I'd been in love before and it never felt as fucked up as this. Love, obsession. I just didn't know.

I was relieved when Lina left the country; it made it easier for me to cut her out of my thoughts. She went off to be with a woman she loved, which soon turned sour. She has been plagued by a lifetime of rotten relationships, while I continue to love and be loved. That is the only solace I can find in this tale. That and Lina's best friend, a woman in whom I have been developing quite an unhealthy and intense interest of late...

# Electric Shocks/Lesbian Cocks

### TRISTAN TAORMINO

"Closer to God" by Nine Inch Nails blared in the small, smoky club as I slinked down the bar, dressed in a black latex mini-dress shined to the maximum extent of the law. Everywhere I looked there were butches in suits, leather dykes, and lingerie-clad girls. Teasing the crowd, I toyed with the zipper of my dress, which ran from my cleavage to between my legs. Finally giving in to them, I stripped down to nothing but my seven-inch heels. A fire-engine red dick in a red sparkly harness stood at attention between my legs. Gigi appeared in a black vintage bustier and Catholic schoolgirl plaid skirt. She kneeled in front of me, took my dick in her mouth. Her perky bobbed hair bounced freely as the red cock disappeared in the O her lips formed. I pushed her back, grabbed the cock, pulled it out of the harness. Then I dangled it enticingly in front of a cute cowboy from the audience, who graciously began to suck it. Gigi handed me an identical red cock, this one rigged by her with a metal wire running through the middle of it. The tip of the wire was covered in alcohol-soaked cotton. I slipped it through the O-ring of the Wonder Woman harness. With the strike of a match, the end of the cock burst into flames. Then she got down on her knees again. In one motion, she deep-throated the cock, swallowing its flaming head to the amazement of onlookers.

Her fiery red hair is a perfect match to her fetish—Gigi loves fire. And the hot blow-job number was just the beginning. Later, she used two wire-and-cotton torches to seductively run flames along her arms and stomach. She deep-throated the torches, just like the dick, all to Eartha Kitt purring, "I'd rather be burned as a witch, then never be burned at all..." She told me that the torches actually do scorch her, proudly showed me the little red bumps forming on her sensitive, creamy freckled skin. She smelled vaguely of burnt flesh.

The fire was just a prelude to another sizzling act: electricity. I've only done electricity play once, with a TENS unit (an electronic device that sends currents through the skin to stimulate sensory nerves). Medical TENS units were originally designed for people suffering from certain injuries and chronic pain; kinky people have borrowed them for their tingling sensation. The TENS unit, even in the context of a scene, still reminded me too much of my trips to the physical therapist as a child equestrian with bad knees. I've never played with Violet Wands before, but you know I am always game.

The Violet Wand certainly is violet, but not much of a wand. It looks more like an old-fashioned set of clippers, with a hole at one end for various attachments, an on/off button, and a dial to control the intensity of the charge. Funny how there was no indication on the dial which way was up and which way was down—a masochist must have thought of that.

Like the TENS unit, Violet Wands were developed as a medical tool, but it's not clear what they were supposed to cure. Most of the attachments are glass, gas-filled bulbs (in the shapes of a pronged rake, a medium and a large glass ball, and a silver-dollar sized knob). When the bulb comes in contact with the skin, a glowing violet spark appears (that's how it got its name). As the bulb gets near, the spark jumps from the bulb to the skin, and you feel a hot, buzzing, tingling kind of shock; if it is pressed against the skin, the violet spark still happens, but the shock is gone. There is another attachment that you tuck into your clothes and that turns *you* into the voltage conductor—the spark comes right out of your fingers and shocks whatever you touch.

Gigi liked the rake attachment with the three prongs, and Rachel opted for the small knob that looked like a vibrator attachment. I went for the large glass ball, which looked like a crystal ball or one of those static lamps. We ran a shock down arms and legs, zapped nipples, even sent some voltage to clits and pussies. It felt like a quick shock and prickly heat on the skin, or when you dragged the wand, a buzz dragging across flesh; to me, it had all the erotic charge of running into a bug zapper. But the partygoers were really into it, so we encouraged them to join in.

When one girl got her hands on the wand, she enticed her cohorts to try it out. Another woman, rumored to be a lesbo virgin, pulled her pants down as two goth girls went to town—one wand on her nipples, another on her clit. She gasped and groaned with each zap. Two other women pushed their shirts up, ready to try the fascinating feeling. It all broke loose then: women with shirts slid up, nipples poking out of bras, pants pushed down, undies shed, bare skin glowing and sparking. There were hands on breasts, wands on hands, fingers brushing across stomachs, buzzing and zapping, legs intertwined, and violet sparks flying everywhere.

These sizzling scenes—oh, and so much more—were captured on film. Unfortunately, what was the high point, for me, of an outrageous evening didn't even make the final cut. But those are the breaks when you're only the subject—or object—of the game. This particular game is known to all you TV viewers as *Real Sex*. When an HBO producer first approached me about doing a segment for the cable network's documentary-style show, I had mixed feelings ("Hooray! Mainstream media attention!" and "Yikes! What am I getting myself into?"). Of the few episodes I'd seen, one—the piece on porn star turned performance artist Annie Sprinkle—was smart and sexy. Most were goofy (like the so-called "masturbation club meeting," which looked more like a bunch of swingers to me) or blatantly salacious (clips of author Lou Paget's workshop on how to please a man featured repetitive images of women practicing blow-job techniques on lifelike dildos). One was simply ridiculous: the story of a couple who together have "sex" with the high-priced, custom-made "Real Doll" was cheesy and obviously staged with actors.

While the producer was interested in documenting (as documentaries do) some "real" aspect of my sexuality, she definitely had her own agenda when it came to the focus of the story. Of all my interests that we discussed in preliminary meetings—anal sex, S/M, porn for women, lesbian gender identities—she seemed particularly focused on my casual mention of dykes and strap-ons. She zeroed in on that topic as tenaciously as my Boston terrier pulls at the leash for a stray chicken bone on the street. As a lesbian herself, she loved the idea of explaining the complexities of the sapphic sausage and putting those ugly penis-envy myths to rest once and for all on national television. Her phallic preoccupation ruled, and by the time the cameras were finally rolling, my friend Gigi and I were hosting a lesbian strap-on party, playing with electricity (which neither of us really do), setting stuff on fire (which Gigi loves to do), and giving sound bites about why we love cocks. Ah, the magic of television!

Before you think I was railroaded into this exposé like

some *Real World* cast member prodded into a temper tantrum, Gigi and I did get to squeeze in a few of our own fetishes. We wooed the crew early in the day, and after seeing two girly girls like us, I think they expected our friends to show up for the party later that night wearing G-strings and pumps. Since both of us adore butches (and believe that positive representations of them are sorely missing from mainstream media), we packed the club's audience with some fine examples of female masculinity, much to the complete confusion of the entire crew. Instead of lipstick and push-up bras, they got chaps, three-piece suits, and crew cuts. I could see the marketing team months later wondering just what they had on their hands. I mean, a show about lesbian cocks is one thing, almost palatable and certainly titillating when those plastic penises are strapped to superfeminine women. But when we match tomboys and women who look like men with the not-so-gender-neutral attachment, we've got a horse of a different color on our hands. Is Middle America ready for butch dykes in a show about lesbian cocks?

Well, it had better be, 'cause here we come! The best part about doing the HBO special was the chance it gave me to make a little history: When will I have another prime-time opportunity to educate the masses about a particularly crucial but mostly misunderstood aspect of lesbian sexuality like strap-ons? Dildos, in one form or another, have been part of lesbian sexuality for a long time. During the '70s and the dreaded sex wars among feminists, dildos were considered by separatist and anti-porn crusaders to be representations of penises and therefore literal tools of the patriarchy. Never mind that they felt really good sliding inside our slick pussies—their shape and all its implications made them more politically incorrect than shaving your legs. Today, we're thankfully past all that, and dildos are one of many different sex toys available to women of all sexualities. From the most realistic peckers with balls, circumcised heads, and veins to lavender goddess and kitten dildos, there's something for everyone. We don't need a man to get some dick, and hey, we can actually have as many cocks—from slim and curved to thick and meaty—as our little cunts desire.

A long way from those days of dick-bashing, lesbians now have much better relationships with our penile friends. We embrace our cocks, reclaim our cocks, and, yes, wear our cocks out in public. Dykes are finally proud to say, Yeah, I've got a dick; actually, I've got several. Sometimes I want it to be real; sometimes when I am wearing it, I imagine it is. Other times, it's simply another pleasure tool to get the job done, and I'm happy to toss it on the shelf after it's served me well. And the idea that anyone, regardless of gender or genitalia, can have a cock has the potential to definitely shake things up. It makes those of you equipped with one at birth seem so...limited. You've just got the one. I've got an entire drawer full of them.

# Kim

### ROSALIND CHRISTINE LLOYD

I met her at a mixed club. You know those mixed dance clubs where the straight women look gay and, strangely, vice versa. We noticed each other instantly through the darkness, like mystical twins or kin from some far-away fantasy dimension of tall, strong, dark Amazonian women with a heightened sense of awareness of their surroundings and everything in it.

Her deep-toned skin radiated even in the dark. Her profile was distinctly female, feminine. A long elegant nose and lips thick like foreign fruit from some richly dark continent, she was tall and regal—her back so straight as if bound by an invisible corset. Her hair was cut so close to her head that I could only imagine running the palm of my hand with feathery fingertips all over—back and forth, front to back, side to side, and round and round what I innately believed would be a beautifully powerful mind.

A tight trendy mesh top allowed me to see she was a nice size until my eyes traveled lower to hips that expanded to a heavenly bounty of womanhood. I, a woman of narrow dimensions (no hips—I've been called boy realness in the way Levi 501s layer my long, mildly muscular ambiguous legs), have an affinity for women with real Nubian hips and real Nubian asses. I like more than enough but not so much that I would ever neglect anything. This sister fit the bill perfectly.

It was something in the way she moved when she danced.

Reckless but controlled, more sensual than sexy. She would dive down deep when she felt a beat, jerk with a rhythm, swagger like a thug, then rise up, lifting her entire body in the air, toes lifted completely from the dance floor like an angel in a gospel trance, head thrown back, mouth open wide in an arch that mimicked Billie Holiday belting out some heartfelt blues.

It was difficult to pretend I didn't notice her. I wasn't looking. For anyone. I've done the relationship thing. I've done the whore thing. I've stretched the lesbian dating limits to the point where I was bored and disinterested. I sensed, however, that this was about to be something very atypical.

Our eyes followed each other. Expressionless. No words were spoken.

I touched her. I don't remember where, but the one movement sent a current through me while she froze in place.

"What's up?" The only two words I could find.

"You." Her voice was deep and womanly.

Introductions were made, and she gave me the once-over with distant recognition. I felt stiff, rehearsed. We kept telling each other how beautiful the other was.

Her name was Kim. She was in town on business. Her line of business was fashion, urban fashion. She used words like "merchandising," "concept," "design." Enjoyed dancing. Didn't know too many people in New York and would like to have the opportunity to take me out for a drink. Quick and thorough. Neat.

Engaging, even charming, her game (if I may be so bold to call it that) was airtight. As disinterested as I was in meeting anyone, she convinced me that my wishes were contrived and that I should be more spontaneous and surrender to fate. So I did.

Three, yes, three days later, Kim called (no, I didn't have the number to where she was staying, so I couldn't call her even if I'd wanted to). When the first day went by, I laughed it off. The second day was a minor threat to my insecurity. On the third day I practiced forgetting her, but I was quite breathy and close to guarded submission when I heard her voice on the other end of my cordless, a voice with origins deep in the chest. Raspy like a smoker's voice and unbelievably erotic.

All she said was, "Are you free for a drink tonight?" No "hello." No "How are you?" No typical greetings full of protocol. I was embarrassed by my availability, but she was flying out the next day. If I had any desire to see her again—and I knew I did—I would have to accept her invitation.

"There's a lounge I know, near my office, called Noire," I suggested.

"I'll meet you there in an hour." And it was set.

The unpredictability was awesome, and the clock just so happened to strike midnight.

It was 1:05 when I walked into the bar. Kim sat there with a giant martini before her, five plump olives floating on the bottom. She sucked on a cigarette like I'd expected her to. A woman with vices—obviously not afraid to live, not afraid to die. When she saw me, she took a very long drag from her cigarette, almost as if she were trying to inhale me. In contrast, I held my breath before I sat. Despite the somewhat cool forecast, she wore a tank top, the top edge of it resting on top of gumdrop-size nipples (have you ever sucked the sugar off a gumdrop?). A long sheer wrap skirt draped those hips and thighs of life. Her neck was long and vulnerable.

We hugged. Mine was awkward. She pulled me in closer, pressing herself into me so hard I was compelled to look her in the eyes—she captured my glance and my lips. I resisted. Some might refer to this as a missed opportunity—resisting the lips of an extraordinarily attractive woman. I could only allow myself to linger there for a moment. To me, she was still a stranger. But those lips sent me to both heaven and hell.

Kim smiled at me, almost delighted in my hesitation and resistance. We exchanged pleasantries. I ordered a cocktail. I couldn't relax, as I had the distinct feeling of being mentally undressed. She was fucking me with those eyes, and I had no control over it.

Six more cocktails between us later, we were outside. It was freezing: New York City, dead of winter. The streets were isolated. Those who knew better sought the warmth of the indoors. We didn't know better. Or did we?

As we walked quickly with no designated destination, our footsteps smacked against the concrete sidewalk, stiff and hard, cold beneath our feet, echoes bouncing against the granite walls of stiff skyscrapers. Saying nothing, she burrowed herself into me, careful not to disturb our pace but validating herself.

Stumbling upon an alley, Kim suddenly turned really aggressive. She bum-rushed me, flinging me against the wall. Shocked, I wasn't exactly sure how to react. Partly amused, largely turned on, I decided to comply. My lined leather jacket (a vain choice strictly unsuitable for the weather) did nothing to cushion my back against the bricks that pounded against my body. A ribbon of pain stretched like lighting across my back. Acting as her accomplice, the cool November wind whipped my face so hard it stung. Her eyes, locked in an intense stare, held me tighter than I imagined her muscular arms could, threatening me, warning me not to move. And I didn't.

Breathing hard, she flung her bag to the ground and slowly approached me. Gripping my throat with soft but strong hands, she pressed herself against me as hard as she could, her crotch crushing mine harder than the bricks against my back. Her breath quickened against the side of my face and in my ear as she shoved her thigh between my legs, followed by her tongue between my lips. Both angry and aroused, I couldn't move, as she had me expertly pinned.

Her hips moved against me while her hands busied themselves opening my jacket, shoving my turtleneck up and exposing my naked breasts to the elements. Grunting approval, Kim anointed them with those juicy lips that I didn't want to stop kissing. Her tongue teased the tips of my nipples before tracing tiny circles that turned into wider ones. Her wet imprints created chill bumps across my skin. As she worked my nipples, I was soaking my jeans (no undies tonight). Madly aroused, I squirmed while she ravaged me before clamping her perfectly straight teeth on the meatiest part of my breast. I sucked in air between my own clenched teeth, not able to suffocate the bitch scream that escaped from my throat. Inside my head, I told myself not to make any more incriminating moves or else it was highly likely she would unleash some wicked shit on me.

She started to travel lower, placing tiny kisses and nibbles along my stomach, her lips pulling hard on my navel piercing, which made me squeal yet again, before she ripped my 501's open in one quick movement. Now on her knees, she forced my jeans down around my legs. I was no longer aware of how cold it was outside, no longer aware that it was 3 in the morning in some dark alley in Manhattan. She smiled at my shaved pussy, now dripping. Slowly she dipped a finger in and out of me, then stuck that same finger in and out between her big juicy lips, tasting me, approving of my flavor. I didn't move, although my thighs were trembling.

"You want more, huh?" Kim whispered. "Sure you want more of me?"

Yes, Ms. Thing was a rough little femme, and I wanted nothing more than to put my mojo on her. I wanted to work those hips. Damn, did I want to be up in that ass. But she didn't have anything on my agenda in mind. She was in charge. Dipping her finger back inside me, she worked a rhythm on me so fierce and hard, I barely noticed the ball of her fist nearly lifting me to the skies; or maybe I did notice because I rode her like a neglected nympho. Oh, yes, I did want her to reach in and tell my soul something. Every time she thrust herself inside me, going deeper and deeper, I thought I would lose myself.

Just when I thought I was about to collapse, her long thin index finger quickly shoved its way up my ass from behind, followed by her tongue licking my clit with slow thirsty cat curls that sent me over the edge in five tumultuous minutes. And she didn't stop there. Pressing her lips farther into me, she sucked me until my entire torso trembled violently with orgasm after orgasm after orgasm. I was still propped against the wall, my thighs straddling her shoulders, wrapped tightly around her. If anyone walked by, we didn't notice. If it was 30 below outside, we didn't feel it. I just gave myself to her. Whatever she wanted she took. By then I was too exhausted not to come. She had turned me inside out.

Pulling herself away from me, she quickly got herself together as if she suddenly realized the time. I thought we were just getting started! I was barely pulling my jeans up, and Kim was bundled up and nearly out of the alley.

"Thanks for the drink, girl. Got a plane to catch. I'll call you next time I'm in New York," she hollered before vanishing into the night.

She didn't have any plane to catch, I thought. Did she just play me for some pussy?

Going back into the chilly New York wilderness, I knew even if I never saw Kim again, she did something to me in one night most women couldn't do in a lifetime. So if you're reading this, Kim, I'm still waiting on that phone call. I've got something for you.

# Fist First

RACHEL KRAMER BUSSEL

When I agreed to meet with Sarah, I honestly hadn't planned on anything more complicated than cooking dinner with her, which for me is a big enough task in and of itself. We had mutual friends, and when she heard I was going to be in town she suggested we get together. I was looking forward to a nice, quiet evening; I'd been to a wild sex party the night before and wasn't looking to get laid. I knocked on her door, and a tall, athletic, serious-looking woman in a Charlie's Angels T-shirt and shorts greeted me. Like so many people I e-mail with before I meet them, she was nothing like I'd expected.

She'd decided on gazpacho for our meal, and I took over some of her duties when the onions became too much for her eyes. We ate the cold, spicy soup and talked about writing, politics, and the dyke scene. She seemed pretty conservative to me, and I felt a little out of place. I got the distinct impression that while she was cool and interesting, any prospects of us getting it on were foolish. I was OK with that, even though I'd started to wonder what she'd be like in bed.

Afterward, I indulged my secret fetish: doing dishes. She stared at me while I did them, not talking, and I felt a little uncomfortable. For all my forays into exhibitionism, one-on-one eye contact often makes me nervous. So when the dishes were done and she asked me what I wanted to do, I asked her to take me home. That's the polite thing to say on a "non-date," even if the truth is that you want her to kiss you.

She drove me back to my friend's apartment, stopping the car in the middle of the street. I reached over to hug her goodbye, and our faces brushed against each other. I felt her skin and her breath, and I leaned in and kissed her. She kissed me back, and soon our tongues were seeking each other out, not so much rough-and-tumble but sweetly exploratory. Which is why what happened next was so shocking. She reached over and grabbed a chunk of my long hair at its roots and pulled, hard. I had to stop kissing her as my head fell back, my neck exposed.

She continued to tug, in short, sharp pulls that left me spinning and gasping. I started squeaking, making those little breathing sounds that are all I can do when I feel on the verge of orgasm. I crinkled my face up as if I might cry, and that's how it felt, like I wanted to cry or scream or plunge her fingers into my cunt. I was lost in my hair and her hand, and every time she pulled I felt myself get a little wetter and my pussy ache just a bit more. I spread my legs wider in the seat, making my plaid skirt run up the tops of my thighs. She stroked a finger across my throat, and I really felt like I would explode at any moment. I wanted to hike up my skirt and continue, but I couldn't forget that there was a big streetlight shining down on us.

We returned to her apartment, after I left a mumbled excuse on my friend's machine about why I wouldn't be home. She led me to her bed and I knelt down. I felt like I was shaking, but I think I was pretty still. She petted my head, told me I was being a good girl. Again she pulled my head back by my hair, and my whole body spasmed in response. It was the most erotic thing that had ever been done to me, both more subtle and more direct than any other kind of stimulation. It was a simple action that sent shivers throughout my entire body. My cunt felt so wet and open, gaping wide, the marionette to the strings of my hair. She drew her index finger over my lips, and I opened my mouth. She slid it slowly in and out, and I eagerly sucked on it, savoring it like it was her cock. Then things changed, and I was no longer the active one; instead of me sucking her finger, she was fucking me with it, strong back and forth motions toward the back of my throat. Now it was two fingers, then three, then four. It hurt a little as they hit the far reaches of my throat, but I liked it. Whatever part of me she wanted to fill up was fine. I opened as wide as I could for her, wanting as much as she could give me.

She moved me onto my hands and knees on the bed and hovered over me. While one hand worked my mouth, the other stroked my pussy. I felt like my cunt was out of control, beyond arousal to pure, almost scary, need. She murmured words that floated over me; only her strict tone resonated. She pulled my thong up so the fabric stroked my pussy and asshole, causing me to arch against it, before pushing the wet fabric aside to touch me. She slid two fingers in and out, and I spread my legs for her. I felt more pressure, more tightness. She took her fingers out of my mouth and laid herself on top of me. I spread my legs as far as I could.

Her body pressed me into the bed so I couldn't move, and I liked it. I loved every move she made to make me hers, every inch I gave up to offer myself to her. Her fingers became increasingly insistent. And then she stopped—not fucking me but moving. I felt something solid and big and full stretch me out, and I knew it was her fist. Fisting: something I'd seen and heard and read about, but had never experienced, and all of a sudden in a matter of 15 minutes I was getting fucked in the most intimate way possible. I lay there, taking her in, my mouth opening but no words coming out. I wanted to cry, not from the pain so much as the exquisiteness and newness of it. She lightly touched my clit and I clenched her so tightly I was worried I'd hurt her hand.

I felt a little scared, a little vulnerable to let her be in me so deep, so fast. I tried to make the most miniscule motions I could, while she found new ways to move inside me, navigating my pussy's most tender spots. I came quietly, almost gently, nowhere near equaling how I felt inside. My last thought before falling asleep was one of amazement that not only did she manage to get my cunt to open for her, but I still had all my clothes on. Imagine that.

# In the Mood

THERESE SZYMANSKI

I walked into the bar. Its flashing lights bathed the joint in an otherworldly ambience. Ear-splitting music rocked the floor beneath my feet. I felt it pump through me, taking over my heartbeat, invading my soul.

I glanced around the place, my leg finding the pulse of the beat and rocking of its own will.

She was sitting at the bar, wearing 4-inch black come-fuck-me-pumps, black stockings, a black skirt cut an inch above her knee, and a tight black sweater. A wineglass half-full of a pale wine was balanced between her graceful fingers.

I stopped. A grin slowly crawled across my face, curling one corner of my lip into a snarl. I was a sleek jungle cat looking for its evening meal. And she was the prey.

I was in my element.

She looked up at me, a cascade of her short blond hair falling over her face. Her vivid green eyes slowly appraised me, taking me in, inch by inch, from my black-booted feet, planted a foot or two apart, up my tight blue jeans encasing my muscular legs, to my hard-packed crotch, bulging my jeans out. She paused there. For a while.

Then she slowly skimmed over my white T-shirt, glowing from the iridescent lights, and black leather jacket. She stopped again at my face, noting how a lock of my brown hair fell casually over my forehead before meeting my eyes, her eyes playfully challenging me.

That look told me she wanted to be taken, hard. She wanted me as much as I wanted her. I looked around the bar, slowly assessing the playing field. There were only two other women in this Saugatuck disco on this Thanksgiving weekend.

I reached down, grabbed the hard one I was packing, and adjusted it within my tight blue jeans. My black silk boxers, holding my hardness in place, were strangely soft against my skin—much as I imagined her skin would be. I planted a cigarette between my lips, pulled a Zippo from my hip pocket, and flicked the fire to my smoke.

Glancing up at the bartender, I sat down on the stool next to the woman. "I'll take a Miller Lite, and another one of what she's having." I looked at her. "What is it? White zinfandel?"

She smiled at me. "Yes, it is." She turned to face me, her uncrossed legs brushing against mine.

I laid a few bills on the bar, picked up my beer with my left hand, and took a deep gulp. Then I placed it back on the bar, keeping my hand firmly around it, enjoying its coldness. I ran my other hand down her leg, enjoying the smoothness of cloth over her hip and the satiny feel of stockings over her well-shaped leg.

I glanced back up into her eyes, feeling more like a predator than ever before.

Taking her hand into mine, I released my beer and stood up. I led her to the dance floor, telling her without words what she was to do.

And so we started dancing, at first laying into the beat and enjoying it for the strength it had over us. I showed this luscious femme all my best moves, displaying my athletic prowess like a peacock proudly showing his plumage.

I was grooving and moving, knowing all the tunes, and

making them all into a courtship of her as I fell onto my knees and dropped onto my back, still a part of the beat that overwhelmed me and made me a part of its merciless throes. But then...the beat changed. It transmogrified into one I could use in this seduction scene.

I pulled her into my arms, pressing against her, then grasped her hands, carefully leading her away from me. I gave her my beat and she followed. I raised our right hands to shoulder height, and lightly placed my left hand around her waist, allowing myself to dip lower, to taste heaven, if only momentarily.

I swung her out, swing dancing her to music that wasn't meant for this sort of dancing. In circles she went, around and about, in and out of my arms, held tightly around her and then releasing her. She moved with me, and I occasionally allowed myself the pleasure of holding our bodies tightly against each other.

But at one point, when we stood apart, not touching, I realized... I looked at her and understood that...

Underneath the black sweater (which really didn't restrain her hard-as-ice-pick nipples), not hidden under that nice, soft skirt, and not concealed by those firm-leg-hugging stockings...she was wearing nothing I could not see.

Which is to say, all she was wearing I could see. There was nothing more.

Oh, yeah, this babe wanted it, and she wanted it hard and bad.

We returned to the bar, needing liquid. Once there, we spared a few moments to enjoy our refreshments. I ran my cold beer down her neck, sending a shiver through her. She shivered with enjoyment, a shiver that was, thankfully, not lost on certain already-chilled portions of her anatomy.

"Excuse me," she said, just loudly enough to be heard over the music.

I watched as she went to the lady's rest room. Well, for now, it was a lady's rest room, but in a moment it wouldn't be. I suddenly realized that the chances, in this boy-laden bar, of anyone interrupting us were infinitesimal. Perhaps they'd be greater if the bar was packed, but it wasn't. I picked up my beer and stood. I adjusted myself, and then I walked into the bathroom.

She was in the handicapped stall. How convenient.

I leaned against the stalls, watching her shadow underneath her stall. I paid attention to what she was doing, where she was, and what she was about to do.

When she unlatched the door, preparing to leave, I was there.

I pulled it open, out of her hands, causing her to cry out in alarm.

I smothered her cry with my mouth.

I pushed her against the wall, thrusting my tongue into her mouth, ceasing any cry that might have come through her throat.

Her lithe figure was pressed into the tiles of the wall, her back curving around the steel bar that ringed the edge of the handicapped stall. I pressed her against it, thrusting my thigh deep into her, into her crotch, causing her to arch herself against me.

Visions flashed through my mind.

She had worn this same outfit for me before, the first time we had dinner with Dan and Charles. There was no tablecloth, and through the seam of the two tables pressed against each other, the boys probably saw me realizing that she wore no panties under her skirt. They probably saw me fingering her gently, until she pushed my hand away. She later told me she would have come if I had entered her then, under that table, in secrecy.

I pushed her up onto that steel bar in the handicapped

stall. I used it to hold her weight while I spread her thighs wide and pulled down my zipper. I pulled out my long, thick tool and teased her swollen clit with its tip. We both knew it was soon going to be inside her. I would soon be fucking her with it.

I reached into her sodden pussy, coating my hand with its heat and fluid, and then drew that beautiful liquid over my hardened tool, so it'd be easier to slide up into her. I placed her hand under mine and slid our joined hands up and down along the length of my eager dick. Plus, it was just fuckin' hot to have her give me a hand job, sliding her hand up and down me.

I let her know what her teasing was doing to me.

I pushed it all up inside her.

She gasped.

I slowly eased it out, almost all the way, and then thrust it back up inside of her. I looked deep into her eyes, while I was deep inside her, and then took a firm grip on her exposed hips before withdrawing and then plunging into her again, hard. Her gasps told me I had been right: She liked to be fucked, hard.

I rode her hard, thrusting into and out of her, riding her like a wild mare in heat, taking her like an animal... Just like she wanted to be taken.

I remembered our first kisses, out in a cool, fall parking lot. She'd staked her claim on me that night. That night our tongues had darted in and out of each other's mouths, and she staked her claim, and I accepted. But now, tonight, I was in charge, with my jeans and shorts down around my thighs, and my hard pack deep inside her.

I was taking her in a public place. Anyone might enter, anyone might see...

...see me with my hard dick stuck in her pussy. Thrusting

it in and pulling it out; using her like a piece of rubber. Fucking her, with her sweet ass up on a piece of steel, like some slut I'd picked up tonight at the bar.

I remembered being inside her. Feeling her clenching my fist within her, and her body bucking against this invasion. She loved every minute of it. She liked getting fucked.

This was as much her fantasy as mine. Me taking her in an unknown rest room in the middle of the night.

I fucked her hard.

# The Sailor

### Diana Cage

From the back she really looks like a sailor. Tight white pants. Broad shoulders. Short cropped hair. The nape of her neck is bare and sexy. The uniform fits her very well, and I pretend for a moment that she isn't dressed up in some very obvious costume at a party that feels like the fetish prom. From the front she's very much a girl. Freckles, thin nose, high cheekbones defining a decidedly feminine face that I'd bet is the bane of her existence.

The room reeks of propane from the fire show. Earlier, two women danced around each other in a way that was supposed to be sexy. They swallowed huge silicone cocks with flaming ends, made a big show of their tattooed bodies, and pretended to fuck each other. They had everything going for them—beauty, style, even enthusiasm—but it was too staged. They were too black and shiny and clean to be having real sex. They looked like a movie. Like some teenage witchcraft rip-off straight-to-video bullshit. "Stop trying," I said out loud. "Put your rubbery clothes back on and go back to your co-ops." Even the girls on the dance floor, in their PVC outfits and bondage gear, looked bored. They need rape scenes or foot fucking—murder and mayhem. Something spectacular to get them off. A little half-assed flaming sword-swallowing doesn't get anything going for this crowd.

Girls were coughing from the thick greasy air. And a few

had passed out on the dance floor like little latex canaries—only to be escorted from the building by EMTs who assured us they'd be fine and told the rest of us to go outside and get some air. All the good beer was gone. The music was bad. I was feeling lightheaded and loose, and looking for trouble. For a moment, my sailor disappeared from sight and I panicked, thinking I wouldn't get a second chance. But she resurfaced amongst a group of tranny boys, all huddled together away from the girly-girls, like little kids at recess. Her beautiful face looked just a little bit mean even though she was laughing. Looking at her made me feel sexy, and I wondered what it would take to get a girl like that to fuck me. Then I remembered that we all want to fuck someone.

The club I'm in is normally a gay men's porn theater. Live jack-off shows, the works. But tonight it's been rented out for a lesbian fetish party, and latex-clad enema nurses are chatting with Catholic schoolgirls. I came with my girlfriend, Steph, who likes these parties more than I do. She's having fun, chatting up the cute little boys and girls. All of our friends are here. Every once in a while she brings me a beer, pats my head, kisses me, and then goes back to our circle of friends. Normally I'd join her, but tonight it's boring to me. Same people, same outfits. The beer helps some, but not enough. I've just been hanging around the bar staring at everyone. I don't even feel like dancing.

I head outside and bum a smoke from a group of shrieking, silly girls in marabou boas. A gorgeous redhead in a pink plastic skirt offers me a cigarette, which I accept, but I decline her offer of a light. Instead I go looking for some solo leather-jacketed type with a well-worn Zippo. Hey, we all have our fantasies. The truth is, I don't even smoke. I just want something to wrap my lips around—something to keep my mouth and hands busy.

When the sailor walks outside, my spirit lifts. She notices me standing there expectantly with unlit cigarette, and I feel a little obvious as I hold it up to be lit. We don't say anything. Up close she's even prettier. Blue eyes, black hair. I'm too tense to flirt with her so I just look down at my hands.

"Are you having fun?" she finally says to me as she holds her silver Zippo to my cigarette.

I grasp her hand to steady the flame and she winks at me in a gesture that's both boldly flirtatious and totally cheesy. "Not really," I answer.

"Seen it all before, huh?" I can't tell if she's making fun of me, so I shrug and we stand there smoking in silence for a long moment. Then she stubs out her cigarette and walks back inside.

I feel a foreign sensation as she leaves. I can't place it. And then I recognize it as desire.

Her smug face, her perfect stance, all of it both pisses me off and makes me wet between the legs. I don't know what it is about attitude that can get my panties so in a knot. But give me a cool babe over a nice one any day. I crumble.

As I'm finishing my smoke, Steph comes outside looking for me. She offers me another smoke, and I take it. Still feeling warm and riled up, I study her face closely. I can pick 'em, I think. She's really gorgeous. "Handsome" is a better word, I guess. Her sandy brown hair keeps falling into her eyes. She's so relaxed and happy and sexy that I feel a twinge of guilt for taking her so for granted. Then she puts her arm around me and protectively walks me back through the door.

There's a stairwell to our right, one I have yet to explore. Suddenly I'm curious. "What's downstairs?" I ask her.

She says, "Private video booths where you can watch porn and jack-off, and rooms with curtains for anonymous sex."

"You're kidding," I say. And then I blush at how naive I must sound. Of course that's what's downstairs. I'm at a sex party, in a porn theater. What the fuck did I think was down there? Storytelling hour? She looks at me quizzically, trying to gauge my interest in getting fucked before she says, "OK, babe. Let's go."

It's cooler downstairs. The air is fresher. And it's much quieter. Steph is holding my hand, playing tour guide. She's telling me about the glory holes in the video booths, but I only half hear her. My thoughts are on the sailor. The way she lit my cigarette, the way she looks from the back. The way she walked away from me. I am dimly aware that Steph is dragging me into one of the booths. "Let's watch some porn," she says. "Come on, baby." She leads me in and shuts the door. "Don't worry, the doors lock."

*Oh, how handy*, I think.

She puts some quarters into the slot and the screen lights up. The boys on the screen are really young. Barely 18, I'd guess. They are pretty and hairless so I pretend they are cute butch girls pretending to be fags. One girl is bent over a chair getting fucked. She's moaning. Her cock is rock hard and she's stroking the hell out of it. Steph slips her hand under my T-shirt and pinches my nipple so hard I hiss. I feel the throb in my clit.

My cunt becomes a liquidy place, like my head.

When Steph and I fuck, I think about her hand in my cunt. I concentrate on the sensations, the rhythmic circling or the pounding, the feeling of her skin on my skin. I think about how happy she makes me. But on this particular night I can't concentrate. My mind is too cluttered. I imagine the young boys on the screen. Their asses, their hard cocks. I'm overstimulated. Steph's hand is working me, playing me. She knows how. She's so good. She's knows just where to stroke and how hard. She's doing it so right. Just like she did to me earlier, just like she'll do to me later. But it's no good. I can't come. I'm not even close. "Come for me, baby," she whispers in my ear. "Show me how much you love me."

Frustrated, I turn away from her and face the wall. She follows me and pushes me down toward the small stool in the corner. I start to protest, not wanting to be on my knees on the floor of this booth where random guys have sucked random cocks, but I catch a glimpse of something through the glory hole that makes me change my mind. My sailor is in the next booth. She's leaning against the wall with her pants unzipped. She's not doing anything really, just staring at the screen with a blank expression. I position myself for a better view and this makes Steph happy because she has better access to my cunt. I feel her hand run down the crack of my ass before she pulls it back and smacks me hard. She does it again and this time I lean into it because it's something I can feel.

I can see my sailor clearly. She's staring intently at the screen. I wonder if she's watching the same two young boys I was looking at a few moments ago. The video is still playing. I can still hear them groaning. Her blue eyes are half-closed and her hair is a little messy, like she's run her fingers through it a few times and broken up her hair gel. She looks better this way. Hotter. Looser. Something.

She slips down her pants and briefs and slides a hand between her legs. I watch her fingers disappear into the vertical folds of her cunt and reappear glistening, over and over, making that slick *tic tic* sound. Her face is expressionless; she's just staring at the screen, jerking off in the most perfunctory of ways.

Steph is still fucking me, but suddenly I feel her more than I did a few moments ago. A cloud has lifted, and now my swollen crotch demands attention. "Fuck me harder, baby, please," I say to her and she does, taking the opportunity to slide another finger in. She leans over me, presses her body against mine. Fingers buried to the hilt in my pussy and her teeth nuzzling my neck. I adore her so much. She's an amazing lover and a loving girlfriend, but right now I'm thinking about the stranger in the next booth and Steph's hands on my body.

Steph is really turned on. I can tell from the rough way she's pushing into me. It must be the porn working its magic on her as well. I'm hot, too, and very close to coming, but I hold on for Sailor Boy's sake. When I feel Steph's thumb at the opening of my cunt, I gasp, ready to take her whole hand. I love it when she fucks me like this, so raw and so forceful-ly. And the sensation of her pushing into me brings me back to where we are and who she is and why I love her so much. "What are you thinking about, baby?" she says. "Where are you? Come back to me. I want to feel your cunt on my hand."

I can see Sailor Boy's hands moving faster over her clit and I badly wish I could reach her with my tongue. I groan and push back against Steph shamelessly in a way I know she loves. My sailor's mouth is open. She flicks her clit a few more times and tenses up, pressing her fingers down into a pussy I didn't get to touch or taste. It's enough, though, and it pushes me over the edge and I gasp as the wave of orgasm hits me.

Steph stops moving momentarily, her fingers still inside. The sweat that's collected between our bodies has dried and our skin is stuck together. "Don't move," she says to me, and I obey. We stay like that for a few moments, and when I look again my sailor is gone.

# I've Got a Tube in My Pocket

REGGIE GRANWALTER

I met Eileen in January. I was looking for a real estate agent to help me buy a house and some mutual friends referred me to her. We talked briefly on the phone about what I was looking for, then made plans to meet over the weekend. Before she arrived I created a detailed list of what I needed, wanted, and didn't want in a home. This left us with not much work to do when she arrived, so we ended up spending about an hour talking about the different places we'd lived.

I learned Eileen had lived most of her life in New York before moving to California and now Oregon. She learned I'd grown up in Portland and I was now buying my first house. We had other differences. Eileen was 5-foot-4, thin with short reddish hair, and 71 years old. I was 5-foot-8, heavy with long brown hair, and 35 years old. Despite our differences, we got along like we'd known each other for years.

During the next couple of weeks, Eileen and I spent several evenings a week and most of the weekends touring neighborhoods and homes. We had a great time—even if we didn't find a house for me. Actually, I was kind of glad we didn't; it meant I could spend more time with Eileen.

I was going on vacation at the end of January and was really excited about the trip, but I hated that I wasn't going see or talk to Eileen for a week. In fact, I'd be missing her birthday! We talked for a couple hours the night before I left. I hoped that would sustain me through the week.

Once at the airport, I learned my flight was delayed for hours due to snow. What to do? I decided to call Eileen. I just felt I wanted to share this with her. I wanted to share everything with her—big things and little.

While I was gone I tried to buy Eileen a birthday card, but I couldn't find one I liked, so I sent three. As much as I enjoyed my trip, I missed her. It amazed me that I could miss someone I'd only recently met so much.

I didn't understand the feelings I was having. I'd never been in a relationship before, but I knew this was more than just a friendship or business relationship. I discussed it with my best friend, but she thought I was making too much of it.

I decided I would see how Eileen felt about seeing me outside of her job. So when I returned from my trip, I invited her over to my apartment for dinner. She accepted, and we spent the evening eating and talking. It was difficult for me to concentrate. I was looking for an opening in the conversation so I could ask her how she felt about me. I wasn't really sure what I wanted to say. Finally I just said, "So, do you fool around?"

You should have heard the stammering as she tried to recover from my question. It actually surprised me, too! When she got her composure back and the blush on her face had faded, she asked me what I'd meant by that. Now it was my turn to blush. I said I wondered if she was into having a relationship or maybe just sleeping with someone.

"I've done the casual sex thing in the past," she said, "but it just wasn't that satisfying. I prefer waiting until I'm in a relationship." I told her about my sexual experiences thus far; that took about five seconds. I said I also wasn't sure about whether I could be involved with someone sexually without being in a relationship, but that I was willing to give it a try.

No plans were made, no decisions were reached, but our cards were on the table. Would something come of it? I didn't know.

It was nearing Valentine's Day. Neither Eileen nor I had any plans for that evening, so we scheduled a couple house tours for the night of the 14th. Since I had missed Eileen's birthday, I knew I couldn't miss doing something for her for Valentine's Day. What could I do that wouldn't be considered too romantic but might give her a hint where my interests lay?

I decided to make her some chocolate candies, since I knew she loved chocolate. I used a small mold shaped like a gift box wrapped in a ribbon.

Usually we met at my apartment and then drove together. That night I picked Eileen up, because she lived in the same neighborhood as the houses we were visiting. She lived in the upstairs of a house of a mutual friend of ours, Terry. She called it her "penthouse." I drove to Terry's after work and came in and visited with them for a bit before giving Eileen her chocolate box. I'd never seen anyone so excited.

After visiting a bit, we headed around the corner to the first house. As we pulled up in front of the house, I was shocked to see that it looked very new. "Actually," Eileen said, "it's brand-new."

I toured the house in amazement. I couldn't believe I could buy a brand new house. Your first house is supposed to be a fixer-upper, I'd thought. I just walked around and around, thinking, *I can't buy this. It's new.* But it was within my price range and had almost everything I wanted. Then I realized the one thing this house had that I probably wouldn't find in another—it was around the corner from Eileen.

We decided not to visit the other house and instead went

to a funky restaurant down the street. Neither of us was really hungry. I was scared, excited, and nervous. I knew Eileen was excited for me; she thought it was the perfect house. We sat for an hour or so just picking at our food and talking about the house.

I remember looking across the table at her and noticing her eyes. I hadn't noticed before how much they lit up her face. They were so expressive, reflecting her emotions. I could have stared into them for hours.

But it was getting late and we decided to call it a night. We hopped back into my truck, and I delivered Eileen back to her "penthouse." She promised to write up the offer that evening so I could sign it the next day and she could present it to the seller that evening. We said our goodbyes, and just before Eileen stepped out of my truck, she leaned over, told me congratulations, gave me a kiss on the cheek, and walked up to her house.

*Wow,* I thought. *What just happened? What kind of a kiss was that? What did it mean? Eileen is my agent. It couldn't possibly mean anything.* But I wanted it to mean something. I went home that night and tried to sleep through the excitement, and I don't just mean about the house.

The next day Eileen and I talked briefly in the morning, and I met her at lunch to sign the papers for the offer. Neither of us talked about the kiss.

After I found out that my offer on the house was accepted, we went back over to the house from time to time so I could make floor plans, measure for curtains, even work in the yard. Eileen let me have my own personal open house so my family could come and see it.

Over the next month, we spent most of our time talking about the house and how nice it would be to live around the corner from each other. I was a bit distracted with packing up my apartment, so time flew by quickly. Finally it was March 15, the day the house closed.

I went to the closing, signed a ton of papers, and the next thing I knew the house was mine. Eileen and I went out and had a celebratory dinner. I have no idea what we talked about that evening; my head was running out of control trying to deal with the reality of owning my own home and what was I going to do about Eileen. All I remember is getting lost in those magnificent eyes.

The next day was Saturday, the big moving day. I had my family and friends over to help me. We got everything packed up and unloaded at the house in a few hours. Afterward, while I was feeding everyone, Eileen came over to see how it was going.

I took the week off from work so I could unpack and get settled. Most days were the same; I called Eileen from bed as soon as I woke up. We would talk and talk. She came by at least once a day to see how my unpacking was coming along. We went out to dinner a couple of times, and I kept getting lost in those eyes. Next thing I knew it was Sunday, almost time for me to go back to work.

Eileen and I had decided to have dinner at my new home and then watch a movie, *A Chorus Line*. We'd both seen the stage version, but neither of us had seen the film. We had a nice dinner and then moved to the living room. We both made ourselves comfy on the couch, and I started the movie. I don't know who made the first move, but after a few minutes we started holding hands.

As the movie continued our fingers slowly and tenderly caressed each other's hands. I remember moving even closer to Eileen so that our legs were touching. Our hands moved up onto our laps. We talked on and off during the movie, recalling some of our favorite parts and songs.

We both continued to caress each other's hands, but as time moved on my hand moved onto Eileen's thigh. The movie continued to play in the background; I don't know how much of it we actually saw or heard. I felt Eileen's warmth emanating through her jeans onto my shorts and bare leg. It was exhilarating. I didn't know where this was heading, but I didn't care. I was living in the moment.

As we became braver, our caresses moved farther up and down each other's thigh. We were content with this for a while, but as we became more aroused, the movements of our hands increased. Our hands swept down the outside of the leg before returning up via the inner thigh. But we weren't content to let our hands have all the fun. We looked into the other's eyes, and Eileen leaned in for a kiss.

At first it was just a little kiss on the lips, and then another and another. I found myself becoming more and more aroused. I heard Eileen moan softly and knew she was as aroused as I was. Our hands were now running up and down each other's bodies. I found Eileen's breasts. I knew they would be exquisite and couldn't wait to caress them.

We were so close to each other, but it still wasn't enough. We both knew what we wanted: the touch of bare skin. I felt my body flush, blood coursing through my veins, and I knew there was moisture between my legs. I'd never felt this way before, and I knew I had to make love to her. It was then that the tape in the VCR clicked off.

I turned to Eileen and said, "I want you now. Let's go upstairs." She agreed. When we got upstairs, she asked for a T-shirt she could put on and a washcloth so she could clean up. I happily set her up in the guest bathroom then went into the master bathroom. I curled up in bed, leaving a small light on in the bathroom.

A couple minutes later, Eileen stood in the doorway wearing my favorite T-shirt. She scurried into bed and under the covers with me. We turned to each other and I kissed her deeply. It only took a few minutes for us to continue where we'd left off. Now we had so much bare skin to explore. My hands moved up under her shirt to cup her breasts. They were silky smooth with firm nipples that stood up to meet my fingers. I couldn't imagine what I'd done to deserve such beauty.

Eileen's hands moved to my breasts, pushing up my shirt. I removed it, inviting her even closer. She responded by placing her mouth on my breast. Oh, my God, this was what I had been missing. I was in heaven. She used her tongue to encircle my breast, stopping to nibble the erect nipple.

I reached over to slip the T-shirt off Eileen. A little light from the bathroom shone onto the bed and allowed me a glimpse of her beautiful breasts. I laid my head on her chest and kissed her wonderful pink nubs. My hand slid over her stomach toward the center of her womanhood.

Eileen had left her panties on and they felt like silk. My fingers traveled down to massage the damp area between her legs. Her breathing was getting faster and faster. My fingers slipped under the edge of Eileen's panties, and I felt the wonderful warmth and wetness of her most tender part.

At this point, Eileen stopped me and said, "I've got a little tube in the pocket of my coat. Would you please go downstairs and get it for me?"

"OK," I said. I assumed she was talking about her asthma inhaler. I didn't have to wait very long to find out. In her coat pocket was a small tube of KY Jelly. I practically ran back upstairs.

While I was gone, Eileen had removed her panties. I lay down alongside her, breathing in her aroma. My hand returned to slide down her stomach then stopped to twirl her soft hairs between my fingers. I slid my fingers between her legs and teased her clit, occasionally slipping a finger inside her. I wanted more. I was drawn in by her feminine scent, wanted to taste her essence.

I knew she was ready, so I began my descent toward the source of her femininity. I moved slowly down her body, replaced my mouth with my hands on her breasts, kissed her stomach, teased her maiden hair until I reached my reward.

I reached in with my tongue, my lips wrapping around her clit, gently nibbling it. I used my tongue to trace her slit, tenderly probing inside to taste her. Eileen was becoming more and more aroused and was starting to lose control.

I slipped my finger inside her, resting it there while I teased her with my tongue. I ran it up and down the inside of her thighs and her wet, soft slit, occasionally nibbling her clit. When she started to come, I stayed between her legs, gently touching her tender areas, relishing her generous juices.

After a bit, I curled into the crook of Eileen's arm while she recovered. Soon her hands were roving my body, and I knew she'd find me wet and ready. She drew my hardened nipple into her mouth and slipped her hand over my stomach.

I spread my legs slightly to give her fingers access to this aroused spot. She slipped in easily, her finger delicately massaging it. She continued to circle it and rub my clit while sucking my breast. I was so turned on, it only took a couple minutes before I was coming, too. My thighs gripped her hand as she continued her gentle massage.

Eileen and I wrapped our arms and legs around each other and held each other for a long time, not talking or moving, just loving each other. I finally turned to her and said I thought we should call and tell Terry that she wouldn't be home to sleep in her penthouse tonight. She agreed.

We made this night, March 24, our anniversary. Eileen passed away of lung cancer five weeks before our sixth anniversary. This story is dedicated to her, a gift for our anniversary.

# Insert Three Fingers Here
## ALISON DUBOIS

It started as a dare. Toby, Linda, and I, the three muske-
teers doing our usual Friday night thing at Elongo's, which
consisted of downing all the buffalo wings we could eat and
all the bourbon shooters we could wash down. I always knew
eventually something would change, but I thought it would
be more along the lines of one of us developing peptic ulcers.

Like most nights, there was a healthy crowd milling
through a blanket of smoke. Two couples danced on the small
dance floor under a spinning strobe to Melissa Etheridge's
"I'm the Only One." One of the couples, both blond, seemed
to be holding each other up more than dancing.

Off to one side stood a pool table where half a dozen
butches were playing. A thin, wiry woman with dark hair and
a buzz cut stood poised with a $10 bill sticking out of the
chest pocket of her sleeveless jean shirt. She held her pool
stick suspended, getting ready to play.

I turned my attention to Linda. She looked at me
through her caramel brown eyes and pushed a mass of
auburn hair away from her face, then exchanged looks with
Toby. Simultaneously they looked at me, eyes sparkling
with mischief.

"So, Ally, how's your love life?" Linda said, nearly laughing.
I watched her fish a cigarette out of her T-shirt pocket. As if on
cue, Toby extracted a beer-bottle-shaped lighter. Linda's cigarette flared red. Unlike Linda, Toby was short but muscular.

Pale blue eyes looked at everyone as if she were studying them. She noticed me watching her and smiled.

"It's wonderful. Thanks for asking. How's yours?" I asked. They both snickered. Then Toby pushed the classifieds from *Willamette Week* my way. The folded paper lodged between my drink and Linda's.

"Well, we've got a solution," Toby said. I stared into her smiling blue eyes. What was she up to? I knew that look, I knew her well enough to know she was hiding something behind that dimpled smile.

"What?" I could hear my own cynicism. Toby gestured at the paper again. I picked it up. There was an ad circled in red.

The caption read: "Insert three fingers here." Just the thought of it opened doors to several seedy scenarios, all of which I was curious about. It was an invitation from two women to come play.

At age 42, my wild days had consisted of fooling around with a few married women. I had never been anything but monogamous in my relationships. And now, with my newly given freedom, I was once again left to my own devices. Ménage à trois was a segue into a lurid world I had no knowledge about—but one that had always piqued my curiosity.

I laughed and washed down the last of my drink. Then I pushed the paper back toward Toby. "Get serious. If you think it's so hot, why don't you call?" I challenged. Toby circled the rim of her glass with an index finger. Her eyes held mine, but there was a secret smile behind hers.

"I've had two women. You're the one who's curious," she retorted.

*Damn!* Sometimes honesty *wasn't* the best policy. I looked at Linda as she put her hands up dismissively.

"What does that mean?" I imitated her gesture.

Linda's smile filled her face. "It means I'm not interested and you're on your own." She stared at her drink.

For a few minutes I was speechless. The idea was preposterous. I had 20 good reasons not to do it, but Toby probably had just as many why I should.

"How about a friendly wager?" Toby teased.

"Right on!" Linda slapped Toby's hand in a high-five. I just looked at them.

"Hey, I didn't say I would. If you two are so eager to part with your money, why don't you just float some this way?" I opened my palm, looking at them expectantly.

"Twenty says she won't," Toby started.

"Nah...Ally will do it. I'll make it 30. And if she doesn't, I'll kill her myself!"

They clinked glasses in a make-believe toast. Their arrogance was starting to tick me off. I knew I had to watch myself; such egging on usually got me into trouble.

For the next 20 minutes the two of them kept upping the ante. Finally I'd had enough. I grabbed the paper and lumbered to my feet, only to flop back down. It wasn't quite as easy to stand as it had been to swallow the shots. A dizzying whoosh of being under the influence and moving too fast left me feeling shaky. I held on to the table to steady myself but the room was still spinning.

Going home was a blur; getting undressed was even more hazy. My first clear memory was waking with an extreme urgency to pee, as if my bladder was going to burst. Sunlight danced along the carpet in weird shapes where it managed to spill in through mostly drawn curtains. I'd survived the night. Bully for me.

For a while I didn't even remember the dare. But then I saw it, that same paper with drink stains and red ink that had bled into the accompanying ads, resting on my nightstand.

Could I really do it? Before I could answer, something made me dial the number in the ad. With each ring my heart skipped. When a machine clicked on, I was relieved. A soft feminine voice left instructions. As soon as it beeped, I spoke.

"Yes. This is Ally, sorry I missed you...I'd like to connect. Call me." Just as hastily, I left my number. For a while I sat on the edge of my bed, stunned, holding the phone in my hands. What the hell was I doing? I started to worry about sounding too desperate or eager. But then, as I started to put the handset back in its cradle, I heard a voice.

"Hello?"

"Hello?" I answered, fumbling to keep the phone in my hand.

"I was hoping to catch you before you hung up. Your message was so short...and I was just stepping out of the shower..." she said. Oh my God, it was *her*! My head was twirling simultaneously with my heart thudding in my chest; even my clit was twitching. I was a mess emotionally, but mesmerized. I listened to her laughing into the phone.

Images of her being naked floated in my mind, and it didn't matter that I had no idea what she looked like. In my mind's eye, she had dark hair, dark brown eyes set off by long lashes, and full lips. Complete with the body of a goddess: full breasts and full hips that lead to a dripping wet, juicy pussy waiting for me to pick like a ripe peach.

"Well, I'm glad you did...catch me, I mean," I said, hearing my voice drop an octave, the way it always does when I get excited. She told me her name was Marcia, then laughed some more.

"Well, I'm glad you're glad! So, Ally, what do you look

like?" she asked, purring into the phone. Feeling a tad hesitant, maybe a little insecure, I described myself, then paused and waited. Had I met her specifications?

"And you?" I asked. Now it was her turn to sweat. She took a breath then proceeded to describe an image not far from what I'd imagined, sans the goddess part. "Whoa…I've *got* to meet you," I told her, hearing myself starting to pant.

"Yeah?" she taunted. "When, Ally? Do you want to play now?" she cooed. My heart thumped in a thunderous roll. I did.

"Where?" I asked.

"Oh, baby, you *are* ready." She giggled. "Know the Royal?"

"Yes."

"Room 104. Bring whipped cream," she instructed before giving me the dial tone.

Whipped cream? I shuddered.

Of *course* I knew the Royal. It had once been known as the crème de la crème of gay and lesbian hangouts. I'd just never had the guts to go there. These days, though, it was in sad need of repairs.

As I pulled into the Royal's parking lot, my brain hissed, *It's not too late to turn back.* I parked and sat. Across the lot I saw room 104; the curtains were drawn. Was she looking for me? Was she looking at my car now?

I got out, feeling scared. Would they both be there? Marcia hadn't said anything about the other woman or *if* there would be another woman. What was I walking into? I began to wish I could send Toby in my place. After all, she was the experienced one. Standing in front of the burnt-orange door, I felt my courage wane. I was about to set the bag containing the three canisters of whipped cream by the door when it opened. A frightening chill shot through me as I faced the deepest chocolate-bar-brown eyes I'd ever seen.

Another shiver tingled my spine. Her red velour robe was barely tied, making her Rubenesque figure very apparent.

"I see you remembered the whipped cream," Marcia said with a broad smile, stepping aside. Cautiously I entered the boudoir, wondering what adventures lay ahead. Once inside, my senses kicked into a hyper alert mode. I was trying to take in all the details of a place I knew I'd never visit on my own and would probably never see again. A king-size bed swallowed most of the space in the drab room. Only two simple end tables and a single lamp accompanied it. A lonesome TV was anchored on the wall next to the bathroom. Everything from the curtains to the carpet was done in tacky shades of orange and red. It was nothing like I'd imagined.

Marcia closed the door and drew the curtains, which made me feel closed in. My thoughts were getting fuzzy. On one of the tables were three glasses and a bottle of wine. My heart leapt. Did that mean what I thought it did? Was there someone else here? As if in answer to my unspoken question, I heard shower water. I looked at Marcia, who seemed to be reading my mind.

"She'll be out shortly. Want a drink?" She picked up a bottle of chardonnay.

"OK," I said shyly. She poured a glass and handed it to me. Our fingers brushed, and I gulped.

"Relax, Ally…we're gonna have a good time," she said, casually spreading out on the bed. Her robe opened halfway, giving me a full view of dark Southern curls and a round ass. When she caught me looking it made me blush. I felt myself perspire. She'd been watching me; obviously she didn't share in my discomfort. And why should she? After all, she wasn't the ingenue here. Yet I felt myself instinctively going toward her. Cold hands drawn to a flame. I welcomed the heat.

With a small sip of wine rolling on my tongue I left the glass on the table and went to her. Kneeling on the bed, I reached for the tie on her robe. Her eyes watched me undo the loose knot and push down the sleeves, freeing her voluptuous breasts and hips. She pulled me into a kiss that left me horizontal and gasping. Equally quickly, she proceeded to unbutton and unzip. Soon my bra was open and my own curls were showing, jeans and underwear in a heap at my ankles. I kicked them loose as I sat up, freeing myself of my shirt. Her lips grazed my breasts, softly drawing on a nipple. It gave me a rush.

"Hey, are you starting without me?" a voice said behind me. I turned to see a statuesque woman with pale features and catlike green eyes. They twinkled when she spoke, looking at us hungrily. She was a slender woman with blond curls on her mound and head. She had small, taut breasts, and when she moved every muscle in her tight little body strained. "Ally, meet Julie." Marcia did the perfunctory introductions. Julie's eyes ran the length of my body and settled on my face. Then Marcia said to Julie, "Come and get yourself some of this." I quivered.

Julie nuzzled my neck as Marcia tweaked both nipples. I groaned. The incredible pleasure was beyond the realm of anything I'd ever known. I felt Julie's pert little boobs against my back like two nubs pressing against me. She reached under my breasts, cupping them. She held them out like an offering to Marcia, who accepted the invitation, sucking one, then the other, while Julie continued to nibble my neck, exploring my shoulders. They laid me down, sharing wicked smiles with each other, a secret code between them. They'd done this before. I had no idea what was to come, only that I was more than willing to comply.

Suddenly Marcia kissed me, deep and full, probing my mouth with her tongue. I returned her fervor. But then just as abruptly she moved away, leaving me dazed as Julie's lips continued the kiss. And on they went, over and over, first one, then the other, leaving me breathless and wanton. They started on my breasts, each taking one to thoroughly work over. And just when I thought I would go crazy they turned up the heat by taking turns dipping a finger or two into my sobbing cunt.

"Please…" I begged, my hips rising with each stroke.

"Need something? Hmmm?" Julie hissed in my ear.

"Oh, she's a bad little pussy, isn't she?" Marcia mocked, trailing a finger from my cleavage to my inner thighs. I moaned, gyrating. I did need it; I wanted one of them or both of them to finish. My clit painfully languished. "Spread your legs!" Marcia commanded. My legs fell open like pins dropping in a bowling alley.

She looked at me hungrily, then glanced at Julie. "What do you think?" she asked her.

"Open your cunt," Julie instructed. Desperate for release, I swallowed and obeyed. Closing my eyes, I parted my lips. After a series of catcalls and vulgar cadence, I felt a shift on the mattress. Someone had moved, but I wasn't sure whom. I stole a look and saw Julie whisper to Marcia. I released myself, feeling lightheaded and overwhelmed. I began to sit up, but Julie stopped me. I lay there with my heart racing as fast as the room was spinning. "Don't move," she said. Then she straddled me and started fucked my face hard, her slick pussy sliding over my mouth. I grabbed her ass to steady her and heard her shriek with delight.

Distantly, the scent of cinnamon wafted through the room. Was it incense? It melded with scents of baby powder, herbs, and her musky juices. Julie's breath came fast and short, her cries less and less discernible as her hips continued to thrust and grind against my hungry mouth. Her clit was a hard bead against my tongue. I sucked for all I was worth. Suddenly she grew silent, holding her breath, hips motionless, as she arched back and let out a long cry. She sounded like a wounded animal as she continued to spasm, sprinkling my face and hair with her juices. I tried lapping every sweet drop but couldn't. She eased off, making a thud into the space beside me, still sweaty, panting. I wanted to protest her departure, but before I could Marcia had mounted me.

"Hey, cowgirl, ready for a *real* woman?" she taunted.

"Hey!" Julie scoffed playfully.

She lowered her bush to my lips as I slid my tongue inside her groove, tasting her distinct flavor while still savoring Julie's; it was a cornucopia of female nectar. She moaned, starting to buck, finding her rhythm.

"Think you can keep up with me, big girl?" she jostled. I sure as hell was going to try. I clutched her perfectly shaped ass and held on as she shoved and pumped her pussy into my face. There was a point where she was oblivious to anything but my tongue exploring and plunging inside her.

Just as her whole body was meatier than Julie's, so were her cunt and clit. Her cunt swelled, seeming to double in size. Her pussy was so saturated from my saliva and her own lubrication that it was a fight to hold on. But as she jerked unevenly I knew she had nearly reached her destination. She was grunting openly and gutturally. Then, with one final thrust, she convulsed in orgasm. Her heavy breasts bobbed haphazardly as she slowly returned to us. She let herself collapse next to Julie. I scooted over to give them more room.

Marcia lay there draped in perspiration, looking absolutely gorgeous, her chest still heaving. I watched her mammoth breasts rise and fall, rise and fall. "That girl can suck!" she exclaimed between breaths. Julie just laughed.

"I know!" she answered, kissing Marcia. The gesture started a chain of events; I watched them kissing and rolling together, totally engrossed. There is nothing more beautiful than two women kissing. It made me wonder if they were a couple. They seemed to be so in sync with each other, and it excited me to see them frolicking. Gingerly, I started to stroke myself.

Abruptly, they disengaged. Simultaneously Marcia batted my hand from my throbbing pussy and took her place between my legs. Instantly I felt her tongue on my aching clit. I was ready to come, but she wasn't going to let me, not yet. She thrust her tongue into my wetness and the sensation seemed to go straight to my soul, bolting a line of blue electric ecstasy through every nerve ending in my body. Julie joined in, licking along my hips, pinching my nipples, and stroking my body with delicate caresses. Suddenly she started kissing me so fiercely it left me breathless.

"Ohhhhhhhhh..." was all I could say, feeling one wave of pleasure overlapping with another, then feeling a hot jolt from my lips through my nipples as Julie continued to tug, tease, and torture them while Marcia munched, licked, and sucked. I couldn't hold back any longer; Marcia's tongue was working me into a frenzy. The sweet release whirled me into the cosmos of my soul as I heard my voice cry out like the trail of a comet I was chasing. I felt my hips bouncing on the bed and both of my lovers flopping with me, until only joyous slivers were left. Marcia stayed, dutifully licking up my come.

"Hey!" said Julie. "Don't be so selfish!" she scolded.

Marcia rolled off to let Julie climb on. Marcia seductively

wiped the last dribble of come from her chin with her fingers and sucked it off as her eyes held mine with a piercing intensity. The sight of her eating my come made goose bumps form all over me.

"Ready for round two, big girl?" she asked, leaning in to kiss me.

"Round two?" I gulped, dizzy with just the notion of it.

'Hello...?" Julie chuckled between my legs before diving in. I grunted in mild protest.

"I can't so soon..." I confessed, wriggling under her. Marcia took my face in her hands, quieting me with kisses.

"Just let it happen, baby," she said, happily sucking on a nipple.

"No...you don't understand..." I was trying to force Julie's face from my cunt, which burned with a strange mix of fiery hot and cool slushiness. But Marcia pushed me back on the bed, filling my mouth with one of her large breasts. I tried to close my legs, but Julie would have none of that.

Marcia pulled away, then they collectively rolled and drew me onto my unsteady knees. I felt like I was on a merry-go-round, going faster and faster. I glanced over my shoulder and noticed a lavender dildo in Julie's hand. Just the size of it made me want to retreat. She grinned unabashedly at me, smeared lubricant all over it, then crammed another gob in my cunt. I quivered and held my breath, then winced as I felt it go in so deep I was sure the tip would come out my mouth. Sharp shards of pain resonated all through me. I squealed from the exquisite sensation, half pain, half pleasure. I had never known such delight.

Instinctively I followed her rhythm, slow at first, then faster and faster and harder until I was aware of nothing but those powerful strokes. In between thrusts, she was sighing and grunting, growling things like: "Have you ever seen such a pretty pussy? So hungry?" And: "That's it, baby, just take it in." I was trying, feeling my vaginal walls expanding and contracting, straining to comply.

From the corner of my eye I saw Marcia watching Julie fucking me. I wondered what was going through her mind at that very moment, what she was feeling. She squirted jelly on her right hand, then signaled Julie to step aside and withdraw the dildo. Immediately I felt the void. Now what?

Marcia carefully inserted three fingers and gradually her whole hand as she explored my cunt, the tight fullness sending waves of pain and unfamiliar ecstasy all through me. I shook violently, sensing that something very new was about to happen.

Just as quickly, a rush of juice erupted from within the deepest recesses of my being. My body convulsed as if it had a mind of its own, leaving my brain somewhere else. It had abandoned me and taken along with it my ability to be cognizant. Primitive groans, cries, and utterances had replaced speech. Marcia and Julie not only knew this secret language; they were its creators.

Slowly Marcia began to unearth her hand from my female cavern; simultaneously I tried to relax the muscles that would allow her freedom. At first it felt like my soul was being birthed as she withdrew. She shook her fingers briefly. The strong, intoxicating odor of pussy and come pervaded my senses. I sniffed the scent, drew it in deep as if taking a hit from a joint, wanting every last remnant. During all this time together, no one had used the whipped cream. As I lay slumped in a ball in the center of the bed, my ass still in the air, I assumed they'd either changed their minds or had forgotten. Wrong!

Julie pushed me on my side, then Marcia rolled me on my back. By this point I felt like a human Gumby doll; they could have done anything. My mind was screaming: *They can't really have more in mind?!* I was utterly exhausted, hopelessly trying to regain some of the composure I'd lost not so long ago.

But Marcia popped the cap then handed it to Julie, who proceeded to decorate me as if I were some giant Christmas cookie. In a syncopated dance they licked, slurped, and smeared cream all over me. My nipples grew painfully hard as Marcia continued to suck and slurp them to attention, doling out her own brand of delightful torture.

We were a menagerie of tongues, arms, legs, breasts, asses, all over, playing with one another as we began a new tempo of loving. I was struggling to endure, wondering *How did they do it?* I'd always considered myself an adept lover, but I was in awe of them. Julie settled between my legs, rubbing the whipped cream into my bush, around my labia, in my hole, along my clit. She surfaced wearing a dab above her upper lip.

All of a sudden her lips closed hard around my sore clit. It made me cry out as she worked my bud so deliberately and intensely. Yet, to my complete amazement, she managed to coax not one but a series of orgasms from my wracked, spent body. It left me bewildered and reflective; she'd accomplished in one night what I had failed to do in 42 years of living. After the thrashing finally subsided, Marcia moved away, colliding into Julie sprawled next to me. I'd never felt so utterly drained. There was no doubt these women were pros.

After a long moment Marcia started to gently make circles on my shoulders. She eased me onto my stomach. I complied, wondering where this was going, but then, as if she were once again reading my mind, she whispered, "Relax, I'm just going to massage you." And she did. Julie stood by the bathroom door drinking a glass of wine. Her eyes glossed over in that familiar way of lovers after a good fuck.

"Hot water?" she asked Marcia as she rolled off the bed.

"Hot water!" Marcia returned her frivolity. In unison they looked at me. "Come on, Ally, join us!"

And that's how our romp together concluded. A shower together, washing come and whipped cream off our bodies. We exchanged brief kisses beneath that stream of divinely hot water. For a moment I thought and perhaps wished it was going to lead to a different crescendo, but then Julie winked in a knowing sort of way and I understood.

Instead we were content to dry one another. Playful pats using big, fluffy red towels. I felt strangely bonded to these women. We came together for a final kiss before I departed, leaving my paramours and a part of myself behind. When I stepped into the coolness of the night air, it felt like culture shock. I'd been in there a long time. The night had slipped away. For a moment I wondered if our motel neighbors had heard us, but then just as quickly I shrugged it off.

I sat in my car, suspended in the experience, wiping condensation from the windshield, letting the car warm up. My body was still tingling. I gave one last fleeting look at the burnt-orange door of 104. I'd never forget that number.

# The Girl on the Stairs
ANNE GRIP

I hadn't been to a sex party in more than a year. I always got too stressed over what I was going to wear, much less what I was going to do, which was all too often nothing. But when my girlfriend, Jeep, and our friend Opn invited me to drive into New York City with them to go to a new play party, I couldn't refuse. It would be a good one, they assured me, lots of cuties, very friendly and welcoming.

It sure was a sexy space. Other nights the place was a gay men's sex club, except for this once-a-month night when it was women-only. The place had a good vibe. There were two main rooms with lots of oversize furniture for play and a cozy back room for fucking. Much to my delight, they also had slings. For the pretend faggot in me that was the sexiest of all. Boys did nasty things in those slings—butt-fucking each other like crazy. It gave me a little shiver thinking about all the raunchy sex that must have gone on there night after night.

I was wearing jeans, a T-shirt, my leather suspenders, and a leather cap. It was my butch look, or as butch as I get. I dress butch when I want to be anonymous and blend in. When I want attention, I go as a girl, but this was my first party in a really long time and anonymous was just fine by me. I was nervous and shaking a little on the inside. It's hard to flirt and make eye contact with girls you don't know when all you can think about is how hard it is to put one foot in front of the other. This sex-party stuff sure got me worked up.

After exploring the space, my girlfriend and I loitered next to one of the slings. I looked at my girlfriend and looked at the sling, then looked at my girlfriend again. We grinned at each other, knowing exactly what the other was thinking. I tilted my head. "You wanna?" It's a hard offer to resist for wanna-be faggots like ourselves.

She took her pants off over her boots and saddled up in the sling, throwing her legs over the chains on either side. I took a puppy pad out and lay it under her to catch any dripping lube. I unzipped my jeans and pulled out my cock, rolled on a condom, and greased it up. I was nervous. This was a different kind of nervous: performance-anxiety nervous. At least I didn't have to worry about staying hard, but...well, have you ever tried to butt-fuck your girlfriend in a sling? It looks really easy in the porno movies, but it's kind of not.

First of all, what was missing was the mood. We were right out in the open, more or less, and were doing this without much warm-up, and not much else was going on this early in the night. And then there were all sorts of logistical issues, like getting the right angle with my cock. The height of the sling was up a little high, so I had to stretch up a bit on my tiptoes. And of course one hand was gloved and lubed and useless and the other was struggling to pour out more lube, because boy, do you need plenty of lube. And of course you don't want to touch anything in a public sex club.

But my girlfriend was a good sport. Perhaps I wasn't the stud of her dreams giving her the ride of her life, but she let me know what felt good and what didn't. We made jokes and went slow and tried to work up some heat, but, well, we were out in the open. Perhaps it was just too early in the party to really let loose. Well, at least we tried. I leaned over her body to kiss her deeply, then she went off to the bathroom to clean up and get dressed. I washed up, cleaned our play space, and surreptitiously looked around to make sure no one had noticed what a bad lay I was.

Across the room I saw our friend Opn talking with a couple of women. I went over to say hi and prove that I knew someone and wasn't a total loser. She was happy to see me and gave me a big hug and a smile. I should have recognized the smile as an "I have plans for you" smile, but I was still kind of shaky and wasn't paying close attention.

"Anne, would you like to play with us?" she asked. *Us?* That would be her and the blond standing next to her.

"Yes," I responded without thinking. At this point I was open to suggestion. I had just played and had a little taste, and now I was revved up. I wanted more. I knew Opn would take good care of me; she always did. Anyway, from the calculating look in her eye as she sized up this girl, I wasn't the one with anything to worry about. My friend Opn is one of the sweetest ladies you will ever meet in your life and also one of the most sadistic tops I've ever encountered.

The blond girl kept staring at Opn expectantly. She looked as though she was about to say something but just kept biting her bottom lip and fixed her attention on Opn. I took this for good submissive manners, but there was definitely a gleam in her eye as she nodded her assent to the terms of play and they finished their negotiations.

Opn decided we would use the basement for our scene. We went down a set of concrete steps into a small space lined with tiny lockers, where the boys usually check their clothes—useful for your jock fantasies. Behind us was a heavy door that looked like a meat-locker door. I felt removed from the rest of the party; I could barely hear the pounding music upstairs.

Opn ordered the girl to undress as I watched. I did it in such a way that it was clear that I didn't want to watch her and wasn't interested in the fact that she was taking off all her clothes right in front of me. But at the same time I wanted to be polite. If she wanted me to watch then I would watch her. But I didn't want to be disrespectful or ogle her just because she was getting naked in front of me.

Most likely I was blushing, because I felt warm. The girl was very matter-of-fact as she stripped down to her thong and garters. She was wide-hipped with a curvy rump. My mouth was a little dry. Then she took off her bra. She had lovely and large breasts. She stood there in front of Opn and just waited. The girl looked calm, no longer expectant. I marveled at how self-assured she was, standing nonchalantly in front of strangers without her clothes on.

Opn had recruited a third woman to top with us, and the three of us touched the girl's exposed flesh. We stroked her and caressed her, lightly scratching and rubbing her skin. Our six hands, some using sensation toys, all focused on this body placed between us. The trip had begun. I kept my attention on the safe places: arms, legs, thighs, shoulders, belly. We were all getting a little high from the contact and the sensuality. The girl's breathing had slowed and was now deeper, interspersed with small sighs.

The basement only had a small area of free space, and Opn wanted to start some serious play. She looked around and thought about it for half a minute. Coming to a decision, she positioned me on the stairs, legs spread apart, four steps up from the bottom. Then she had the girl kneel on the second step and lean forward into me for support. Her full breasts pressed into my torso; I was very aware of this contact. I looked into her face to find her almond-colored eyes staring into mine.

Now I was an entirely different kind of nervous. The kind where your cock is hard and you don't want the girl to feel it against her leg. My cock was hard. The girl wet her lips with her tongue and kept her gaze locked on me, which made me even more nervous. I had nowhere to go, nowhere else to look—I had to stay put. I didn't know this girl, and I had forgotten her name. Wait, did I even know her name? But it was too late to panic. Instead I smiled. She smiled back, slow and flirtatious. This was OK. If a naked girl was lying on top of me and I got turned on, well, wasn't that why I'd driven all the way down here in the first place?

Blows started to fall on her back, heavy, solid blows from my sweet femme friend who was also a wicked top. I felt the impact of each stroke. It was a little frightening to feel someone get hit that hard. The girl's mouth would open and then she'd exhale sharply. The inhale would be slower and her eyes would close a little. Another blow would fall, her breath would rush out, and a startled look would cross her face as her eyes widened. Her body melted further into mine. I was supporting her full weight. The concrete stairs pressed into the leather of my suspenders in a sharp line across my back.

Another blow landed, then another. Her eyes sought mine, and I held her gaze. Her expression seduced me. Each new wave of pain brought something deeper out of her, and the most amazing thing was that she was giving it to me. I was riveted by this exchange. And I was most certainly getting off. I'd made a decision to accept what she was giving me, to trust that it was being given freely, and that nothing more was required of me but to stay with her every moment, to witness and to appreciate.

So I lay there and tensed my body and cushioned her and watched her closely. I loved how she lay there and took it. I loved how badly she was being hurt, even as I couldn't believe how much she was taking. My dick was rock-hard, but I wasn't too worried about that. Somewhere along the line I'd gotten permission to touch and hurt her breasts. My own hunger surprised me as I pinched and rolled her nipples into large erect mounds.

Before I'd been content to just watch her be hurt. Now I knew how badly she needed to both give and take this pain. I understood something about this girl, and I marveled at it. I saw her fearlessness and her raw sexuality. I felt desire pour out of her and cover me like sticky nectar. As close as we were, our bodies pressed against each other, I wanted to go deeper—I wanted to go inside. She was feeding me, and I wanted more.

But every scene must come to an end. Our cries and laughter had drawn quite a few onlookers at the top of the stairs, including my girlfriend, who was perched on a step with an amused look on her face. The girl and I disentangled our bodies from each other. Her blond hair was all disheveled. The four of us who had played all hugged each other. The girl got dressed. I went to fetch a couple glasses of water. After drinking one down, the girl went up to smoke. Opn packed up the toys and chit-chatted with some of the onlookers.

I was so happy with how my party had turned out I decided to tag along to the next one. I don't remember what I decided to wear; it didn't seem like such a big deal this time. On the ride down we were cruising in on the West Side Highway of Manhattan when Opn turned to me and said with a grin, "Someone's looking forward to seeing you again." *Oh, yeah,* I thought with a wide smile. *Now, that is sweet.*

# Ode to a Stranger in Red

RACHEL MEDLOCK

I'm a pretty wholesome girl: I'm a near-vegan vegetarian, an athlete, a teacher. I don't do drugs, I don't smoke, and I drink so rarely—and so little when I do drink—that I'm thinking of giving it up entirely. You could almost mistake me for one of those concerned-about-the-environment, granola, Birkenstock dykes, except that I'm not that concerned about the environment, I don't like Grape-Nuts, and I don't own any Birkenstocks. Besides, I'm too butch to be a granola grrl. Who needs Birkenstocks when you've got Doc Martens? The black leather dotted with yellow thread seems to go with everything in my wardrobe.

I'm every incurable, good-natured tomboy you've ever met—I'm the one screaming at the TV during March Madness, the one wearing blue jeans in mid-July, the one playing third base when August rolls around. I'm the chivalrous, old-school type who can't bear to open her own car door until she's opened her date's. I'm the loyal, stable, relationship type. The serial monogamist type. The one who'll own three dogs by the time I'm 40. The affable but hard-to-get-to-know token gay friend, the politically correct lesbian-girl-next-door type.

I've never been *that girl,* the one leaning casually against the bar, winking at the girl next to me, and doing my best *Hey, baby, what's your sign?* I can't bring myself to do it. Maybe it's an expression of the vestiges of junior-high-school-dance-party insecurity, but I think it has more to do with my tastes—approximately 96% of the lesbian population completely turns me off. No, I'm serious—I'm neurotically picky about my women: I can't do too butch. Neither can I do too tall, too short, too plump, too skinny. No one much older than me, and no one much younger. No big boobs, no excessive makeup, no excessive perfume. No blue eyes, no leopard prints, no vinyl pants that don't quite fit. No gray eyes, flannel shirts, flare-cut jeans, oversize soccer jerseys, or tattoos of flowers and/or cartoon characters.

When you add together all my idiosyncrasies and neuroticisms, it would seem rather unlikely to find me fucking a complete stranger's brains out in the backseat of a rental car, wouldn't it? I have to admit I found it all rather surprising myself. Let me tell you how it happened:

I landed in the northeast because I was in love. It was one of those crazy, intense, passionate, U-haul lesbian romances that burned itself out even faster than it had begun: We moved in together after three-and-a-half months; it was all over at six. And when the dust cleared, I rubbed my eyes, looked around me, and realized I was living not just in a new city but a brand-new region of the country—other than my ex, I didn't know a single queer person in a 100-mile radius—actually, more like a 500-mile radius.

At first I didn't mind being isolated from my familiar queer world. If anything, I needed a break from it. But gradually it started to wear on me. I went one month, then two, then three, four, and five months without a date. Maybe you know what I mean when I say there's only so many times you can flip through a *Best Lesbian Erotica* collection or an issue of *On Our Backs* before they start losing their inspiring qualities. To add insult to injury, my ex had started dating someone new—a cute, butch rugby player who sometimes went by "Tommy." (She sort of looks like a "Tommy," actually.) I was happy for her, but her dating success only reinforced the fact that I hadn't had a date since we'd split. I was beginning to think I'd lost my touch.

Then, out of the clear blue sky, serendipitously descending angel-like from the heavens to rescue me, a lesbian coworker from my new job called and asked if I wanted to go out with her and some friends. (We'll name her "Jen"—she looks like one of those athletic, abbreviated-name girls.) I was surprised to hear from her—I knew she was gay and assumed she knew I was gay, but since our respective job duties didn't often bring us together, I'd never had much opportunity to chat with her. I'd wanted to corner her and ask her about the local queer community, but how would I broach the topic? Sidle up to her desk, lean in, and say, "Hey, baby, what's your sign?"

(Now, I know what you're thinking, and no, I didn't fuck Jen's brains out in the backseat of a rental car. Get your mind out of the gutter—that's not where this story is going.)

In the end, she saved me the trouble of figuring out how to break the ice.

"So… I don't know if you like going out," she said tentatively on the phone. "I mean clubs and dancing and whatnot…but some of my friends from college wanted to get together this weekend, and I was wondering if maybe you'd like to come."

I said sure.

And that's how, on a Saturday night half a year after I'd moved to the northeast, I found myself in a bar I'd never been to, shaking hands with women I'd never seen until that evening.

Jen's friends were all nice, wholesome girls—mostly athletic girls with abbreviated names. Each of them vaguely resembled the other, and as soon as Jen introduced me, I promptly forgot all their names. It was shortly after the round of introductions, while I was discussing queer cinema with one of Jen's friends ("No, I haven't seen it, but have you ever seen *Chutney Popcorn?*"), that I saw HER.

You know who I'm talking about. This is the woman who makes you forget what you're talking about in the middle of a sentence. This is the woman who, even if you don't take her home, will be making surprise guest appearances in all of your best erotic dreams for the next three months. This is the woman who makes you throw all of your high granola ideals, along with all that other "wholesome" crap, out the window.

She had the walk. Perhaps it was the motion, caught out of the corner of my eye, that made me turn my head. And then—oh, sweet Jesus—my jaw dropped despite myself. I had to close it quickly before anyone noticed me gawking at her.

You have to picture her: black, patent-leather boots—nearly up to her knees, leaving tantalizing inches of visible leg before the skirt started. The black skirt matched the black boots, following closely the line of her thighs, the curve of her hips, the shape of her ass. The skirt's split ran straight up the middle. But what held my attention was the red—where the skirt ended, the red velvet began. The sleek fabric ran up her belly, around her chest, and tapered at the top into two spaghetti straps. The straps crisscrossed down her back and disappeared into the black skirt. Her hair was even shorter than mine—and I should explain to you, in case you didn't know already: Besides Sinéad O'Connor and Demi Moore, only a few very special, very bad-ass women can carry off a nearly shaved head with a mini-skirt and remain completely feminine. This woman happened to be one of them.

I suddenly wanted to be part of that red velvet—I wanted to be its smooth underside, the layer that slid along her skin when she moved, the layer that was tucked into her skirt, pushing against the elastic band of her thong with every black, patent leather step she took. I wanted to be the top seam of that red velvet—I wanted to be the red edge that ran under the perfect line of her collarbone, under her smooth neck; I wanted to taper into two thin spaghetti straps and run down her back so that I could feel her shoulder blades ripple and her ribs expand and contract as she laughed. I wanted to crisscross all the way down, ride up on her hips, tie together, and rest in that magical indentation in the small of her back.

Jen's friend said something to me. I snapped out of my reverie.

"I'm sorry...what?" I said.

She was still on queer cinema. She repeated, "Did you ever see..." But the woman in red was on the move again. She prowled out of my field of vision toward one of the far bars, and I had to drag my attention back to the conversation.

"Um, no, I don't think so," I answered, unsure whether I was telling her the truth since I hadn't actually heard the movie title. *Focus, Rachel,* I told myself. I didn't want to blow it with the first group of queer women I'd met since moving north. No need to lose all composure just because of a little eye candy. I refocused on our conversation, at least temporarily. But my eyes were still wandering. I watched my woman in red as she meandered from her crowd-watching station on the wall, to the bar, and back again.

My visual stalking went on like this for at least 20 minutes. At one point she walked right behind me and the women I was with, turning sideways to squeeze past us. I held my breath as her shoulder brushed past my back with less than an inch of clearance. A chill ran down my spine. Returning to the far bar, she leaned forward and ordered a drink. The gay guy behind the bar said something and she laughed. That's when I first saw her beautiful, warm, perfect smile.

I felt a decision happen inside me. It was an involuntary, physical reaction, like some sort of hormonally induced muscle spasm. I finished my beer in two long swallows and turned to the other kids.

"I'm going to get another drink," I told them. "You guys need anything?"

They all shook their heads in succession.

I headed toward the bar without the faintest clue as to what I'd do when I got there. Like I said, I'm not your typical bar-roamer; I didn't have any cute comments lined up, I didn't have a joke ready or a pickup line in mind, not even a compliment prepared. What would I compliment, anyway? "Uh, you've got cool boots." I'd sound like a tool. All I knew was I had to do *something,* had to muster all of my tomboy courage, had to wrestle my tongue back from the cat and find *something* to say. As for what that something would be...well, I'd work that out when I got there.

A slow-motion walk across the room. A tentative butterfly fluttered into my stomach. A few feet away—wondering: Should I look at her, make deliberate eye contact, pretend to be surprised, pretend I hadn't been checking her out since I walked in? But I didn't have time to decide; she met my eyes and gave me the half-smile, half-nod. I reached the bar, leaned toward the ear of the bartender, and ordered a gin and tonic. He mixed it quickly, dropped in a lime, pushed it toward me, and said he made it "with the good stuff" at no extra charge. I laughed and thanked him, left a dollar on the bar. And the woman in red, her elbow two inches from mine, who had overheard his comment, turned to me, flashed that beautiful smile again, and said, "What's the point of drinking gin if it's not good gin, right?"

(What's the point of sin if it's not good sin?)

I made some clever remark about gin. She laughed. That seemed like it might be my cue. I offered her my firm handshake and introduced myself.

"Rachel," she repeated, "I'm—" But the music drowned her out.

"Sorry, what?" The dance floor was beginning to fill up, and the music was getting louder. She had to do that club trick where you lean all the way into the other person's ear just to be heard. Her lips tickled my ear. "Allie," she repeated. (Her name wasn't really "Allie," although she did sort of look like one.)

I should pause here for a moment to say how instantly impressed I was with Allie—and this time I don't mean her red velvet tank top. I think that if Allie had turned out to be an insipid, vacuous, or just basically uninteresting person, I would have said "nice to meet you" after a couple of minutes of chatting and walked back over to rejoin the queer cinema conversation with my coworker and her friends. But as it turned out, Allie was anything but insipid. She wasn't just stunning, she was stimulating. After five minutes of conversation, I realized that she was as smart as she was sexy— sexier because she was smart—with a mind, wit, and humor that were all as sharp, subtle, and appealing as the way her skirt fit around her hips.

We talked at the bar for almost half an hour, the conversation bouncing from Plato to mountain climbing to queer politics and our favorite gay men. And then, before I had a chance to protest it or suggest it, she took me by the hand and pulled me onto the dance floor.

I love the dance floor. I love surrounding myself with a hundred hot and sweaty women, I love the thumping bass that crawls under my skin and down my legs, the way the lasers and strobe lights interrupt the darkness, the music, and the movement itself—I love the combination of all of them, mixing together indiscriminately into a decadent, sweet soup of smoke, liquor, sweat, and sex.

And I loved the feeling of Allie's body pressed against mine. One of her hands anchored itself on a belt loop of my jeans; the other roamed up and down the back of my body, now following the movement of my hips, now crawling up my neck. I let my own hands land lightly on her hips, my fingers playing in the rippling creases of red velvet. I moved my thigh between hers, feeling the fabric of her skirt stretch and slide to accommodate my leg. She dug her fingers into the short and spiky hair on the back of my head.

After we'd had enough of our bumping and grinding and sweating on the dance floor, enough flirting and teasing each other with vertical foreplay, we took a break. We grabbed a couple cups of water from the free-gin bartender, then headed to one of the tables surrounding the dance floor. I set the water down on the table and sunk into the chair next to Allie. I was catching my breath, rubbing my sore quads, thinking about how cool the water would feel on my tongue. But I didn't have time to raise the plastic cup to my lips. As I reached toward my cup, Allie reached toward my head and pulled my mouth into hers.

A long, slow, sweet kiss.

The bar, the music, the dancers, the passersby all dissolved and disappeared. I couldn't hear them anymore, couldn't see them, couldn't care less that they could see us. The bar was empty; there was only me and this sexy new friend. My hands found the red velvet again. I felt the contours of her body underneath—soft and firm in turns, the muscles tightening and relaxing beneath my fingers.

She bit my tongue as it left her mouth—softly, but firmly enough to remind me of who she was: the woman in red. The woman with knee-high patent-leather boots, the woman as comfortable discussing Plato as gin and gay men. I felt myself go wet, and now I couldn't get enough of her. My chair teetered forward, threatening to tip over completely and dump me into Allie's lap.

After a few minutes, Allie gently pushed me back. I let all four chair legs return to the floor.

She licked her lips, then cleared her throat. "I should tell you something," she said. "I'm married."

It was like plunging into an ice-water bath. In a split second reality rushed back in: I was in a smoky nightclub I'd never been to before, it was filled with unfamiliar faces, and unfamiliar passersby were looking curiously at me and this stranger in red. Music throbbed all around us. A dance floor was just behind me, filled with women, including the people I'd abandoned an hour earlier.

Finally I found my voice. "To a…"

"Oh, to a woman, of course to a woman," Allie said hastily, as if this fact alone would redeem her and allow me to breathe easily again. When she saw my expression hadn't changed, she added, "The thing is, we're nonmonogamous. I know it might seem strange, but that's just how we are." She waited. But I had nothing to say in response. She said, "I'm freaking you out here, aren't I?"

"Well…" I began, then stopped to think. I wanted to choose my words very carefully; I wanted to make her understand I was the chivalrous, old-school type. The loyal, stable, relationship type. The serial monogamist type. And I didn't want to violate anyone else's relationship (even that of a stranger more distant than the stranger sitting across from me). "I try to be really good to the people I'm with," I said at last. "And I don't want to help anybody else to...not be good to the person they're with."

"I'm telling you," she repeated, "we're nonmonogamous."

"Nonmonogamous," I said doubtfully.

"Yeah."

"Nonmonogamous, as in..." I'd heard rumors of non-monogamous relationships, but I'd always assumed they were tall tales, no more based in reality than *Goldilocks and the Three Bears*. "Nonmonogamous," I said again. "How does that work?"

She shrugged. "It just does. It works for us."

"How long have you been together?"

"Seven years."

"Seven years?" I did the math: She had been with the same woman since she was 18. "And you're nonmonogamous. That's amazing."

Allie shrugged, as if it were really no big deal.

I was still uncomfortable. Nonmonogamous or not, I didn't know if I could be with someone else's girl. "So when you go home, and you say, 'Sweetie, I hooked up with a random girl I met in a bar,' she'll say..." But I didn't know how to finish my sentence. What *would* she say? If I'd been the other half of a nonmonogamous relationship, what would I say?

Allie finished my sentence for me. "She'll be proud of me. She'll say, 'Rock on, good for you!'"

"But she's your..." I rolled the word around on my tongue because it sounded so odd. "Wife." (Is that what you would call her? Is that what I will call someone one day, or will I pick a different word?)

"Yes, she's my wife," Allie said, a note of exasperation creeping into her voice. I could tell she was getting tired of our conversation. "Look, I don't do lies," she said bluntly. "That's why I thought you should know. But it doesn't matter what happens tonight. Tomorrow I'll still go home to my girl. I know that, and she knows that, too." She searched my face. I must have still looked somewhat doubtful. She sighed at me. "I guess what I'm saying is, I'm just looking to have a good time."

I recognized that she was placing a choice before me. Choice one: walk away, find my lesbian coworker and her friends, who were all either with their girlfriends or else too butch, too tall, too short, too plump, too skinny. I'd spend the rest of the night dancing and discussing queer cinema. Which didn't necessarily sound like such a bad thing; after all, hadn't I come out with them to make a few new friends?

Choice two: stay and find out what adventures were in store for me and this beautiful woman in red.

(Would it be the lady, or the tiger? Which was which?)

The music, the bass, the passersby were all dissolving again. I smiled at Allie—although this time it was more of a smirk than a smile. "OK," I answered. "That's fair."

"Good," she said, and we immediately resumed the business of making out.

It's not the publicness of making out at a table in a bar that bothers me—I'm not ashamed of a little PDA once in a while—but the discomfort annoys me. Making out while sitting in a straight-backed wooden chair? It was cramping my style.

Allie must have felt the same way, because she pushed me back again and glanced around us. "Maybe we should take this party elsewhere?" she suggested.

We both thought for a moment. I would have offered my

car, except I had come with Jen and her friends. I explained this to Allie.

"Hmmm, in that case I guess it's 'my place' instead of yours. C'mon," she said, taking me by the hand.

A few moments later we were standing in the club parking lot beside a small silver car. Allie said, "It's a rental," by way of apology.

I frowned. "It's a little small," I said after peering into the backseat.

"Sorry, next time I'll be sure to plan ahead." She unlocked the car, and I swung open the back door. She climbed into the small backseat as best she could, muttering something about her boots as they caught on the edge of the seat. I climbed in after her, closing the door behind me.

"This is so high-school," Allie laughed while we were adjusting ourselves—elbows and knees and seatbelts seemed to be everywhere.

"Except," we said at the same time, "I never got to do this in high school."

There wasn't much time for conversation after that. Our mouths were full of things other than words. At long last I got to do what I'd been waiting to do all night, ever since I'd seen Allie from across the bar: push up that red velvet tank top with the spaghetti straps and claim the smooth, soft skin underneath.

My other hand slipped up Allie's skirt. She giggled.

"What?" I asked, a little indignant at being laughed at.

"Nothing," she said. "It's just that...you're a lefty."

"I'm not a lefty. Haven't you ever seen *The Princess Bride?*"

"Yeah..." She thought for a moment, then suddenly exclaimed "Oh!" once she got the reference.

I won't tell you every last smutty detail of what happened in that car. A girl has to draw the line of privacy somewhere. Even when you have "public" sex, in the middle of a club parking lot, with clubgoers walking past, even then there are some intimacies that are best left untold, best kept sacredly silent.

So I won't give you the play-by-play, but what I will say is this: I love the feeling I get when a woman's body engulfs my hand. I love the initial teasing my fingers do, the way they brush past her without touching, the way they climb up the inner thigh then stop. I love feeling the heat that comes from her. I love that moment of first contact, when I draw a circle around her with my index finger and gently slip inside. I love the way she gasps. I love the way her body gasps with her.

What I love most of all is reading her, riding her as she rides me, listening to her from the inside out. Feeling, knowing, learning to hear the most secret part of herself, the very center of her, the part her body keeps hidden from view. A woman's body is not public like a man's is. A woman's body is subtler. I have to enter her before I can know her. Her flesh surrounds me, and now I am mapping its folds with my fingers, I am measuring her distances as I trace lines inside her. She is an ocean; this is her coast. My fingers rub, caress, push, dig deeper. I can almost take her pulse from here. I can feel her when she responds. I can guess her next move before she can whisper it or scream it to me.

My tongue draws a thin line from her belly button to her nipple, then temporarily rests there. My teeth tease her nipples, helping them to harden into little dark-pink jewels. I kiss her. But my mouth can't stay anywhere for long; it is restless. It roams across her body, hungry, searching for nourishment on her bare, saltwater surface.

We sweat; we slip on each other's wetness. The noises we make are guttural, less human than animal. When I feel her begin to come, she digs her nails into my back and I take pleasure in my pain. This is sex at its best: primal, intense, electric, joyful, together, alone, angry, ecstatic, playful, solemn, fusion.

Postcoital. The peaceful afterglow of sex, warm and fuzzy even with this relative stranger. The windows have all fogged up—it is as close to drawn shades as we are able to get. We lie there quietly, spent, as comfortably as two people can in the backseat of a tiny car. I am vaguely aware that a seatbelt is digging into me somewhere, and that I will probably have bruises the next day.

We talked a little. About her life, her wife, their future, then about my life, my ex, my future. I had a sudden sense of how young we both were, of how much we've each been through already, and how much more we would have to work out. I had a sense that we both needed this, this one-night communion.

Allie started getting dressed, leaving the patent leather black boots, the skirt, and the red velvet top in a damp pile on the car floor. From a suitcase in the front seat, she fished out a man's undershirt, a well-worn pair of jeans, and a pair of hiking boots. Once she was dressed, she looked like a wholesome, concerned-about-the-environment, granola-y, Birkenstock dyke. Not at all the type to pick up a complete stranger in a bar and fuck her brains out in the backseat of a rental car.

I laughed and shook my head. "You just pulled a complete 180," I told her.

She smirked. "I'm known to do that."

In our boots, our jeans, our men's tees, our same-color hair almost the same length, our same-color eyes almost the same shade, we matched. We could have been sisters.

I laughed again, this time at myself and my so-called "standards": If I'd passed Allie on the street this way, I wouldn't have given her a second thought. Too butch. I love being surprised.

We climbed out of the backseat as awkwardly as we'd climbed in and walked back to the club, so that she could use the pay phone and I could find Jen and her friends. As it happened, Jen found me before I found her.

Grabbing me by the elbow as I walked by, she asked, "Where have you *been?*"—as if it were a genuine mystery, as if she hadn't already guessed, as if I didn't have a guilty smirk on my face, like a child caught with her hand inside the cookie jar (even though it wasn't a cookie jar that my hand had been playing in).

"Um," I said. Instead of launching into the story, I asked if they could meet me in the parking lot when they were ready to go. While Jen gathered her crew, I walked Allie back out to her car.

We shared a long embrace in the parking lot, more like the kind two old friends share than that of two strangers who've had a night of raucous sex. I gave her one last kiss, biting her tongue softly as it left my mouth.

"Thank you," she said, "you made my weekend." Then she grinned impishly. "You know," she remarked, "usually I like to at least know a girl's last name before I have sex with her."

For a brief moment—so brief it couldn't have even been a full second—I considered giving her my last name, or asking for hers. Or giving her my e-mail address so that we could continue the conversations we'd started. But it seemed better to let things stay the way they were—perfect and uncomplicated.

I said, "Me, too," and left it at that.

Jen called me from the other side of the parking lot. She and her wholesome friends were standing around the car, peering curiously at Allie and me. I gave Allie's hand one last squeeze and waved goodbye.

That's it, I thought. That's the last time I'll ever see the woman in red.

I went to my ex's the next morning for our weekly ritual of laundry. She and I had once been perfect, and uncomplicated, but now I found it odd to see what our love had eroded into—not even a friendship, but a weekly acquaintanceship based on whites/darks, delicate/regular, warm/cold. As I headed into her building, her new girlfriend, Tommy, was coming out. We smiled at each other cordially in the hallway. Tommy's clothes were rumpled, and her hair was standing on end. I held the door open for her.

Inside the apartment, I greeted my ex with our standard, platonic Sunday-morning hug. She asked me how I was; I said I was fine. I asked her how she was; she said she was fine.

"What've you been up to this weekend?" she asked. "Anything exciting?"

I shrugged. "Not too much. Same ol', same ol'. You?"

She shrugged. "Not too much. Same ol', same ol'."

# What Ifs

MARY DUMARS

The blinking monitors mounted on the walls throughout the train station all said that the train was delayed. She would be late arriving. I looked around for a seat in the cavernous, outmoded lobby, but rejected them all. I didn't like crowds, not even thin ones. I decided to wait outside, let the cool night air clear my head.

Over the past few days, I'd asked myself the same question over and over: "What if we don't like each other...we don't get along...she's disappointed by my appearance...she's a homicidal maniac?" Of course, my friends had encouraged that last one. They figured for me, the quiet, naive type, to agree to meet someone I'd met on the Internet was just plain crazy. I mean, really, what could I possibly know about someone I'd never seen before, some stranger who lived way up in Nowhere, New Hampshire, and just happened to be coming to New Orleans?

Never mind that we'd met not in some dirty little chat room, but through a listserv for lesbians of African descent, a group that included some very prominent figures in the feminist movement of the late 1990s. Never mind that we'd been talking on the phone daily, or nightly to be more precise, for more than a month. Never mind that our families were from the same small hometown in Louisiana. Never mind that we probably had more in common than most couples who've been together for years. Never mind that love was an indiscriminant little bugger that crawled and bit where it pleased, whether it was convenient for its victims or not.

Love? My friends definitely thought I was out of my mind. I, who remained calm through even the most threatening of situations and the heaviest of love scenes, could not possibly be the person who constantly rattled on about this woman I was talking to every night until dawn. I, the always rational and often skeptical one, could not seriously be intending to host this woman in my own home, then drive five hours through backwoods Louisiana alone in a car with her. "Well, at least leave us some emergency information so we can explain to your mother why your remains were never found." What are friends for, huh?

I was in love. I thought of her constantly, wanting to tell her about every little thing that went on in the course of my day. I could hardly wait for 8 P.M. to come so we could talk and I could let all the little conversations I'd had with her in my head finally come out. We talked as if we'd known each other all our lives, and still there was so much to share.

I don't know who made the "first move," but suddenly we were no longer just friends. One night she had been lamenting that she didn't have a full-length mirror. My already feverish mind envisioned her standing before the mirror, a pale cream silk nightgown flowing over her petite body, lace brushing warm brown calf muscles. I saw myself slowly walk up behind her. I enfolded her in my arms, feeling her soft body yield into mine. My lips found the warm curve of her neck as I kissed and licked her sweet fragrant skin. Our bodies slowly swayed together, a mutual dance of desire. Our eyes smoldered in the mirror as my hands caressed and explored her voluptuous curves. My palms moved across her abdomen, enjoying the soft roundness, moving down her sides to lightly brush full thighs. Her moans reverberated inside me with each caress. As my hands rose up her sides to cup her breasts, her back arched slightly, pressing her bottom into me. Her moans of pleasure echoed my own as her already erect nipples hardened in the palm of my hands. I was mesmerized by her smoky stare, her parted lips in the mirror. Then she turned in my arms, and we were face to face, hot, sweet breath mingling as our lips met in a ravenous kiss. I felt the cold glass against my arms as I pressed her against it, my body needing to touch her entirely. As my hungry lips traced the curve of her neck and jawline, my voice suddenly breathed into her ear, "God, I want to fuck you."

Abruptly, I found myself back in my bedroom, curled up under the comforter, holding the phone to my ear. I hadn't realized I'd spoken any of those images out loud until I heard her sharp moan on the other end of the phone line. I felt so embarrassed and apologized for my forwardness. I must have sounded like some deranged sex maniac; I just knew she would hang up on me and immediately change her phone number.

Detailed fantasies soon developed into a heated love affair. She had somehow snuck in behind my prudish veneer and loosed a sexual muse in me. As we spoke our lovemaking late into the night and early morning, we found only temporary relief as our desire for each other threatened to devour us. Her tongue proved to be as honey-dipped as my own had become.

Our relationship developed over the course of the next few weeks. I was in the middle of a move to a new apartment when she informed me that she had scheduled a visit to her parents in upstate Louisiana, and that her train was coming to New Orleans, where she would normally catch the Greyhound to her final destination. She wanted to meet while she was in town. I decided I was due for a visit to my own family, so we could drive up together.

Now the final hour had arrived. After e-mailing me her itinerary, then reiterating the fact that she absolutely hates to arrive at a terminal and have the person picking her up be late, I had hustled to get there early and she was the one who was late.

I went back outside and waited at the front of the station, crouching in a pseudo-sitting position. From there I had a clear view through the glass doors and could watch the train passengers spill into the terminal from the opposite end of the lobby. As I watched, I played with my locks, still wet from a hurried bath.

I had spent the day cleaning my old apartment. I had finally moved all my junk to the new place, but I still hadn't had a chance to set up my room. I told her I was moving and that my roommate was already staying in the new place. She decided she wanted to come to the old place the first day; she didn't want to socialize with anyone that night. So I'd had the crazy task of getting the place ready to vacate yet still presentable for company. The only things left in the house were my chair, bed, and stereo, all in my old room; the rest of the house was totally empty. Not exactly as inviting or romantic as I'd have liked it to be.

The hardwood floors were shiny and clean from a good mopping. The double French doors in the living room were all polished and left open, an invitation to the rest of the house. The bathroom, with its claw-foot tub, was spotless. The kitchen was clean but empty; I had already moved my appliances over to the new place.

After cleaning the house from top to bottom, I had to hurry and get myself presentable. My locks begged for a washing after a sweaty day in a dusty old house. The cool chamomile shampoo felt wonderful against my scalp. I relaxed in the tub a little longer than planned. My body ached a little from all the lifting and work, but I felt strong and fully aware of myself in the warm, sudsy water. When I realized how late it was, I had to rush to get dressed, thanking God I'd had sense enough to iron my clothes before doing anything else. I put on my wide-leg black jeans, thin white shirt, and brown tweed vest, pulled on my polished black Italian shit-kicker boots, grabbed my keys, and flew out the door.

Seeing where you're going and actually getting there are two entirely different things in New Orleans. So, after breaking a few minor traffic laws, I'd made it to the station and found a parking spot. This was another reason I waited outside; having my car towed when I'm supposed to be picking some-one up, especially someone I'm meeting for the first time and trying to impress, would definitely not be good.

I saw the crowd pouring in through the doors from the tracks and checked the watch I kept in my right pocket. Had her train been on time, it would be arriving now, but the monitors said it would be late. I knew better than to trust New Orleans info, so I stood up and sauntered into the lobby just in case.

The woman looked kind of familiar. I knew that her pic-tures, like mine, were at least a year old, so we both had changed a bit. I hate mistaking people, so I just nodded, nearly passing her by. She reached to hug me, and I enfolded her in my arms. She was a little smaller than I'd expected, though my boots make me a little taller than I really am. As I leaned in slightly, my lips were level with her ear as I coolly said, "What's up?" As we pulled apart, she broke into laugh-ter and shook her head slightly. She looked me up and down.

Then she surprised me with the first words out of her mouth: "I would look great in that."

I noticed her struggle with her large green duffel bag and, being the gentlewoman I am, offered to carry it to the car for her. The bag was almost as big as her and probably heavier than both of us together; needless to say I was glad I'd parked close. As I began to pull out of the lot, she asked if the bouquet of flowers in the backseat were for her. I stammered something incoherent about not wanting to be forward, and then said they served a dual purpose, to welcome her and to christen my new place. I clutched the steering wheel with both hands and didn't dare look to see her reaction to that bit of nerdity.

I nearly jumped out of my skin when she touched my wrist to admire the black-and-brown wooden beaded necklace I wore woven around my right hand. I quickly recovered, though, from the bolt of electricity that coursed from her finger, and hardly reacted at all when she buried her hand in my locks to caress the back of my head. I apologized that my shirt was so wet from the heavy hair resting on my shoulders. Then she put her hand on my knee, and I nearly lost it. I knew she was amused, and surprised, by my nervousness after the intimate conversations we'd shared together. I'm not a touchy-feely person, and it quickly became obvious to me that she was. I don't know how we made it back to the house safely.

She sat in the wooden armchair and scanned the restaurant section of the *Gambit,* the free local paper. I stooped next to her, peering over and pointing out places I knew. I was fully engrossed in my own thoughts until she said huskily, "Your voice sounds so sexy." I promptly stood up and moved to a respectable distance, then continued to describe restaurants I'd been to. She finally told me just to pick a place that I liked.

I parked the car on the dark, deserted back street. She slipped her small hand into mine as we walked around the block. I pointed across the street to the old U.S. mint behind the stoic iron fence, looking austere through the tattered curtains of Spanish moss hanging from the trees. I also mentioned that gays and lesbians who inhabited the French Quarter and By Water neighborhoods often frequented this area, the wide tree-lined median of Esplanade Street forming the border between the two communities and serving as a favorite place to walk dogs.

We slipped into the slightly brighter interior of Siam's, a Thai restaurant, the narrow entrance hardly noticeable from the street except for the tiny balcony and the little red rickshaw on the sidewalk. The young waiter seated us at a small, candlelit table, his subtle gayness a comfort on this awkward first date. I ordered Thai tea for myself and suggested she try mine first to see if she liked it. She was fairly new to Thai cuisine, so I described some of the menu items. I already knew what I wanted. I told her about my first experience at Siam's; how I actually cried over the Garuda noodles because they were so good. I was a bit embarrassed admitting this, but she was greatly amused by it.

I was beginning to relax a little. We were getting along just fine, sharing stories about our childhood, just like we had on the phone. As we talked and laughed, I studied her features, her mannerisms. She was dressed in a stylish pantsuit with small black and white checks. The shirt had a solid black front with checked pockets at the hip and a tieback. Her jet-black hair was combed back onto her shoulders. Laughter animated her entire body, and I could tell she liked to laugh a lot. While tasting the tea, she studied me. She asked to see my necklace, and I removed it to pass it to her. As I dropped the silver moon face in the palm of her hand, my fingers tingled from the brush of her skin, and we seemed suspended for a moment. She smiled at me before observing the amulet. She said she liked the simplicity of it and especially the yin-yang on the back; she said it fit me perfectly. She handed it back as the waiter served our food.

We talked and giggled through the entire meal. I felt myself falling in love all over again, her playful eyes seducing me between audible moans of appreciation for the intricate tastes and fragrant spices of each dish. I shamelessly watched as she slowly twirled the tip of her tongue around the spoon of melting mango ice cream. I wished I were the tiny wrapped banana dancing in the hollow of her pink mouth, her full lips glistening with the sweet honey glaze. I had eaten my fill, but she was stoking another appetite in me.

After dinner, we drove slowly through the busy city streets. She asked if there were any parks open at night, so I drove to City Park. As I warned her against the dangers lurking in a dark public place full of trees, I found myself speeding through the quickest routes and soon we were back on the main road. I felt bad that all she'd really seen were big eerie trees draped in gray matter instead of the beautiful majestic giants adorned with lacy moss that graced our city. But I didn't feel bad enough to go back, and I quickly forgot about it as she laughed at my over-cautiousness and firmly planted her hand on my thigh.

When we arrived back at the house, I turned on some music and began to put sheets on the futon. I had picked out a new pair of sheets for this occasion. They were the most expensive set I'd ever bought, but they were 100% cotton and I wanted them. The dark-gray fitted sheet contrasted beautifully with the white flat sheet, both with thin light-gray stripes. The designer called them matrimonial sheets, but I tried to forget that. I sat on the corner of the bed, my legs folded on the floor, and listened to her talk about her train trip down here. My back was to her, so I didn't realize that she was undressing until I looked over my shoulder and saw her pulling on a pair of boxers under her oversize T-shirt. I quickly turned around and put my head in my hands; I felt a headache coming on. She laughed softly as she crawled onto the bed behind me. Then she requested I play the cassette she'd sent to me in the mail.

We listened quietly as Sade's sultry voice danced through the room. She began to trace small circles along my back, and I said, in my best sarcastic voice, "If you're going to do it, do it for real." She laughed again as she kneeled closely behind me and massaged my shoulders. The song switched to "Turn My Back on You." As her fingers brushed higher and higher up my neck, I felt the tension fade and the excitement rise inside me. When her hot mouth opened on the curve of my neck, I stiffened then melted in her hands as a long moan escaped my lips. Her tongue left a trail of flames as she licked and nibbled my skin. My years of celibacy quickly washed away in a flood of desire, and I turned to devour her deep kisses. We both drank thirstily of the long passionate kiss that took us beyond the point of return.

When we finally parted, she sank into the bed and I turned back to the wall. My mind was blank; what do I do now? Two years was a long time to be on my own. I liked the calm, the absence of heartache, the serenity of no more arguments. I wasn't sure I was ready to give all that up. But that wasn't really love, was it? That turmoil was not like this.

This was friendship; this was long conversations that never want to end, laughing at stuff we shared growing up, deep discussions on political issues, a shared understanding of the need to forge working friendships with the exes out of the hurt that threatened to destroy us. This was good. This was more than possible; this was already happening. This was already love. What now?

I snapped back to reality when I heard her voice ask if I was going to get more comfortable. I was still fully dressed, my boots safely on my feet. I could still escape...but I didn't want to. I excused myself to the bathroom, where I slowly changed into my favorite black cotton pajamas with the big jogging pockets and the zip-up top. I washed my face, braced myself, and walked out into the bedroom. I slipped under the cool covers and lay down.

She lay on her side, facing me. We chatted quietly, listening to the music. She moved a little closer to me and laid her head on my shoulder. I put my arm around her. As I talked about nothing in particular, I noticed her hand move to my chest, playing with my zipper. She smiled and began to slowly unzip my top. I kept talking. She slipped her hand above my left breast. I kept talking. She cupped my breast, squeezing my nipple. I looked at her and said, "You don't waste time, do you?" She laughed and then took my breast into her warm mouth. I watched her face as she licked and sucked, eyes closed but eyebrows expressing the pleasure her moans confirmed. My own eyes glazed then closed, savoring the sensations coursing through my body.

This woman I had imagined making love to was finally here in my arms doing all the things I had fantasized about. She kissed her way around my bosom, exploring each mound in turn. She buried her face in between my ample breasts and inhaled deeply. Her tongue circled each nipple, slowly climbing higher until she reached the peak of each hardened knoll. I gasped each time her hot mouth closed over me then released me from a hard tug to cold air rushing over the sensitive tip of my swollen nipple. Her fingers mimicked her tongue as she moved from one breast to another. She cupped both breasts and held them close. She began to suck both nipples, flicking her tongue around and between them. My body flamed; I had never felt anything like this before. I was riding a tide of molten passion. My body strained toward her, my skin needing to feel her every touch. My only thoughts were of the strong waves of pleasure washing over me. I was drowning, gasping for breath. I couldn't stand anymore.

I seized her arms and shifted my body. I pushed her back and attacked those full luscious lips. I kissed and nibbled, chewed and sucked my fill. I wanted to devour those lips, drink that sweet tongue, bruise that honey bottom lip. My moans mingled with her own. My body covered hers, moving in a wild synchronized dance of desire. Her hands were buried in my wild locks, holding me close to her. I explored her soft curves with my own hands, feeling the dip of her pelvis swell into solid thighs. I wanted her.

My mouth explored her jawline, earlobes, kissed the line of her neck, my tongue flicking the hollows of her collarbone. I licked a trail between her round breasts. My tongue curved perfectly along the underside of each melon. A moist spiraling path led me to an erect and pulsing peak. I relished the changing texture of each enlarging nipple, swelling in my mouth like tight buds straining to bloom inside me. I pulled back to look at her face, saw the intensity of her longing.

I slowly moved down the length of her body, hot kisses trailed by long locks softly sweeping over lightly scented skin. As I neared the sensitive underside of her lower abdomen, I looked up to see her lips parted, anticipation on her face. I looked down at the swell of her mound, dark crinkly hair reaching down between slightly parted thighs. My body tightened pleasantly at the sight of dampness clinging to the hair near her dark plum-colored lips. I traced light hearts across her belly and in the hollows above each thigh. My body melted in the sounds of her torment.

My hands caressed her waist, my tongue slowly trailing closer and closer to her moist entrance. I moved down the inside of her thigh, flicking the back of her knee, nibbling chiseled calf muscle, then reversed my way back up again. Her writhing hips beckoned me; I could barely contain myself. I wanted her. I wanted to feel her wetness, taste her flesh, and know I caused this.

Grazing the crinkly hair with my teeth, I breathed hot breath over her wet lips. Feeling her body tighten, I carefully licked the damp hair, enjoying the coarseness against my flesh. Slowly, my tongue touched the tip of her opening, paused for her answering moan, then slid firmly down the inside of her waiting lips. Wetness rushed through me as I slid up and down the smooth thickness of her. She tasted of salty sweet melted butter. Each stroke of her erect nodule sent waves of heat over us both. I pushed deeper into her, her hips rising to meet my force. My eager tongue wrapped around her swollen clit, caressing it to fullness. The sweet creaminess of her passion flowed over my face as she rode the crashing waves of a powerful orgasm.

Her strong hands held my head still as she fought to recover her jagged breathing. She pulled me up to a crushing kiss, as she flipped me over onto my back and began to explore my body with hungry hands. As she slipped eager fingers into my wetness, I felt myself release with a deep sigh. I was already full of her; I held her hand to my breast and inhaled the sweetness of her breath mingled with the musk of our lovemaking. As we drifted off to sleep in each other's arms, I admired her soft honey complexion resting against my own mocha cinnamon skin. Honey and cinnamon. We belonged together.

The next morning I awoke to find her curled up next to me. I got up to get ready for work. Before I left, I leaned over her serene face and slowly licked her full lips. She awoke and smiled at me with dreamy eyes. I said goodbye and went to work.

At break, my friends and I sat at the local coffee shack and sipped tea. They were anxious to hear all about my date. All I could do was smile a silly grin and sigh. Suddenly I remembered clutching her back as she sucked my breast, feeling the thick muscles working under my hands. I shook my head in wonder and exclaimed, "Her back is so solid." They fell out laughing. That was enough for them. Five years later, we still laugh at that story, my honey baby and me.

# Kitten

## Stephanie Taylor

Stones crunching underfoot, stiletto heels sinking into the gravel, I strolled up her driveway. The setting sun broke through the clouds above the roof of her house, glowing blood red as it sank slowly toward the horizon. The streaky clouds around it burned a multitude of reds, oranges, and yellows, with an occasional smattering of deep-blue sky.

Reaching her porch, I rang the doorbell, then leaned against the wall nonchalantly, waiting for her to answer. I peered around the garden in silence, noting the well tended flower beds, the trimmed lawn, the shining black BMW sports car parked in front of the house.

This was to be our second meeting. The first had ended—as they all did, it seemed—with me feeling unfulfilled, very bruised and battered, and her frustrated. At least she had talked to me afterward, given me a drink, and asked about my well-being. In fact, I liked her, but I was not going to let her know that.

When I was just about to depart the club, in the wee hours of Friday morning, she had handed me a small piece of paper. I had scrunched it up without reading it, stuffed it into a pocket, and wandered away without a word. I'd forgotten about the note until the next morning, when I found it while hunting through my jacket for some change for the bus. I pondered over the creased message on my way to work.

*I want to see you again.*
*Come over on Sunday, around 9 P.M.*
*I'll be expecting you.*
*—J*

Turning it over, I saw that her address was written on the back. One of the more exclusive parts of town, I noted, grinning to myself.

As I traveled across town, the old lady in the opposite seat glared at me. I grinned back like Alice's cat. It still amuses me when I think of the expression on her face when I winked at her seductively before returning to mull over the note.

I hadn't wanted to come, of course! There was so much else to do and, to be frank, I didn't think my body could take another scene. My ass, the backs of my legs, and my back were streaked with welts and bruises. And yet I had thought about nothing else all weekend: I just couldn't get her out of my mind.

The door swung back and there she stood, looking me up and down. Even though I'm 5 foot 8, higher in heels, I had to look up into the eyes of this majestic 5-foot-10 blond mistress. Her hair cascaded down her back like a waterfall of glimmering honey. The tight-fitting black trouser suit hugged her slim figure perfectly, and the cuffs and collar of her cream silk blouse contrasted with the dark wool of her jacket. I felt the same rush I'd experienced the first time I saw her, a feeling of awe, almost of wonder.

"Hi, Joanna," I said, offering my hand, concentrating on keeping it steady, trying to ignore the butterflies that had taken flight inside me.

She smiled; she knew from the last time about my attitudes toward submission. "Hello, Stephanie, my dear. How are you this evening?" She took my hand and squeezed it, gradually increasing the pressure.

I tensed mine in return, also heightening the strength of my grip. But she was stronger, and I felt my fingers being crushed. Smiling, she released me. In frustration I kicked at the stone lion beside the door, leaving a black scuff mark on its rump from the sole of my shoe. I glanced down at my feet, not giving her the satisfaction of looking into my eyes. "Oh, I'm OK. A little sore, nothing serious."

"Good. Well, come inside. There's a good girl." She pulled away from the door, and we stepped inside.

The wooden floor of the hallway gleamed—not a speck of dust anywhere. But then she had people to do it for her—and not paid servants either. My boot heels clipped on the floor as we entered the house, passing several closed doors, until we reached an oak door besides the staircase.

"Oh, baby, I'm going to really enjoy making you my pet." She smiled as she pushed open the door.

I just sniggered, having no intention of being anyone's pet. I was in this for the ride. I wanted to feel the rush of adrenaline from a good scene and the intensity of endorphins as they rushed through me.

The room beyond was sparsely decorated but cunningly designed, with a few pieces of highly functional furniture in a selection of gleaming hardwoods. All of the walls were bare wooden panels, apart from a few choice items that hung on hooks. The greatest benefit of this room was that it had no windows, only one door, and had been sound-proofed. This meant she could control time by making it light or dark whenever she wanted. The combination of soft yellow wall lighting and strips of bright spotlights convinced me of this.

"Now let me have a look at you," she said as she took in my clothing.

As always, I wore skintight leather pants, laced up at the sides. It was quite warm out, but I still wore my leather jacket too—in defiance, I guess. Under the jacket I wore a black singlet, and a small G-string under my pants. Apart from my boots, that was it.

"Very cute you look, my pet. Very sweet. Now take off that jacket of yours."

I slipped it off and looked around for somewhere to hang it up, but couldn't find a place. So instead I tossed it into the corner, hearing the dull thud as it landed on the wooden floor and the slight scrape as it slid to a halt against the wall. Returning my gaze to her, I stood with my feet slightly apart and my arms crossed. The air was filled with the smells of beeswax, polished wood, leather, and a hint of latex. I scrunched my nose slightly, never having liked that smell.

"Hmm," she muttered. "I have many pets already. Real pets. Three cats, a dog, and the horses and rabbits outside. I have a Shetland pony too. Cats, though, they are my favorite, and that's why I like you so much—you're just like a cat."

In my mind, I was trying to work out where this was leading. I had always had an affinity for cats, sure. But me, a cat? She must have seen me grinning again, because she approached me then, saying, "You're graceful of movement, elegant of stature, proud, independent, cool, serene, and very intelligent. But there's also curiosity within you, which may or may not be your downfall. But," and she paused for a moment, her green eyes boring into my dark brown ones, "I want you to know this, you will be my pet, Kitten!"

She was close enough to touch me now, and her hand drifted out and caressed my right shoulder. My eyes closed immediately, and I shivered under her touch. "And cats loved to be stroked too, don't they, Kitten?"

I took a breath and composed myself against the feeling of her fingertip on my shoulder. It was hard to control myself, though. The backs of my shoulders are sensitive at the best of times, but now, covered in welts...I took another deep breath as she stroked me, her hand slipping beneath the material of the singlet to touch my bare skin.

She had found this spot the last time we'd met, in the club. I'd been standing on with my arms out against a frame, back naked apart from the straps of my black bra. She was standing behind me using a vicious-looking flogger on various parts of my body, to see what reactions she could coax. Once she had found this spot, my shoulder, she was intrigued that any contact there made me squirm and wriggle.

I hadn't been prepared for her to step up beside me onto the frame. With no warning at all, she bit hard on the epicenter of sensitivity. The feeling of her moist mouth on my burning skin was too much for me to resist, and I shuddered instantly in climax. I smiled inwardly, remembering the shock she'd had when I'd climaxed from that one touch.

"Yes, Kitten, I know what this spot does to you," she continued, as one hand drifted across my shoulder blades. Her other hand reached around, and in two or three smooth movements she had undone my belt buckle and the fly buttons. She slowly eased my pants down. The hand that had caressed my shoulder moved away only once, to get the leathers over my hips.

My head lolled forward, and I felt my body giving way. Eyes shut, I was breathing shallowly, trying hard to regain my senses, to resist. When my jeans were around my ankles, I felt her hand slide across my chest and abdomen and then touch the front of the G-string. I thought I would die on the spot.

"Yes, that's wonderful, isn't it? Now, I have a rule for you. You can get as excited and aroused as you like, but you are not to come until you ask permission. Do you understand?"

I nodded. I had done this before, of course, and had never begged. I'd been driven almost insane a couple of times fighting it. I've left a few too many scenes and needed to dive straight into an alleyway or behind a bush to bring myself off. But I have never asked to be allowed to come.

"Answer me, Kitten."

"Yes, Mistress," I breathed, the sound almost getting stuck in my throat.

She smiled at me. "That sounded almost like a purr, Kitten." She giggled.

A Mistress giggle? I'd never heard anything like it. I opened my eyes and looked around but couldn't see her. I felt her presence behind me. What happened next took me completely by surprise. I half-expected a whip or crop, but what she did brought me to my knees.

Kneeling down, she licked the back of my knee. I toppled forward, my legs buckled, and I barely caught myself with my hands before my face hit the wooden floor. Now, I know I hadn't told her about that spot! My heart pounded and I felt aroused already from her caresses. My other weak spot—how the hell did she know?

Positioned on my forearms and knees, face pressed onto the wooden floor, she leaned and pushed down on my ass cheeks. She licked the back of my other knee. I groaned and writhed; her tongue trailed mellifluously in circles over the sensitive skin. I had only been in the house a few minutes but wanted to come right then and there. Both of them? Both of my weakest areas, one after the other? *Shit*, I thought.

"My, you are so easy, Kitten. Are you ready to ask yet?" I shook my head, incapable of sound, as she continued to alternately stroke my shoulder and lick and kiss and nibble the backs of my knees. "Well, then you cannot come."

I wilted a little inside. *How long can I hold back?* I groaned to myself. The feeling of arousal, of an orgasm wanting to burst forth, was worse in some ways than the pain I was used to. Lost in the battle with myself, I didn't even hear the swish as she brought a cat-o'-nine-tails down swiftly on my ass.

I bucked slightly; it wasn't a light blow, and it cut across the welts from the last scene. I drew in a breath through gritted teeth, clenched my ass tight, and tensed for another blow. It followed quickly, but not where I'd expected. The leather tendrils whipped harshly across my shoulder hot spot. My gasp was audible. My head dropped with such force that my forehead and nose struck the floor. A second blow landed on my shoulder, then a third, a fourth, and another. I lost count and was writhing, eyes watering from the bang to my nose, the nerves in my shoulder rifling an assault on my brain.

She sat on me then, her weight on the small of my back to stop me crawling away. Blow after blow rained down. I tried to curl up, to shrink away, but she held me firm, her weight pinning me to the spot. Her hand snaked out and pulled back on my hair, bringing my shoulders up from the floor. Still the blows hailed down incessantly onto my raw shoulder. I felt myself weaken. I was biting down so hard on my bottom lip to keep back the sobs welling in the back of my throat that I tasted the coppery tang of blood.

I felt her weight shift, and then her mouth bit the dreaded shoulder once more, teeth dragging across the inflamed skin. The burning warmth from the cat-o'-nine-tails blows still glowed on my body. I was fighting myself, not her. My body was screaming for release, but I couldn't give in; my pride wouldn't allow it, not this easily anyway. Her jaws snapped shut on my shoulder once again, taking in a large fold of flesh and sending jolts of pleasure and pain shooting through my body. My mouth opened, and a high-pitched scream left my mouth as I fought it.

"No!" she yelled, releasing her bite on me momentarily. "You cannot come, Kitten. Say it! Come on, baby, say it, and know then that you are mine. That I have bested you."

"I...cannot," I stammered through my clenched teeth.

Her fingertips drew a snaky path down my back, working their way from my shoulders to ass, then slowly back up, Her nails dug into every cut, every welt, as she found them. Her mouth released me, and she sat upright astride my back. I felt the warmth of her body on my skin; the heat from her sex through the wool of her trousers as it pressed into my naked back. The swish of the cattail was more audible this time, but where she struck again caught me totally unawares. With the fingers of her one hand still trailing softly on my back, the leather cut into the backs of my knees.

I jerked with such force that I almost lifted her from my back. "Please..." I whispered, "No more...please!"

"Then. Say. It. Tell. Me. You. Are. Mine." She demanded, a blow accompanying each word. On my shoulders, my knees, my thighs, the blows landed with staggering force. I wriggled and squirmed, tears welling, confused by the blows that were combined with her delicate, stroking fingers.

Suddenly it all stopped, and she climbed off me. Her heels clipped on the floor as she walked away. I lay there, my body awash with so many sensations. I used this time to regroup, to regain control of my senses. I was barely aware of where or who I was, and fought desperately with myself to get my composure back.

"Come. Come with me, my pet."

I turned my head to look up at her and realized for the first time that my face was covered in sweat. My long dark hair was matted and knotted to my wet forehead. I'd been so lost that I hadn't noticed just how hot it was. A bead of sweat formed on my eyebrow, then dropped onto my nose.

I staggered back to my feet but fell forward almost immediately, catching myself against the wall. I looked down and saw that I still had my leather jeans around my ankles.

"Take them off, my pet."

Without objection, I bent down, took off my boots, then pulled the leathers over my ankles. I stood now in only my G-string, and I felt how wet it was. My hand slipped down between my legs. *Hell*, I thought, as I drew away fingers glistening with the wetness. I looked up at her; she was smiling.

"I've only just started, baby. How much can you take?" She held out her hand and I took it, following her back into the corridor, then toward the rear of the house.

Padding along the wooden floor, I felt the varnish sticking to the soles of my bare feet. She opened a door and I peered inside, expecting some sort of dungeon. Instead it was a plushly carpeted dining room, resplendent with a large mahogany table with three chairs down each side and one at either end.

"Stand there a second, baby." She walked to the table and moved the end chair to one side. "Now come over here and stand against the table."

I did as asked. Her hands pushed me forward so that my torso lay flat on the table while my feet sank into the carpet.

My ass was exposed as I was bent over the table. Her hands slipped inside the g-string and pulled it down my legs. Finally, she pushed her foot against the instep of each of my feet in turn, easing my legs apart.

"Now stay still while I get something."

In front of me a large vase with red and pink carnations filled the room with sweet scent. Where the playroom was wood and leather, this room was soft and floral. The playroom was functional and harsh; this was inviting and comforting.

I didn't see where she'd gone, or hear her leave; the carpet muffled her footsteps. I heard a sound, like a cupboard door closing, somewhere in a room to my right. Then a whirring like a microwave, which lasted for maybe twenty seconds, before a ping. Yes, it was a microwave. My damp body stuck to the table; the thick carpet tickled the soles of my feet. My hard nipples were crushed against the tabletop, throbbing painfully beneath me.

My heart was racing with anticipation, nervous energy welling up inside. What was she doing? None of my arousal following her first assault had been lost. I was still in need of release, and the tension inside was almost unbearable. Mingled with it was the frustration that I'd have to endure whatever she had in store for me. I could never give in and ask to come; I had to resist.

"Good, you're still there," I heard her say behind me. The swish sound came barely a moment before the cattail struck once more on my shoulder. I tried to stand up, but her hand went to the back of my neck and pushed down, forcing my face hard onto the gleaming tabletop. The cattail cracked again across my shoulder. My orgasm threatened to flare up again, even stronger than before.

"Shit!" burst from my mouth before I thought.

"Now, now!" She giggled again and slapped me playfully with the cat-o'-nine tails.

"I'm sure you heard the microwave, Kitten. Well, this is what I have for you." She held a little vial, like a nail-varnish bottle, in front of my face. Inside, a brown translucent liquid flowed around a small brush that was suspended from the cap. "This," she said, "is warm oil. Keep still, and remember, if you want to come, you have to ask."

She disappeared from my vision while I tried to work out what she was doing with the oil. My shoulder was on fire now, but that area is so erotic to me that the burning pain only increased my arousal.

I felt her fingers on my sex, parting my lips and exposing me to the air and her mercy. What followed next felt like a thousand hairs run across my clitoris, leaving a warm sensation. It was the bristles of the brush. I gasped so hard that my body shook from the pressure of breathing so deeply. Again the brush slid over my clitoris, covering me with warm oil. I'd never felt anything like it. Every sensation in my body was focused around my clitoris. It was the center of all the feelings and emotions and energy I had left.

All that went through my mind, as she brushed me once more with oil, was that this was unfair: not using pain, not battering me into submission. She brushed me with oil twice more; each caress felt more intense than the previous one. How I resisted I still have no idea; I wonder now if I was too delirious to come.

I heard the bottle being laid on the table next to me, followed by a slight rustle. Her hot breath blew on my wet sex.

"Oh, my god," left my lips in a sharp rush of air. I shook when she pressed her tongue to my clitoris, circled it slowly, and lapped at the sensitive nubbin of flesh. Two fingers slipped easily inside, the muscles of my vagina contracting around them as they pushed in deeper. They curled sharply and found my G-spot with ease.

"Say it, honey. Be mine, baby," she cooed. "Don't fight it. Submit to me, submit to pleasure. Come on, Kitten." Her tongue flicked against me, swirling around my clit and lapping the warm oil from my body. Her fingers deep inside me, her breath on my wet sex, she nibbled on my lips, sucked them, swollen as they were, deep into her mouth and pinched them between teeth and lips. Her tongue snaked around as tears ran down my cheeks.

I could stand no more. I was crying, tears of frustration mixed with tears of surrender, a surrender I knew was coming. Smoothly she stood up, her fingers still massaging my vaginal muscles, fingertips pressing my G-spot and rocking gently back and forth. She lay down on my back, her breasts—still clothed I noticed—pressed against me. Strange, the thoughts that come to mind when one is nearly delirious. Her mouth sought out my shoulder; she licked it once and then bit.

My whole body tensed; I had to come. "No, don't!" she screamed. "Submit, damn you, or I won't let you come! Tell me, Kitten! Tell Me!"

The scream I let out was high and piercing. I sobbed, tears falling easily onto the table and pooling on the varnish. "Please, I have to come, please!" I pleaded.

"Say you're mine. Do it."

"Yours…I'm…yours…your pet…"

"Say you're my Kitten. Tell me your name." She bit my shoulder then, to emphasize her control.

"Your Kitten, Mistress…I am Kitten, your pet…please…"

"Come, Kitten. Do it. Now, Kitten." And she bit me again, harder still.

I orgasmed so hard, for what seemed like an eternity. My thighs were wet with come, and the pressure that traversed throughout my body made me feel faint. I continued to cry as wave after wave flowed through me. The tension in my head forced my eyes shut, despite the tears. The muscles in my neck went taut with the force of my orgasm; my tongue tingled in my mouth and my ears felt like they would pop.

I couldn't move. I went totally limp; I was totally spent.

Her arms encircled me, lifting me. She carried me to a small couch nestled against the wall and laid me down. She lifted my head and chest, then eased herself down, letting my head fall back on her lap when she was settled. Her fingers stroked my hair, wiped tears away, and brushed damp hair back from my eyes. She murmured softly all the while, calming me, soothing me. "Good baby, shush. Be quiet, love. Be still, Kitten."

We sat like that for ages. Slowly I came around, and eventually my eyes opened. She looked at me, her face calm and serene.

"What now?" I asked hoarsely.

She giggled again. I still wasn't used to this—a Mistress giggling. "Well, by rights, you're mine, and I could do with you as I wish. But you hate collars, don't you?"

I shut my eyes; half afraid and half excited about what she planned to do. When I opened them again, she held a red leather collar, rhinestones set around its length, fur lined, but still very functional, with three D-rings attached. "I could make you wear this." I looked at her, wondering what she was going to do. "But I won't. It's not my style, baby."

My eyes took her in, her face, the high cheekbones, the blond hair tied back, clear green eyes. She was beautiful, and she had bested me, at least a little bit.

She must have been aware of my thoughts, because she added, "I want you to continue to try other Mistresses, Kitten. I want you to seek what you yearn. You know where I am, should you wish to meet me again. I will be here." And with that, she took the collar, and dropped it over the arm of the couch, out of view.

She raised me up by my shoulders, and I stood. "I have to go to bed now," she said. "I have an appointment early tomorrow." She eyed me up and down. "There's a shower through the door on the other side of the hall. Clean yourself up, then let yourself out."

All I could do was stand there, numb. I wanted so much to be with her. She had just torn my being asunder, ripped through my psyche, and founds parts of me I didn't know existed. I wanted to make love to her, scene or not. I wanted to kiss her, please her, wanted her to come. I wanted to say thank you. Yet here she was, almost kicking me out of the door.

I had been tamed—even if only briefly—for the first time, made to beg for release, and was now being discarded like a used toy. She bent down, picked up the cat-o'-nine-tails, and hung it neatly on a hook behind the door. No, worse than a toy. She cared more for that whip than she did for me.

"No, I don't need a shower," I spat. "I'll be leaving as soon as I'm dressed." My anger was breaking through the submission and the need to be hers that I had felt only moments before.

"Well, you're welcome to one, should you want one." She followed me back to the first room, watched as I dressed, and handed me my jacket when I was ready to put it back on. She didn't say another word, just watched me. I dressed in silence. I was hurt, confused, and I couldn't understand why she was being like this. She had wanted me, taken me, and then discarded me like trash.

I walked to the door before I even noticed she wasn't with me. "Good night, Kitten. Look after yourself," she called from whichever room she was in. I didn't speak. I opened the door and slammed it behind me as hard as I could, then kicked the stone lion on the other side, giving it a matching scuff.

My boots crunched into the gravel as I worked out my frustration and confusion. I turned back once, when I reached the end of the drive, and saw her watching from an upstairs window. She was naked. Even through the net curtains I saw that her hair was loose, falling around her shoulders, and I felt stirrings inside. Disgusted with them, I turned quickly away.

As I walked to the bus stop, and not for the first time that night, tears ran down my face.

# The Pumpkin Patch

L. Elise Bland

I learned a great lesson in the pumpkin patch: Friends make the best lovers, especially when those friends are perverts. It was the week before Halloween, 2001, in Austin, Texas. The night started out innocently enough. There was a pumpkin-carving party at my apartment complex. My neighbor, Brad, told me to invite anybody and everybody, so I called some people from my women's leather group. I had been in the BDSM scene for about five years. Two of my kinky friends, Rachel and Keri, showed up that night with beer, knives, and a 20-pound pumpkin.

Keri hails from my home state, Alabama. She's a wild Southern girl with short black hair and various tattoos decorating her muscular body. Although Keri and I don't usually talk about much besides kink and redneck heritage, we get along splendidly. She's always up for anything—my kind of woman.

Rachel and I met in the mid '90s at a Texas women's music festival. At that time I was in a desiccated long-term relationship and desperately wanted to experience new things—dildos, games, leather, toys—I didn't care, as long as it was something besides oral sex. I loved having sex with my girlfriend, but I felt that after six years we could stand to rearrange the bedroom a bit.

For months I begged my girlfriend to try out those "cute leather bondage bracelets" I'd seen online, but she always cringed when I brought up the topic. I figured if she wasn't into anything too severe-sounding, we could compromise. Role play also sounded fun and innocent enough. "Why don't you be the lecherous lesbian gym teacher?" I asked her one day as we took a shower together, my hands running down her slippery torso. "You can surprise me in the stall."

I closed my eyes, expecting a kiss or a good grope, but instead I heard, "That's sick!" She tossed my soapy hands away, rinsed off, and went to sulk in front of the television in her bathrobe. She was frightened, and I was getting claustrophobic. I was constantly on edge. Meeting women out and about only made my mind wander more.

Rachel caught my eye at the Lonestar Women's Music Festival. She was a very cute femme with a sly eye—one of my kind, I supposed. I was always happy not to be the only girlie girl in the mix. We spoke briefly but didn't officially meet again until years later. By then I had lost my conservative girlfriend, joined a leather group, and gotten myself into many delightful situations. The night Rachel resurfaced in my life, I was sitting at the feet of a butch, naked except for my leather collar and cuffs. Much to my surprise, Rachel had changed, too. She had chopped off her perky blond bob and replaced it with a crew cut. Rachel was hot before, but she was even more enticing now that I was free to explore. Her pierced nipples pressed through her white tank top, and her thumbs rested inside her studded leather belt. Rachel even sported a bulge in her black 501s. She was a boy with an attitude.

Rachel and I played frequently in the scene but never played with each other. We were always mismatched. When I was into being tied up, so was she. When I was learning to whip, so was she. When I was exclusively into butches, so was she. Instead we became good, platonic friends.

Years later at the pumpkin party, things changed, with a
little help. Whenever Keri comes into town, she inspires the
rest of us to act wilder than usual. Rachel and I got into a
wrestling match on the sofa, and Keri started spanking our
behinds as we rolled around. A frenzied game of random slap-
ass broke out. Hands and butts were flying everywhere.
Finally, Keri had me pinned down to the futon. Rachel was
tickling me, pinching my nipples, and swatting my thighs.
"Stop!" I screamed. "I've got to pee! I'm going to piss all over
y'all if you don't cut it out!"

"Go ahead," Rachel joked. "I've never been peed on
before."

"You haven't?" Keri spanked her again lightly, her eyes
darting back and forth between Rachel and me. Keri had
always been into peeing. The first time I met her was at a
play party. After her play partner had worked her over, Keri
went out on the back porch and squatted in front of all the
partygoers outside. She has no shame. Peeing wasn't a big
deal to her. Orgasming in front of 505 strangers wasn't even
an awkward moment for her. She had done anything and
everything. She razzed Rachel some more: "You're 33 and
you've never had a golden shower?" Keri was 37. I was 34.

"I don't think so," Rachel answered, burying her head in
a pillow.

"Do you want one?" I asked anxiously. I really had to go
to the bathroom, and, between the beer and the wrestling, I
had lost all inhibitions.

"I don't know," she giggled, rather girlishly for a butch. "I
might." Keri and I made her finish her beer then chugged
down ours. We all three tumbled onto the floor, slapping one
another some more and laughing until we were ready to go.

In the meantime, the innocent bystanders milled around

on the front porch with their pumpkins and carving knives. "Hey, y'all! Look what we made!" My friend Brad held a jack-o'-lantern to the window. "Y'all come back outside! You're missing all the fun!" Luckily, Brad couldn't see what was going on inside, and we were most definitely not missing out on the fun. I yanked Rachel up from the floor.

"Let's go." Keri sucked down the last of her beer and played with Rachel's nipple rings through her shirt. "I've got to pee really bad."

We marched Rachel out the front door, straight past the pumpkin people. "We're going to go up front to my place and get some more beer," I told my friends as we waddled off, bladders full. Luckily, my apartment was only four doors away. It was quiet and, best of all, private.

"OK, Rachel," Keri barked as she took off her pants. "Get in the bathroom." We peeled the shirt off of our friend.

"No!" she squealed, pretending to resist. Rachel wiggled her way out of our arms and headed for the front door, but we tackled her and threw her down on the futon.

"I'll hold her down and you take off her pants," Keri ordered. Rachel continued to make noise as I unbuckled her army fatigues. Soon I had exposed a pair of cute cheeks that were still pink from the spanking. I gave her a couple more swats on the rear for good measure. Once Rachel was completely disrobed, she calmed down. She was finally in her element. She loved to be naked and loved attention. Keri and I coaxed her into the bathroom. Rachel was hesitant since it was her first golden shower, so she got on all fours instead of on her back so she wouldn't have to brave the flood head-on. Keri and I faced each other, standing over Rachel with our feet balancing on the sides of the bathtub and our arms interlocked. Rachel's back shook from nervous laughter while our bulging bladders loomed overhead.

I can't say the moment was especially erotic except for the fact that I had two hot naked leather women in the bathtub with me. I had come a long way since those frigid shower days with my ex-girlfriend.

"I can't believe I'm doing this," Rachel mumbled. I couldn't believe I was doing it either, but I didn't say anything. In fact, I couldn't even think straight because I really needed to pee. My gut had swollen to the size of a pumpkin. Keri's strong, tattooed arms held me steady. Before I knew it, a familiar liquid gushed through my lips and arched between Keri's legs. Keri chimed in with her own waterfall. It was hot and wet. My own piss splattered off my legs, and Keri's sprayed everywhere. I'd never seen so much pee at once. It was a shower in every sense. Light, tinted streams poured off Rachel's back and fed into a bigger river that rushed past her feet and down the drain. After a good minute of unbridled pissing, we slowed down until the last droplets trickled from our lips.

"Wait, y'all," Rachel said. "I've got to pee too." Usually the person receiving the golden shower isn't allowed to pee, but we couldn't stop her. She let loose and mixed her essence with ours, laughing all the while.

In no time, it was all over, and I needed a shower—with real water. What had been sexy just moments earlier had become cold and pungent. We washed down quickly but didn't put our clothes back on. Instead we staggered into the living room and crashed on the futon. Before long, my palm was grazing Rachel's crew cut. She was so cute sprawled out next to me. I had always wanted to kiss her, so I did. She didn't seem to mind. I turned to Keri and said, "Rachel told me earlier that she hasn't come in a week."

"Oh, really?" Keri loved a challenge. "Hold on. Let me run out to the car. I think I've got just the thing." I quickly found my gloves and lube and kissed Rachel some more. Her nipples hardened under my mouth, especially when I tugged on the thick silver rings with my teeth. As I moved down her body, I saw that her pussy was still dewy from the shower. I slid one finger inside to test the waters and realized I didn't need lube. She was soaking wet.

"Wow, you sure liked that golden shower, didn't you, boy?" I asked her.

"Yes, ma'am," she muttered politely.

I hadn't intended to mess around with anyone that night— I was supposed to be carving pumpkins—but I had a change of plans. After all, there were two naked women in my apartment, and I'd just had the most exhilarating shower of my life. My entire lower body was throbbing from having peed so much and so feverishly. As I played with Rachel, my ungloved hand wandered to my own pussy. I love touching other women, but I also love to masturbate. It's a treat to feel a pussy without a latex barrier, so I indulge as often as possible.

Keri interrupted us when she slammed the front door. "I've got it," she announced. In her hand was a gargantuan purple dildo dangling from a leather harness. Keri's always prepared; she hauls her dildo with her wherever she goes.

"Oh, no! I can't take that," Rachel squealed. "It's huge!"

"Calm down," I told her. "I've seen you take a fist, so I'm sure you can take that cock." Keri wiggled into the harness and covered the stiff silicone dick with a condom. Even as she adjusted her prosthetic device, she looked natural, as if she was born with a miniature baby doll strap-on and had simply matured into a tall, dick-wielding dyke.

Rachel was on all fours watching me masturbate and kissing

my legs and hands when Keri approached her from behind. Her lean, tan form towered over us both, casting a shadow across Rachel's buttocks. Keri reared back and, with athletic grace and precision, entered Rachel.

It didn't take me long to reach my masturbatory goal once I saw the expressions on Rachel's face. She looked at me with intensity, her eyes opening and closing as she relinquished control of her pussy. Keri was behind her, one hand steadying her hip, the other pressed into her clit. Rachel was in ecstasy, grimacing and moaning. The dog tags she wore as a necklace jingled with each thrust. Rachel was ready to come. Earlier I had gotten her close to the edge with my swift hand, but Keri pushed her right over with her power. She screamed and panted loud enough to wake the old people next door and disrupt the pumpkin party. Her tones filled my ears and my cunt, and I came to the vibrations of her voice. I lay there on my back listening, watching, and brushing my fingers across my swollen lips. I never thought I'd enjoy a three-way. "Somebody might get left out," I always protested. I surely didn't want to be the one left out. Even when I was on the periphery, however, I felt completely connected.

Keri tossed the strap-on aside and kissed Rachel first and then me. Before we could catch our breaths and make our move on Keri, she'd already started without us. Much to our surprise, our ringleader was humping her hand like a poodle on a pillow. She was determined to get hers, too, and fast. She didn't seem quite as graceful once she was writhing on her belly, but we didn't mind. She came hard, jerking her taut ass into the air, and collapsed across Rachel's stomach.

After our adventure, we lay there, kissing, with legs and arms intertwined. I knew I couldn't stay, yet I didn't want to leave. Unfortunately, my other friends were waiting on me. If I didn't go back, they'd come looking for me. I wiggled out from the girl pretzel, put on my clothes, and sheepishly wandered back to the pumpkin party. Some of my friends knew I'd been naughty. It was obvious; I came back alone, with no beer. "Hey, where's that six-pack you promised?" Brad asked.

"Rachel drank it all," I said, smiling.

The next day, there was a big white stain on my futon. Eventually I cleaned it up, but not for a good while. I wanted to remember the night. Rachel also left one of her trademark white wife-beater shirts at my place. I'm not quite sure what she wore home, but I still have her tank top. I wore it for an entire week because it smelled like her. Once it started smelling like me, I washed it. The spell was broken.

In all my years of playing, I've never had an experience quite like the impromptu peeing spree. Rachel is still in Texas, but Keri went back home to the deep South. We all keep in touch, though we never really discussed the pumpkin party in detail, most likely because we got involved with other people afterward. Rachel and I are organizing our next "casual" play date, but it's not as urgent as it was the night we all had to pee. Some things you just can't plan.

# The Watcher

AMIE M. EVANS

I'm in the den studying for my next big philosophy test. The material seems endless, dry, and unimportant. I'm working on my master's degree and love reading philosophy, but tonight I can't concentrate on my books. I don't care about Kant, Nietzsche seems overly grim, and Freud is full of sexual repression. I'm distracted, unfocused, and, frankly, horny. My lover is in the living room, just on the other side of the door, watching TV. What I really want to do is fuck, but we both agreed I had to study tonight. She kissed me on the lips—long and hard, pushing her big, round hips against mine, cupping my tiny ass in her hands, pulling my whole body against hers. The feeling of our bodies pressed together and the smell of honeysuckle mixed with the scent of her skin made my clit stir. Then she sent me to the den with a soda that's now almost empty, a smack on the butt, and firm orders not to return until bedtime. I decide to take my chances and get a refill on both the soda and that kiss. Perhaps we can have a quickie on the sofa as a study break. I'm sure that if we fuck I'll be able to concentrate.

The door is ajar, and I peek out before entering the living room. Through the crack, I can see the sofa but not her. My girlfriend's the hottest thing—thick, dark brown hair cut close to her scalp in a prickly crew cut, deep green eyes, and big breasts. She's wearing oversize jeans that hang low on her hips with a big belt holding them up, her favorite blue-green

T-shirt, and her high-top Doc Martens boots. She's a big butch with a full-size body. We get called "fag" a lot from behind by frat boys. I look like a fag with my almost curveless body, short blond hair cut in a little boy's style, jeans loose on my body, and my almost nonexistent breasts. But her? Anyone not able to see the woman under that butch haircut and clothing is blind. She has the curviest hips, a big, round butt, thick, shapely legs, and a soft, full belly—pure goddess, butch goddess. But then maybe the frat boys know more than we think. Maybe we are more fag than dyke with our dueling dildos and masculine ways of moving our bodies.

I peek out the door from another angle to catch a glimpse of her before I enter the room. I see her on the sofa leaning against the arm, but I know she can't see me. The television's on, but she's not watching it. She's got her jeans down around one ankle on the floor and her other foot is up on the sofa. I have a full view of her hand on her bushy cunt. Her fingers are working her clit and her eyes are closed. I thought I felt want in the kiss she gave me earlier.

I quickly step back behind the door. This has been my fantasy for a long time—to catch her masturbating, to watch her without her knowing I'm there. I take a deep breath. My heart races inside my chest; I try to calm myself down. I return to the crack in the door to watch. Her fingers are still working her clit in small, tight circular movements. She brings her other hand over and slips one finger inside her wet pussy. Her mouth opens slightly, but no sounds come out of it. She pumps her left hand in and out of her cunt. Her hips rise and fall to meet her slow strokes.

I pull myself behind the door again. This is too much. I'd asked her once before, after we'd moved in together, if she'd masturbate and let me watch. She'd said no. I'd begged her, offered all kinds of bribes, and she kept saying no. It just made me want it more, but no matter what I offered, she refused to do it for me. For a while I was obsessed with watching her masturbate. It was the only thing I wanted to do sexually. And no matter what I offered, she said no. Our whole relationship's like that—a big power trip. We're both tops—well, some would argue we're both switches, but we're both tops. We both want to run the sex, control the other's orgasm. Anyway, we compromise—most of the time—let the other have top time, give into bottoming for fantasies. Every once in a while there's a power struggle. That's what this was about—her saying no to me. I go out of my way to make her think I'll be home at a certain time, then show up early, sneaking in quietly in an attempt to catch her masturbating. No such luck. I've even pumped her for information, trying to find out her fantasy of the week, to use it as a bargaining chip. No trades have ever happened. After a while I let it go. Now—here I am, watching her.

I undo my jeans carefully, trying not to make any noise, and slide them down to my ankles. I spread my legs and touch myself. I'm wet already. I'm so excited by the sight of her jerking off I'm sure I'll come quickly. Leaning forward, I slowly turn and position myself in front of the crack to peek at her. I slide one finger inside my wet cunt and pull the juices out. I slide that same finger over the hood of my clit in a slow, light circular pattern.

She's got two fingers inside herself, and her hips rock in perfect rhythm with her strokes. She's rubbing her clit with the tips of her fingers in hard and rough circles the way she likes it. Her eyes are closed, her mouth slightly open. I stroke myself harder, allowing my hips to move in rhythm with my fingers, being careful not to make any noise or bump the door and cause it to open wider. If she catches me, she'll be very angry. There'll be a fight, and I'll be unable to defend myself. I know what I am doing—watching her masturbate without her knowledge—is wrong. I'm know she doesn't want me to do this. I know if she catches me, she'll feel betrayed, and justly so. But I can't help myself, I'm consumed with lust at the sight of my butch with her hands buried in her cunt. My lust is driven by the very fact that she doesn't want me to see her doing this. And that desire is fueled by my fear of her catching me, the terror that rises inside me as each second passes, that she'll see me and I'll be exposed for the voyeur I am. And I'll have no justification for my actions. None. But that's all beyond my control.

She shifts her body, putting one leg over the back of the sofa, spreading her legs wider. She lifts her head, looking over her large breasts and her round stomach at her cunt—one hand pumping fast and hard, three fingers buried deep inside her snatch, the other pressed firmly against her clit, moving in quick, circular strokes. She bites her bottom lip. Her upper body moves in and out with her heavy breathing.

I speed up my own hand, closing the gap between where I am and my orgasm. I slip my finger inside my cunt and pull out more liquid, smoothing it over my throbbing clit and bearing down on my hand to create more pressure. I feel dirty watching her like a peeping Jane and that excites me, sends rush through my body. I feel a surge of power as I view her in secrecy, doing the very thing she's forbidden me to watch her do. My own breathing is heavy and I control it, forcing it to remain shallow and quiet.

She closes her eyes, her head falls back, and her hips thrust forward. Her face contorts into the familiar "I'm coming" expression. She buries her fingers deep inside and bucks her hips. Seeing her climax puts me over the edge. I plunge my fingers deep inside my cunt as the spasms of orgasm hit me. I clasp my other hand over my mouth to hold my cry inside. My body shakes with waves of intense pleasure.

Dazed in the afterglow, I back away from the door. I'm shaking from both the orgasms and the fear that I'll be caught. I pull up my jeans and return to my desk. I can't go out there and get a drink now. I stare at my books and notes and I can only think of her—spread-eagle on the sofa with her fingers buried inside her cunt. I want to rush into the living room and kneel on the floor in front of her. Press my face into her wet cunt, feel the soft flesh of the thighs press against my check as I lick at her wetness, run my tongue around the folds of her labia, inside her hole, and onto her clit. I want to reach up and clamp one hand onto her full breast—feel its softness, then pinch the nipple ever so lightly until it's erect. Watch her wiggle under my touch—squirm in delight. I want to plunge first one then two fingers into her dripping cunt and run them along the soft, moist walls of her vagina, pumping in and out as my tongue flicks her clit and she comes in my mouth. Her body jerking, her hips pumping, her thighs pushing against my face.

But I can't. She'll know I saw her.

I stare at my open book and wonder if I'll tell her I finally got what I wanted—that I watched her masturbate, that she didn't even know it.

No. I think I'll keep it my secret.

# Insert Tongue, Pump Low; Tap High, Straddle Mule

STEPHANIE SCHROEDER

My daddy is trying to fix the TV. It just blanked out. I am pissed. Royally. This is *our* weekend: no TV, no cell phones, no e-mail. But she cajoled 15 minutes of TV time in exchange for me checking my e-mail, so OK. I'm done, but now because the TV has played a trick, she's all over it—instead of me, who's posed quite sexily on the big top-grain black leather chair in my ripped jeans, bare feet, and an "Exotic Dancer's Alliance" baby-doll that's really tight, overlaid with a faded denim shirt that's now sliding off my shoulders.

"C'mon," I say, "give it up. It's the fucking cable. You know the trucks are working out front."

"Damn it," she spews. "We'll miss *Witchblade*." She fiddles a moment more, then says, "Fuck it," finally noticing me. "I know you hate TV," she goes on, "but I like to watch it."

"Hey, man, I've got 45 minutes until I have to leave for my salon appointment. What do you think we could find to do in that window of time?"

"Well, what do you think?" she asks.

"I'm not supposed to think anything," I reply. "I'm not allowed to suggest, say, or name the time we do anything this weekend, remember?"

"Smart-ass. Get into the bedroom."

I follow her from our cozy little living room space into the hidden room behind the facing wall. She lies down. "You can go down on me." She looks into my eyes.

"What if I don't want to?" I retort, hands on my hips and sass in my Midwestern lilt.

"No problem." She starts to sit up. I push her back down and take off her boxers and T-shirt. I kiss her, our tongues mingling with the spicy taste of the salsa we just ate and our own sweet taste that we create when our saliva mixes. Uhhmm. Delicious. I move to her neck, where I know she loves to be bitten, not too hard, the way I like it—no marks for her—but just enough to make her wince. Then down to her breasts, full and heavy, pre-period, and suck her nipples. I tease my daddy with my tongue, using the very tip of it, then suddenly suck her entire breast into my mouth. A glance of pain shoots across her face, which I ignore. I gingerly continue down her large belly, tasting the slightly salty flesh, kissing her hot spots and kneading her soft rolls of flesh with my slim hands. So beautiful, this woman, my big butch daddy almost three times my size, handsome like the devil, strong and powerful at the right times, gentle and kind at others; she even cries in my arms on occasion. My daddy. She says, in between sighs and moans, that she has plans for me. Tonight.

"Tell me," I say.

"After I come."

I slide lower and linger, finger the outline, the crease that separates her big belly from the pubis below, play with the various incredible creases and her bush. I inhale deeply to smell her fragrant scent that I love so much, so sharp and musky, so much better when aged by a day or two without a shower. I run my tongue and fingers along the insides of her thighs, down her thick calves, lick the crease between thighs and hip, then stroke her lips gently through her bush. My stroking gains momentum, and she sighs. I spread her lips and sink to my knees, open my mouth, and position my tongue flat at the base of her perineum, then drag it hard up to meet her clit. "Ahhh," she moans, and I know she's ready.

I pepper her outer lips with little flicks, licks, and kisses, then move inside, taking long, slow strokes with my tongue up and down, moving in and out of her cunt hole, drinking her pearl juice, shucking the oyster, as it were. I go crazy, centering on her clit—not flat on, just under the hood, which in her case I call a jacket because it's so big. It's large enough for the entire tip of my tongue to fit underneath; to stroll through the exotic pussy woods, the field of wildflowers, dilly-dally with my lips, teeth, or tongue—even take a breath, come up for air and regroup, then dive back under her warm, wet jacket. I work my ass off to hit the right chords—a little jab here, a ting there, a flat note underneath, and then the circular motion around the now-engorged nub that brings her to the brink. I leave her there until I once again slide the tip of my tongue under her clit jacket and push hard one last time while she comes loudly, coming, moaning, groaning, and cursing.

"You fucking sexy bitch! Shit!"

I wipe my face on the sheet; even my eyelids are full of her thirst-quenching, tasty, and sticky cunt juice, that special blend she lets flow just for me.

"What's the plan?" I ask offhandedly. "I've got to leave."

She looks me square in the eyes, "Take my credit card and go to the Leatherman and buy a riding crop and a slim vibrator. You must tell them your daddy told you to buy it. And don't forget batteries for the vibrator. If they don't have the right size, go across the street, right next to where you're getting your nails and hair done, and go downstairs to an unmarked store. They'll have it. And don't dally."

"OK," I say as she drifts off into a late-afternoon nap. I rummage though the closet to find my spike-heeled black leather boots, put them on, and take her credit card out of her wallet. "See you in a few," I say, and slip out the door, locking it behind me.

I jump into a cab and try the miniature tape recorder I've shoved into my bag. Shit. It doesn't work. I'll have to buy batteries. I walk into a photo shop on Bleecker and buy two AAs. I put them into the recorder and check over and over: "Testing 1, 2, 3," to make sure it works. This is a bonus, a plus, a present for my daddy. I walk around the corner to the Leatherman, slam the tape recorder on the counter, and turn it on. I look at the little goofy-looking leather guy, who looks at the tape recorder and then me, and say, "My daddy said I have to buy a leather riding crop and a small vibrator. Do you have those two items in stock?"

"Yes, downstairs."

I grab the recorder and walk, almost tripping, down the very narrow and dizzying spiral staircase. Downstairs I find exactly what I want, but see more interesting things, too. The vibrator is perfect: a small one, though I can't for the life of me imagine why she's asked for this. She fucks me with her big fingers, four at a time sometimes, as well as several thick dildos, so what in the hell is a skinny little vibrator going to do? Whatever. I spy the crops. Four sizes: one a miniature, one with a too-small head, one out of stock, and one of my ideal make—medium handle, with a rather large flap. I take it off the hook and am ready to head up those crazy stairs when I see the bullwhips. Oohhh. I finger them, sliding my hands around one or two of them, caressing the long implements and smooth leather. Two particularly interest me: the cattail and another with a kind of elongated diamond-shape tip. "What's the difference," I ask the guy who works on the lower floor, "between the two? I mean, besides the obvious."

"Well, that one cuts," he says, referring to the cattail. "The other is more blunt but can cut as well." I store the information in my head and go upstairs.

"I hope you have batteries behind the counter," I tell Pinocchio, "because I am not going back down those stairs in these boots."

"Sure," he says and rings up my order.

I just make it across the street to my nail appointment. I pay for everything up front so as not to do damage afterward. I even buy some lotion and stuff cash in three mini-envelopes: one each for the manicurist, hair washer, and my stylist, who, on my last visit, gave me the "look" that is getting me a lot of attention in the modeling world. Lena is ready, and I know I want "Lotsa Latte." After four turns under the nail dryer, I'm ready for my hair.

"Come on over, sweetheart. How are you?" My stylist gives me a great cut. "All finished."

"Can you please put some sticky shit in it so it looks good when I bust in on her with the goods?"

"Sure," he responds, rubbing some nice herbal stuff into my locks. Everyone but the receptionist is gone. I pull on my leather jacket, hike my bag over my shoulder, carry out the well-wrapped sex toys, and jump into a cab.

A few minutes later I walk into our loft. Daddy's sitting in the big leather chair. Her mouth drops open. "When did you put those boots on?"

"When you were napping."

"I didn't take a nap," she says indignantly. "I got right up and went grocery shopping."

"So where's dinner?"

"It's almost ready."

"If you weren't sleeping when I left, how come you didn't know I put on the boots?" I challenge as I take off my denim shirt.

"Wait," she says, "get the camera." She takes a shot of me in my jacket. "Straddle the chair." She takes another shot. "Take off the jacket and rest your arms on the back of the chair." Snap again. "Get over here." She shoves here tongue down my throat. Oh, God.

"What's the plan?" I ask.

"We're going to eat dinner, and while you clean up I'm going to strap it on and then we'll watch *The Matrix*. After that I'm going to redden your ass with the crop and then fuck the shit out of you, pump my cock into every hole in your body."

"Sounds good to me." I set the table while she serves.

I adjust myself on the couch and she slides next to me. I finger her cock in anticipation. "How long is the fucking movie?" It's something she's wanted me to see since we met, her favorite and, she thinks, something I'll dig because of my conspiracy-theory/working-for-The-Man ideology. So we watch. I admit that it's interesting, but nothing more. I present her with a collectable Trinity/Carrie Anne Moss action figure I've been saving for this moment. She's very pleased. We snuggle and she narrates. I'm bleary-eyed from the fancy lager I bought for dinner and almost fall asleep. Finally, it's over.

We retire to our bedroom and roll on the bed. "Take off your jeans, but keep the boots on."

"They won't go over."

"Then take the pants off and put the boots back on!" she commands. I comply. I've deliberately worn my plain white cotton Jockey "schoolgirl" underpants. She takes the riding crop and runs it across my body, riding it over every inch of my flesh until it slips beneath the elastic of my underpants. She rubs my bush with the crop; I'm breathing heavily. I'm scared and excited at the same time—we've been working up to this. Me, androgynous and vanilla a few months ago, now high femme and kinky. What a change...

"Stand up."

I act like I don't hear her.

"I said, stand up."

I stand.

"Take off the panties and bend over."

"Make me." Something a friend told me he always tells tops.

"Do it now or you'll just get hurt worse—payback's a bitch."

So I do it. I pull the whites down around my ankles and stay bent. Daddy caresses my ass with the crop. And then a whale. And then another. And another. They start landing harder, with less time in between. I'm pretty good at this game; I'm tough as nails, I've been told, by my daddy. After about 15 minutes, my ass is red and burning with welts, but I haven't blinked. "Shit, you don't fucking budge. Lie down."

I do and spread my legs—wide, ready, my boots teetering on the edge of the bed. She pulls down her shorts and slathers her cock with lube, spits into her hands and moistens my cunt. She guides her cock into me while I pull her closer, and she grabs my legs to complete insertion. Then she goes after it, thrusting full force, huffing and puffing while I moan and groan, yell and scream. "Don't come without asking Daddy," she says, just as I'm clearly on the verge. I manage to hold back for a few minutes.

"Can I come now, Daddy?"

"Not yet." She's pumping me so hard I'm ready to explode.

"Please, now?"

"OK." We're rocking the bed. Hard.

"Again, please?"

"Yes. God, I love feeling you first close around my cock and then push me out."

I can barely breathe; I'm hyperventilating. A minute later: "Again?"

"Yes, if you say 'please.'"

And then I just keep coming. That's my secret; I can come more times than any woman can continue to fuck me. "Can I please have a drink of water?" She hands me the cup on the nightstand, then pulls out. Exhausted, she lies next to me and probes my cunt with her large, wonderful fingers. "Oh, yes," I whisper quietly, as she slides first one, then two fingers inside me and makes me come several more times. Then we're both spent. It's time to go to bed. "What's the vibrator for?" I'm stumped.

"For me, tomorrow."

Shit, she's taken me up on my offer to explore a bit, overstep the butch party line and her own fears. I don't say anything, just kiss her good night, and we arrange ourselves as we do every night: me facing the bathroom with her behind me, and as soon as I get adjusted, her arm rests across my waist.

The next morning I bring her breakfast in bed. We fuck around a little. My ass is no longer red and the welts have gone away, so she orders me to lean against the window and whales on me until I ask her to stop and fuck me. Then we watch another movie, with the same theme. "Why don't you buy my political shit, eat it up, if you like this stuff so much?" I inquire. She laughs. We part, her to read for school in the bedroom and me to work on my manuscript that will change the world. "Wait," I say, "you've got to call your law school buddies to invite them over tonight, but I want to be sucking your cock while you phone them."

"I can't," she protests. "I can't do it straight."

"C'mon," I beg. "It gets me off, the public exposure aspect."

"OK, but I'm not strapping it on, just putting it in my shorts. And *no* noise."

"Agreed." She makes the call while I give her head. Not one of her fucking friends answers. I'm deep-throating, eating her cock alive but not getting off. She leaves messages all over town. Fuck this! I pull the cock out of her shorts, rip open her boxers, and dive into her pussy. She's totally shocked. I just eat. She's still recovering from my aggressiveness, the audacity of the act, shredding her shorts in my lust. She loves me for it, but it also befuddles her and stymies her Italian butch instincts. After she comes, we go about our respective work. I put on music. "Keep it low," she admonishes from the bedroom.

I change the tape a couple of times until Annie Lennox comes on. "Sweetheart...." And I hear her in the other room. "Is it too loud?"

"No, I like it. Come in here so we can make out."

"OK, just a minute, I've got to save this essay on disk." I take my time, spell-check a full-length essay on capitalism, religion, and television. This takes a while, and then I have to turn Annie over. I take off my flannel shirt to reveal the black silk slip underneath and sneak up behind her on the bed and lick her bare ass.

"Hey, I didn't mean make out with my ass!"

"Of course I came to make out with you. I just wanted to lick your ass, seeing how I destroyed your shorts so you have nothing to wear on the bottom." We kiss passionately, bite lips, and gnash teeth. "You could rub your clit on my leg and come."

"Move over so I don't fall off the bed." And we talk while I move on her thigh.

"How's your ass?"

"Still red and bumpy," I tell her. "You did a good job. I'll remember it at work tomorrow when I have to stand up to make phone calls."

"You don't fucking budge. What is it with you?"

"You know, I'm a tough girl, hard as nails, remember?"

"Yeah, we're both tough and hard. That's the deal, I know."

"But," I say, a wry smile creeping across my face even while I'm starting to get wet, my breathing labored, "I know that in the back of your mind you're thinking about what will break me, what you can do to break through, just for a minute, maybe even just a second."

She smiles back. "I just want to try to pinpoint your fears and help you through, let you cry in my arms, comfort you."

"I know. But I've already given it away. You know what my real fears are. You're just working on a plan to tap into them."

"Come right now and go back to work."

"I need another minute, 45 seconds if you push your leg higher up."

"I bet I can shave off 20 to 25 seconds," she counters, and she brings her knee to my cunt and I ride for a few seconds until I do indeed come.

Yeah, I'm a tough girl all right. Hard as nails. But this woman—gentle and wise, hard and rough—my daddy, has shown me new ways of being, both sexually and otherwise. Out in the world I'm an aggressive bitch, a pushy broad, an uppity woman, but here in bed with my butch, I become submissive, soft, and that turns me on! This bottoming thing…it's not half bad: I trust my top daddy to find my deep insides.

# Times Square

MICKY SMALL

Magic happens in Times Square. The energy. The pulse. The center of the city. And the world.

Chris and I had been dating for almost a month. She was the badass stud I'd always yearned for. A punk rock drummer, a writer, and a poet. She entranced me from the moment I laid eyes on her. Shoulder-length dark hair with chunky blond streaks. Slightly taller than me, with strong muscular arms and a sexy, well-toned build. A great smile that transforms into a delicious smirk. Dressed up for work, wearing pants and a suit jacket, she could appear femme, but she was definitely butch. I'm a super femme—long blazing raspberry hair, and a body of well-sculpted hourglass curves that makes both girls and boys turn their heads. Ruby red lips complete the picture. Our combination intoxicated me.

Though she tells me I showed no visible signs of interest that first night, I was convinced the whole world could see my body trembling. My legs felt like jelly; I was amazed I could even stand. As we hugged goodbye near the subway entrance, our bodies touching for the first time, I longed for her to pull me close and kiss me. I wanted her to throw me against the concrete wall, to fuck me like crazy. But my "femme manifesto" forced me to keep those thoughts to myself. Until the next time.

Our next date was at Stingy Lulu's, a bar in the East Village where Chris's friend Toni bartended. After a couple of drinks, I excused myself to use the bathroom. Toni glanced over at Chris and said, "So, do you wanna date her?"

"Nah, I wanna *fuck* her," Chris casually replied, finishing off her beer.

After carefully touching up my makeup and trying to keep myself from jumping Chris at the bar, I nonchalantly headed back to my seat, almost tripping down the stairs. I inched myself closer, trying to hint at what I wanted. She leaned over, looked deep into my eyes, and whispered, "Would it be presumptuous of me to kiss you?" I quickly responded by leaning into her, my beating heart ready to explode. Our lips met, and at that moment I knew spontaneous combustion was physically possible. That instant chemistry led us to her place that night and kept us indoors for the next few weeks. Marathon sexcapades filled our time together, both of us amazed we had met our sexual equal. We found ourselves playfully pinching each other to make sure the other was real.

After three weeks of nonstop sex, we decided to venture out in public together. But whenever we tried to leave the house, one of us would grab the other and we'd end up back in bed. Or on the floor. Or on the stairs. Or in the shower.

My best friend, Jen, was performing off-Broadway, and we figured we could last at least that long in public. That night we spent about an hour having drinks at an Irish pub, the Rolling Stones playing in the background. The sexual tension between us was unmistakable, but Chris was a perfect gentleman and kept herself under control. I, on the other hand, was climbing up the walls, needing release.

Jen bade us farewell and headed off to the theater to warm up. As Chris polished off her drink, she offhandedly commented that she wished there were a cheap motel close by.

With a slight smirk, I pulled my keys out of my bag. "How about making a visit to my office?"

Chris glanced at me with a familiar glow in her eyes. I was definitely going to be ravished soon. Before I knew it, the check was paid and we were walking out the door arm in arm toward the middle of Times Square. As we approached the crosswalk, Chris grabbed me and kissed me deeply. The surge of energy that coursed down my spine could have powered the nearby streetlights for a year. I felt like the whole world was watching. In my mind I compared us to the infamous wartime picture of the sailor kissing his woman in the middle of Times Square. The flood of wetness between my legs drove me wild. I was delirious with need.

We walked quickly toward my office, a tall skyscraper right on Broadway. The neon lights were shining brightly, billboards were flashing, and street vendors were selling their goods. The smell of honey-roasted peanuts filled the air.

I hoped the front door was open this late. A rush of nervousness pulsed throughout my body. What if the security guard could tell why we were there?

I took a deep breath, nervously turned the door handle as beads of sweat wet my palms. When the door opened easily, I waltzed into the marbled lobby with a radiant smile, acting like being there that late on a weeknight was the most natural thing in the world. I signed in, and Chris followed me into the elevator. When the door closed, she grabbed my hair, pulled my head back, and kissed me deeply. Her hot breath on my exposed neck sent a wave of electricity straight to my pussy. My knees started to give out as the door opened.

Walking down the dark hallway toward my office, passion building, I grew hyper-aware of familiar sights and sounds. The door seemed a million miles away, even though it was only a brief walk from the elevator. Our footsteps echoed loudly throughout the hallway. As my office door finally appeared, my hands fumbled with the keys I was so used to handling. Chris pushed her body into mine, almost thrusting me into the door. I could barely keep myself focused. The mix of the fear of discovery and unbridled lust was over-whelming. As soon as the door opened, Chris shoved me inside. Looking around, she checked out the surroundings, exploring the items I used everyday. The bare-bones office housed three employees. Stacks of recycled paper, random supplies, and refurbished office machines filled the cramped space. Makeshift bookshelves that seemed like they would collapse from so many years of overuse lined the walls. The space was so tight that two desks could barely fit side by side. Personal space was at a minimum. The room seemed to close in on me as our longing filled it.

"So this is where your pretty little ass sits all day." Chris motioned for me to sit. She stood beside me, whispering in my ear. "I think it's time to christen this office."

She yanked my short black skirt down past my ankles. The sudden exposure drove me crazy. Then she pulled down my tights and knelt before me, her passion mounting and mixing with mine. The room was so hot I could barely breathe. Then she planted her mouth on the inside of my thigh and began to suck. My back arched, wanting to feel her surround me. She circled my thigh, getting closer and closer to my aching pussy.

Chris moved in closer, kissing me deeply then darting for my open, wet pussy. Her tongue made one long lap across my throbbing lips and started the upward climb toward an impending release. Her mouth lapped, then sucked, then pulled me in closer to her. Darting inside, she swirled her tongue in and out, pulling my juices toward her with the strength of a magnet. She drew me in, and I lost all control. Moaning and writhing, I could not have her close enough. She grabbed my nipple with her teeth and bit gently. I straightened my legs, feeling the full release nearing. She circled faster and faster with her tongue, moving in and out, licking my clit, then sucking, pulling me in closer and closer, feeling me move beneath her touch. I felt her getting hotter and wetter, knowing we could be caught any minute. I climbed higher and could no longer hold on. I exploded, my body convulsing in waves of pleasure, floating high above myself as she kissed me one final time.

She lifted me out of the chair, steadying me. I straightened up and could smell our passion everywhere. Sitting in my chair would never be the same again.

I followed her outside. The cleaning woman came down the hallway asking to be let into the office. She had forgotten her key. I shuddered inside knowing she could have barged in on us. But I simply smiled and let her in. Chris stood behind me, a smug smile across her lips.

Chris and I walked out of the building arm in arm and disappeared into the center of Times Square.

# The Invisible Line
## LA MOONEY

Dykes never take me seriously anymore. When I was bald, stomping around in hard leather boots and a wallet chain, girls believed I was capable of casual sex. I'd walk past you, and I knew by that invasive look at my crotch that you weren't interested in my thoughts on the politically correct topic of the day over coffee. No, that look told me you were thinking about pushing my body up against a wall and force-feeding me your hand. Taking me in a bathroom, with nothing exchanged but smirks over the grunts of heavy public fucking. I was a baby dyke then, and the only heat I ever experienced after those sidewalk exchanges was the warmth rushing over my cheeks. But almost no one gives me that look now. Now that I'm no longer afraid to return your looks with more than an embarrassed smile.

Most days you'll pass me on the sidewalk and think I look like your neighbor child's kindergarten teacher. And except for those of us who get hot for teacher, there's not a huge market in dykedom for the good-girl teacher look. I have the most unassuming features, when cradled by "I work 13-hour days and don't have the time" hair. I'm sure you know the type. We wait at bus stops together, and you look at me, wondering what my life with the hubby and the front yard looks like. You return my glances with the disdain you've saved for those who see you as their voyeuristic target. My days are full, and even though I'd be in high-femme armor 24/7 if I had the energy, I save that ritualized dressing up for nights I know it'll be appreciated.

It had been a while since I'd spent the time to line up the seam of a thigh-high stocking along the back of my calf. But when I got the call from Alex, saying she was back in town, I knew I needed a night where I felt queer as much as she needed to see a familiar face.

After all of our moves chasing girls across the country and back, we've always managed to wind up in the same city when a freshly broken heart needed a heavy shot of bourbon and good company. And now, more than ever, I needed to remember what it felt like to be looked at with lust, even if that look came from the eyes of a person the dyke code of honor has expressly labeled off-limits. We've each got one person in our lives who, were it not for some overcomplicated relationship with a shared acquaintance, would be in our beds every night of the week, and Alex was mine.

We all met at a job raising money on the phone. When you were resting after a rough day of work and got that call with the unrecognizable caller ID at 8:50 P.M., I was the one on the other end of the line pushing you against the wall to agree to a $25 pledge card you'd probably never return.

That was two years ago. My ex had just followed me back from California, after 11 torturous months of breaking up. I was the first to get a house, and since I'm never one to leave anyone to couch-skipping, I let Alex and Erica move in, in what probably passes as my greatest moment of poor judgment.

I was thinking about Erica as I was deciding on something I could wear to work and feel sexy enough in for a night out after four hours of sitting in an overheated basement. Alex and I were back at the phone job again. The only thing that had changed was that Erica was now gone. My own relationship with Erica had finally exhausted itself, and the enduring friendship between Erica and Alex had dissipated, leaving only the constant reminder that Alex was Erica's friend first, and I would be crossing some invisible line if I were to ever feel Alex's hands inside my body.

I decided on the standard femme uniform. I glanced over at the bed, and my cat had already found her way onto the black skirt that I had decided to squeeze myself into for my official resurfacing. It's always humorous to me how I'll plan my evening around my underwear selection. I'll spend five hours walking around with red satin floss between my fleshy ass cheeks when I know no one is likely to see it, just in case. Tonight was no different. It would be inconceivable to me to be caught with my pants down in a pair of cotton panties, and even if I was only going out with Alex, I was determined to exude "fuck me" with each sway of my recently neglected lower body.

The game was on from the moment I lowered myself into the stagnant air of the basement for work. Four hours of sideways glances and smiles with ulterior motives, coupled with the constant rejection from faceless voices on the other end of the line had us both ready to flee the minute the clock's small hand reached 9.

I knew Alex appreciated the effort behind my costume that evening. Her gait slowed as she put out her arm to support my slow, drawn-out sway in large barstool heels. I was wearing the kind of shoes that are meant for sitting at the bar, commanding attention, not walking at a rapid clip.

We ended up at Larry's Blues Bar, our old haunt in Pioneer Square. We took our place at the bar, sandwiched between frat boys and their Barbie-doll dates and rough men who wouldn't be thrilled about a woman in a short skirt draped casually off the arm of a girl who was more butch than they'd ever be. Neither of us had seen the bartender in years, but she remembered us fondly and kept drinks sliding over the counter all night. I'm not exactly sure who paid for them, but the only place Alex's money found itself that evening was in the tip jar.

After three months of vacant looks from butches on the sidewalk, I was thrown into a trance each time Alex pushed her hand between my thighs. She'd grab my legs and prop them over her own bulky thighs, teasing my inability to wear a pair of sensible shoes within a 20-block radius of black boots and 501s. If these actions had come from anyone else, I could have counted on my plans for that evening. But Alex was someone I'd known for years. We touched each other with the common playfulness shared between sisters.

She jokingly told me about the terrible sex she'd had with the last girl before she got back in town. Apparently, the little girl wasn't too fond of the spike jutting out of her labia or her predilection for "unnatural sex." I remember teasing her about the fact that she hadn't yet seen my newest holes (little pink rhinestones hidden under my clothes) before sashaying off to the bathroom as gracefully as possible with an uncountable number of drinks down me.

Before I got the stall door locked, it was pulled from my hands. "Shhh." Alex fumbled with the door and joined me in quiet disbelief, as she realized we were crammed together in a small stall with no locking door. "You know I'm not one to let you walk away with an invite like that hanging in the air."

I propped myself up on the back of the toilet, resting the hard edge of my tall heels against the lid of the toilet bowl. She shoved her thick hands up the front of my shirt, with all the grace of a small child opening a package they'd been waiting for. The door flung open just as Alex had discovered the first piercing.

"Damn it. You have such shitty planning. Why couldn't you pick the locking one?

"I wasn't expecting company. You're a crafty boi—you'll figure something out." A seductive smile graced my lips and she chastised me for being a smart-ass while in such a compromising position, as she jammed her foot underneath the door and resumed her work on my tit.

I sometimes prefer a more seductive way of removing my clothes, but the urgency with which she shoved my pile of shirts and my bra out of her way coaxed my hips back and forth with expectation.

Alex only politely fondled the barbells in my nipples for a moment, and then our history together began to get me into trouble.

"Your favorite part about getting these was probably the searing sting of the needles themselves." I watched her rotate the gems toward the walls until I could see the swirls of taut skin around my nipples. She released her thumbs and flicked her index fingers to create one last jolt before the barbells spun themselves back around.

I could smell the scent of Maker's Mark on her breath as she lowered her mouth onto one of my throbbing nipples. I felt her neck tense under my fingers as the door to the bathroom opened.

"Don't stop, baby." Her eyes looked up to greet mine, without removing her mouth, as she waited for instruction. "Just don't let go of the door." I had never mouthed commands so quietly in the middle of getting fucked, and the challenge only turned my excitement up a notch.

I bit my lower lip to prevent any sounds from escaping as Alex clamped her mouth down on my chest. My hands were tightly gripping her short hair, and all we could hear was the faint sounds of our breathing over the trickle of pee in the next stall.

We heard her leave without incident, and Alex celebrated that triumph by lifting up my ass and sliding my skirt over my hips. At this point I had never been more pleased with my fondness for wearing pretty panties. I felt my body shiver as it encountered the coldness of the porcelain. With my cunt now exposed to the cold air, I could feel how wet the satin had become, just as Alex began to negotiate her way past my underwear.

That seductive smirk changed owners as Alex pushed her hard fingers into me. I caught her smile before my head flew back into the wall. Alex reached up and slid her hand between the brick wall and my now-throbbing head.

With each thrust of her hand into me, it became more and more difficult to resist the spontaneous moans escaping my mouth. Alex pushed her body into me, and I felt the denim covering her thigh grazing my cunt lips. I laughed, knowing that when she left, she'd have me smeared down the front of her pants. Her hand was now completely inside me. I felt like a glove over her, only barely resting on the back of the toilet.

With her hand manipulating me from the inside and her body firmly shoved against mine, she reached down, and I felt our lips together for the first time. Time stood still then.

"What the hell are you doing? Get out!"

Alex had let go of the door, and I jerked my head up to see one of the young Barbie-doll patrons staring at us through the door.

"Use the other stall." Alex didn't take her eyes off me, as she pulled the door from Barbie's hands and closed it with her foot.

With her hand still inside me, she pinched and pulled my clit with her other hand. I looked down to see her hand buried inside me as I used my hands to pull her head back to my face.

"Use the other fucking bathroom. I swear if you don't leave, I'm gonna tell the bartender."

I slid my fingers through her hair and wrapped my lips around her tongue. I felt her knees buckle with the realization of what my lips really liked to do.

"This is a girls' bathroom. That means men aren't allowed in here."

"I'd better go, baby." Alex gently pushed off me, and I felt cold air rush over me where her hand had been just seconds before. She waited for me to pull my clothes on before kissing me gently on the lips and opening the door.

I heard a small squeak from Barbie, as she realized that there were no men in the bathroom stall. I saw Alex grab her own fleshy tits and with a smile on her face reply, "I'm sorry. I don't generally use the men's rest room. After all, it *is* the men's rest room, and girls aren't allowed."

Barbie escaped her embarrassment by entering the other stall, as it became free. I finished up and went out to the sink, only to encounter a woman who appeared to be in her 50s making eye contact with me in the mirror.

"Did you finish, sweetie? That friend of yours was cute." As I looked at her, it was obvious that she was family and that she'd had her own flashback as Alex and I surfaced from the stall.

"I'm sorry if I inconvenienced you at all," I replied. My face became flushed as I had a flashback of my own. I remembered my grandmother walking in on me while I was making out for the first time ever.

"Not at all. You don't worry about that little tart. She's just jealous because her boyfriend doesn't get that hot for her." She pulled out a tube of lipstick from her purse and handed it to me. "For a little touch-up. You don't want to look like you just had sex in the bathroom!"

We smiled at each other, then returned to the bar.

Alex had hailed a cab and had my coat waiting for me at the door. I glanced up and saw Barbie exit the bathroom. I blew her a little kiss and slid my arm around Alex as we strolled out the door.

# Family Gathering

JEAN ROBERTA

"Mom and Dad, this is my friend Julie," I smile, trying to sound gracious. I hate having to call her my friend, but I can't think of a more accurate word that would make sense to them.

Julie smiles too hard, trying to charm them. They can see that she is short, stocky, and native-looking. I'm hoping they can't see that she's a dyke who dropped—or was pushed—out of high school at age 16. She is now 20 to my 30, which would seem much too young to them. How little they know. I hope they won't ask her any questions.

I can hardly stand living in my own skin. I've brought my 4-year-old daughter to my parents' house for them to baby-sit. I know I'm taking them for granted, and their raised eyebrows show me that they wonder why I'm so eager to go out with this unusual new friend. I can't tell them that I met her in the gay bar a week ago when I went there for the first time. I'm not in the habit of lying to my parents or anyone else, but I knew before I seized my courage in both hands to enter that place alone that my coming-out process would require the skills of a secret agent.

Julie and I smile our way out the door. I slide into the passenger seat of her car as she smoothly starts the ignition. This gesture, like everything else she does, looks sexy to me. I know she could turn me on as easily as she can turn on a motor: *Vrooom*. As she would say, it would be a piece of cake.

Our relationship doesn't make much sense, even to me, although I dreamed about such things all through my short and nasty marriage to a drunk, through the two years when I lived with my baby in the smallest bedroom of my parents' house, and then through the months since I moved into the co-op for low-income single parents and lucked into a temporary teaching job at the Indian college. Last week I decided to stop dreaming and go looking for real live lesbians. So now the one who noticed me and struck up a conversation is taking me out on a date.

"Your parents have a lot of books, eh?" she asks, making conversation. Sometimes she seems so childish to me.

"They've both taught at universities," I tell her. "Most faculty families have a lot of books."

This amuses her. "I bet you have a fuckin' library in your apartment." She laughs. For a split-second I'm tempted to fight back. I could call her an ignorant piece of trash in words she has never heard before. But I quickly control my temper. "Yep," I answer calmly.

We're going to see *On Golden Pond,* starring Katherine Hepburn and Jane Fonda. I'm not sure why Julie invited me to this movie. It's supposed to be about elderly parents and their grown daughter, not an obvious choice for a lesbian date. She probably thought it would be "philosophical" enough to impress me.

She pays for us both, and I don't insult her butchness by arguing, even though I know she's living on unemployment insurance. I make a note to myself to remember this date: March 1, 1982. I have a feeling that my life will be different from today forward.

Julie rests an arm on the back of my seat, then clutches my shoulder and pulls me close to her. She radiates heat, and I feel like purring. None of this has any connection to the family melodrama on the screen—not that I can see, anyway.

I like the clean smell of Julie's short black hair. I know I look slim and white compared to her, but we could be distant cousins. I once saw a family photo of my grandfather's grandmother, a Mohawk woman with two long black braids. Julie doesn't know any of her biological relatives because she was taken from them and placed with a white foster family when she was a baby. That happened a lot here on the Canadian prairies in the 1960s.

Julie's warm fingers graze the back of my head, combing my fine brown shoulder-length hair. She doesn't seem to care who might be watching, so neither do I. I could just melt. I'm glad that my being a teacher doesn't scare her. I wonder if she'll ever be my student. I can't tell how she's reacting to the movie, but I can feel her eagerness to touch me. I feel smug because she's here with me instead of with her ex-girlfriend who wants her back. They were together in the bar when I met them. I'm not even sure I believe Julie's claim that they broke up some time ago, and my common sense tells me not to get too involved. But my hungry pussy is telling me something else.

As the credits roll, we wait until the theater is almost empty before we stand up. "We'd better go pick up your kid," Julie reminds me. I'm grateful and anxious at the same time; I can't afford to push my parents' patience too far, especially if I'm in the starting phase of a long-term relationship. But why is Julie so willing to pick up my little chaperone?

When we go back my parents' house, my daughter is sleepy and resentful. I explain to my parents that I need to get her home to bed as soon as possible. They seem to approve of my responsible attitude, and they don't demand a critique of the movie.

When we approach the co-op, I invite Julie to come in for a while. I carry my dozing child along a slippery path in the half-melted snow. The sound of Julie's boots crunching beside us is as comforting as the sparkle of moonlight on ice and windows. This village of broken dreams, of sad women and confused children, looks enchanted at this hour.

We enter my modest apartment, and I wonder if she thinks I'm a slut, or if she thinks I'm trying to pressure her into the role of a dyke husband and stepfather. I only want to feel her arms around me and her warm mouth on mine. I don't know how to tell her this.

"I'll just put Emma to bed," I tell her, "and I'll be right back." In the meantime, Julie can browse through my fuckin' library. It wouldn't hurt her to do some reading.

Emma doesn't want to sleep in her bed with a stranger in our place. "Mom, I need a drink of water. Come and sleep with me." I know now why I shouldn't have done this. I bring her a glass of water and tell her to go to sleep. "I'll have nightmares," she whines. "Mom, why can't you come sleep with me? Why can't that man or lady go home?" I lose my temper and tell her she's old enough to sleep alone. Her voice rises in a wail. I'm terrified that Julie will be so turned off by my lack of parental control that she will leave.

When I finally emerge from Emma's bedroom, Julie laughs aloud. "Did you get your kid to sleep?" she smirks. I feel myself blushing. I must be too hungry, too easy to read, too awkward at all of this.

"Kids," Julie laughs, her gaze penetrating my eyes. "You gotta love 'em. Mine does that, too." She has told me about her own girl toddler, conceived when Julie was passed out drunk at a party. Julie's Catholic foster parents are raising her, having rescued her from Julie's attempt to give her up for adoption. I realize that Julie and I have one thing in common: a ton of baggage, some visible and some harder to see. But her past, unlike mine, was a lesbian adolescence crowded with women; men only screwed her when she wasn't conscious enough to stop them.

She wraps her arms around me as though she's been doing this forever. She seems to be wearing men's cologne, and its breezy smell mixes with her sweat. Her full lips find mine. Oh, my goddess, her tongue pushes in between my teeth and makes itself at home in my mouth. I don't think I can remain standing for much longer.

"Where's your bed, babe?" she chuckles into my hair. She, who seems so savvy, hasn't found it.

"The chesterfield pulls out," I explain, ashamed of the tackiness of sleeping in my front room every night. The picture window that extends from there into my kitchen is almost 12 feet wide, and there is a high-rise apartment building across the street. Traffic sounds waft in without a pause from the major intersection outside. My curtains seem like thin protection for our privacy.

"Pull it out, honey," she orders softly but with authority. If she said, "On your knees, bitch," would I obey? Probably. But I won't go any farther down this imaginary road. I focus on the task at hand.

My sofa is soon transformed into a lumpy double bed, big enough for my guest and me. No one but me and my daughter has ever been in it. Julie unbuttons my shirt, exposing my skin to her sight. I shiver, even though my apartment is always overheated. "How did you do it with your last girl-friend?" she asks, making me squirm. "What do you like?"

I feel unbearably stupid. "I don't know," I squeak, my voice sounding young and nasal in my own ears. "I've never done it with a woman before."

The grin of a proud and lecherous bridegroom spreads across Julie's face. I could faint from relief. I'm offering her something I can only offer once, and she appreciates the gift. I feel like a shining snow maiden, blessed by moonlight. "Oh, I'm gonna love this, baby," she brags. "I'll show you what you don't know."

I want her to make me hers, even though I don't really believe this is possible. I want to save her from her life, and I want her to save me from mine. I know none of my desires are politically correct or psychologically trendy. I feel like the reckless heroine of a 1950s pulp novel about the doomed and the damned, poised on the edge of a cliff. I doubt whether she can handle my weight, but I trust her to catch me when I jump.

I'm sitting on the edge of my bed. I pull off my shirt and bra and toss them onto the floor. Julie lowers her mouth to one of my hard nipples as she kneels between my legs. Every familiar thing in the room looks different now. "Ohhh," I moan as she sucks, holding me in place. She comes up for air, smirking possessively.

"I see goose bumps," she teases.

"You made them," I sigh. In some sense, though, I am making her. I can almost see her rising like bread dough, growing into the dyke who can change me into something new. Watching her, I can catch that spirit.

She sucks my other nipple, pulling and nibbling it like a spoiled child, overdue for weaning. I'm tingling from head to foot. I tug on her tartan shirt, and she obligingly takes it off. She unhooks her bra, revealing girlish breasts that don't go with the wolfish image she tries to project. I'm moved almost to tears by the evidence that she's actually a girl.

She stands up to take her jeans off, and she's all business. Her tight panties follow, and she steps out of her clothes as though she'll never need them again. I let her unbuckle my belt and unzip my pants. I know instantly she'd rather have slipped her hands up my legs under a flowing skirt. Next time I'll dress to please her, I think.

She explores my flat stomach with her hands, running them over the straight scar that runs like the shiny track of a snail between my navel and the edge of my curly brown bush. "Did you have an operation?" she mumbles.

"I had Emma by Cesarean," I explain, wanting her to know that I'm not ashamed or touchy: I wear my mother scar with pride. I was one of the last mothers to be cut vertically, so I'm wearing a trademark of classic obstetrical surgery. I hope it doesn't turn her off to see I've been changed by others in ways she could never change me. Baggage.

Her instincts are sound, and she kisses down the scar. In a classic gesture, she spreads my legs, releasing my warmth, my smell into the air. Before I expect it, she's entering me with a sly, cunning finger. It makes room for its neighbor, the finger that signals an insult. I'm getting fucked, for better or worse. I'm so wet I'll probably leave a puddle on the bedspread.

She's working up a steady, demanding rhythm as she watches me. I'm so moved I'm afraid I'll go into convulsions. But she wants me to lose control, so I cautiously let out a groan.

We are like ice and molten lava: She watches coolly as her fingers come to know me inside, and I respond with the frenzy of one who has been damming it up for 15 years. This is what I never got from my teenage girlfriends, never gave to them. This magic is what white women were burned to death for knowing, and it's part of the reason why Julie's ancestors and mine were labeled "savages," converted or destroyed. Cultures, like people, carry baggage.

She prods and tickles and strokes me inside. "Do you like that, honey?" she purrs, knowing the answer. Her words are the last straw, as they tickle my ears and my mind in sync with her fingers. My clit can't hold out, and I come and come, squeezing her fingers like a hearty dyke shaking hands. My moan almost rises to a wail or a howl, the opening bar of a coyote serenade. "Sshh," whispers Julie, flattered and alarmed. It's too late.

"Mom!" calls my kid. "I'm scared!"

I gather my breath. "It's all right, honey," I call back. "Go back to sleep."

The baby demon is enraged. "Mom!" she shrieks. "I'm scared! I heard noises!" Julie is rolling around with laughter, watching my desperation.

"Damn!" I whisper. "I have to go." As I stand up, Julie swats my ass. In the absence of a listening child, she would probably give me a resounding slap that would make my cheeks quiver.

I try to soothe my child back into a trusting sleep. She's no fool, and she knows something interesting is going on behind her back. "Mom, why can't your friend go home?" she demands.

"Grown-ups can stay up later than kids," I remind her, pulling rank. "You have to go to sleep."

"I heard noises," she complains. "I think a burglar is in our house. Or some kind of animal that made a noise like *uh-ahh-oohhh!* People don't talk like that, Mom," she lectures me.

"There's no animal here," I tell her, though I'm not convinced. "Think about nice things, and you'll have nice dreams."

Julie still looks amused when I come back to her. "You'll have trouble having a relationship with anyone," she predicts with relish. "Your kid is gonna drive them away if you don't stop her from demanding your attention all the time." My naked guest seems to like seeing me trapped and grateful to the one dyke who can put up with my child. I feel as if I'm cheating on a spouse, but I'm not sure which of them it is.

I can't stand her condescension, and I need some control over someone. I hold her, enjoying her solid flesh. I kiss her and enter her mouth as she jerks in surprise. I push her down on the bed and lazily grasp one of her breasts, squeezing it into a rounder shape. She moves uneasily.

I'm lying on her without guilt, knowing she can carry me. As if anticipating what I will do, she grabs and offers me her other breast. "You need this more than I do," she jokes, as though she still has milk to offer. I descend on her nipple and suck it like an addict getting a needed fix.

I run my hands over the bulge of her midriff, a roll of warm fat in a place where my skin barely covers my ribs. Her body is a foreign country, and I want to discover every hill and bluff and little ravine.

Her slit seems to be throwing off heat, like a crack in the earth that leads to the thermal source of all life. I follow the heat and the scent to a coarse black thicket of hair and part it like a curious animal. She moans before I can even touch her inside, but she squeezes her legs shut and grabs my trespassing hand. "You're not supposed to do that, honey," she explains, reciting the rules of the sorority.

"Why not?" I ask in as steely a voice as possible. "You did it to me." I have a feeling that I'll someday accuse her of this in public, and there will be no turning back for either of us.

"You know," she mutters in embarrassment. "You're the woman. I'm bringing you out."

"That's stupid," I retort. I remember how my kid reacts to adult impatience with her fears, and I decide to soften my tone. "Look, I'll never tell anyone," I assure her. "It's none of their business anyway. It doesn't matter. I've waited a long time for this. Don't you want me?"

She won't answer this question in words, but she's stopped fighting me and her thighs spread apart slightly. Nose first I approach her heat, like a bloodhound. I carefully open her lower lips, afraid any sudden movement will make her change her mind. I stretch out an experimental tongue and begin licking pussy for the first time. I'm delighted to note that I don't have to overcome any revulsion to the smell or the taste.

Julie rolls like the ocean, or like something that has always lived in its rhythm. She is shamelessly wet and craving more, soaking my mouth and chin and my fingers. She spreads her legs as wide as possible, as if to get as much attention as I can give her. I had no idea I could inspire this kind of response, and I'm almost afraid that I can't bring this symphony to the kind of climax the audience is expecting.

Julie is on a roll, and I can only hang on and wait. Before long, she jackknifes into a fetal position, trapping one of my hands between her big thighs. She gasps and grunts in a way I have no trouble interpreting. I stroke her gently until she seems to be finished.

We both rearrange ourselves until we're pressed together, breathing in each other's skin and fluids and hair. I feel as if we're both hanging on to avoid drowning. "That was heavenly," I tell her, feeling like a prim schoolmarm who can't bring herself to use earthy words. "It was good," I revise my statement, hoping to strike the right tone so that she'll let me do it again sometime, even if this is against the rules of the sisterhood I now belong to. "I hope you can spend the night."

She rises up in mock-righteousness. "Well, I guess!" she retorts. "I hope you weren't thinking of throwing me out after that. Bitch." She makes it sound sexy. I laugh, imagining Emma's indignant reaction to Julie's presence in my bed when she bounces into it in the morning. I wonder how soon my parents will be informed of all this. Best not to spoil the moment by thinking about it now.

The precious moment is always a hard thing to grasp in memory. At this time, the early morning of March 2, 1982, I can't even imagine how the saga of my first lesbian affair will develop: with a trail of clues showing what Julie did with her ex-girlfriend while I was out, with arguments and reconciliations leading to a threesome in my bed, with Julie's desire to watch me enjoying her male drinking buddies while they enjoy me, and my desire to give her everything she wants for reasons I don't understand.

Later on, the games will turn darker and I will be naively surprised. In that phase, even Julie will seem bewildered by our reactions to each other. Thinking everything of mine belongs to her, Julie will drink up my nest egg from teaching, and I will threaten to report her to the police for stealing it. Her visit to my ex-husband and his new wife, to discuss the possibility of helping them get Emma away from me, will kill some part of my feeling for her. Strangely or not, my body will never stop responding to her open smile, her clean female smell, the sound of her sexy voice.

In the opening act of the opera, I'm holding a luscious

young woman in my arms, and she feels like the embodiment of spring. I think she is all the woman I could ever want. I know now that my life will never be ordinary again. I have no regrets. Now that she is in my life, I look forward to my future. I am certainly living in interesting times.

# Overtime

JULIE LEVIN RUSSO

Like good dykes in search of adventure, Clyde and I set off
on a motorcycle. I wasn't wearing underwear. She was packing. It was Saturday night, and the downtown business district
was deserted, like some post-apocalyptic ghost town—all
clean, immense angles of glass and steel. Entering the atrium
of her building was like crossing into an indoor city: The esca-
lator was dwarfed by marble columns, and it glided us off in a
vast lobby, tastefully vegetated and complete with its own
café and newsstand (now barred up for the night). The only
sign of life was a security guard stationed unobtrusively near
the elevator, which you needed a magnetic ID card to operate
after hours. Clyde pressed me against the wall and sucked on
my bottom lip as we rode up.

Clyde is a techie wage slave at a gigantic bank. I'm an acad-
emy brat raised by doctors. When she unlocked the door to
her office and showed me into a long, featureless bunker over-
grown with a maze of cubicles, I was struck dumb with glee-
ful awe. I really hadn't imagined such efficient, beige geome-
try actually existed outside of sitcoms and Dilbert. I'm sure
that, for her, the glamour had more than worn off, but I felt
like I was walking onto a movie set. Most of the modular walls
were only breast-high, and the lack of privacy was titillating.

I know exactly when I started having fantasies about office
sex. I was visiting family for the holidays, and my aunt let me
stay up to watch TV with her: one of those late-night lawyer

dramas that I was old enough to know most grow-ups would think I was too young to watch. But my aunt was hipper than other grown-ups. I probably had a little crush on her. So I played it cool when one virile suit, working after dark with the new secretary for company, reached to unbutton her blouse, laying her out across his desk in her black lace demi-bra and pushing her skirt up past the tops of her stockings to fuck her. Even at my tender age, I knew this scene was hot, and I can still visualize the breathless, forbidden kisses, the décolleté glowing in the dim light, and most of all the possessive caress-es and submissive writhing that for years were staples of my adolescent masturbation. I am unabashedly un-PC when it comes to fantasy, and I cream at the vision of being hired for my short skirts and virginal naïveté, objectified and manipu-lated on the job, ultimately coerced into sexual servitude by a honcho with the power to fire me. Now, with a willing and appropriately employed partner at my side, I was on a clan-destine mission to make this wet dream a reality.

Clyde showed me her desk, where I know she sits every day imagining me stashed underneath as her covert cocksuck-er. I asked her if she wanted me to wiggle down there now.

"I do, baby," she said, "but we've got an important meet-ing to go to."

We headed for the conference room, just past the obliga-tory coffee maker and copier zone. It was completely filled by a massive burnished-wood table that could probably seat 30, and bordered on two sides by continuous windowpanes. Even as a naive ingenue, I could see no meeting was immi-nent in the darkened room. I stood at the far end and hid my imaginary trepidation by looking out over the city. I'm scared of heights, and from the 28th floor the twinkling lights took on a vertiginous swirl that pulsed right to my cunt. Clyde came up behind me, wrapped her hand around my neck, and pressed my cheek flat on the cool glass. I felt her hard-on against my ass as she slid her other hand up under my skirt. Uh-oh.

"Well, aren't you the little slut, showing up at work with no panties on?" she crooned into my ear. "You think you can come in here every day and tease me, shake that pretty ass around in front of me, and never give me any?" She turned me around, lifted me onto the window ledge with my back leaning on the ether, and kissed me hard. "Now I think it's time for you to suck my cock."

Clyde had warned me that, in her more legitimate experiences working odd hours, she'd noticed that the security guards downstairs kept track of who's in the building and always showed up within 45 minutes to make the rounds. If we got caught, she could lose her job. We were listening with one ear for our anticipated visitors and playing under a thrillingly real-time constraint. It wasn't long before I found myself spread out on my back at the head of the table, with my skirt around my waist and a big butch cock sliding into my pussy.

"You like being my little office slut, don't you?" Oh, did I ever. "I think I'm going to bring you in here every day and make you take my cock during my lunch break. We only have a few more minutes before everyone else comes back, so you'd better hurry up and come for me if you want to keep your job." I rubbed my clit while she plowed me, and I floated right up to the corporate headquarters in the sky.

Afterward, we cleaned up the evidence carefully—making sure to collect the empty packets of lube and rub my face-print off the window—and zoomed off into the night (with a nod to the security guard on our way out). I can enjoy the prurient satisfaction of having another adventure under my belt, but Clyde's the one who gets to sit at the end of the conference table in a meeting and trace the outline of my ass on the polished wood. It's so divine to make a fantasy come true.

# Ungentlemanly Behavior

### Khadijah Caturani

"All right, bitch. Get on your knees and suck my cock like the hungry little slut you are."

I froze.

For the first time in our two years together, these words did absolutely nothing. My cunt didn't twinge, my ridge didn't moisten, my cheeks didn't ruddy, *nothing*. The words "bitch," "slut," "cock," "suck," "fuck," "cunt," "whore," "ram," "ass"—none of them did any more for me than the words "toast," "audit," or "reorganize." Probably even less.

And what's more, the whole mean butch-daddy-top thing wasn't even really working for me anymore. Amanda's sneer, bad posture, wife beater, slicked-back hair, and 10-inch black cock (which she was stroking like it was made of gold) had stopped reading as dangerous, sexy, and subversive, and now were just...same-old, same-old.

But the thought of expressing this to her filled me with the kind of dread otherwise reserved for admitting one's lost virginity to the woman who birthed you. My butch only had a temper when we were in the safe confines of a scene. Otherwise, she had something more like a dark abyss of self-hatred, guilt, and shame. This matter had to be handled delicately.

I crawled my way across the kitchen floor to her, forcing my most cunning and mischievous smile, and placed my face worshipfully below her silicone spear, teasing the inch or two of phantom cock aura between us with my tongue. She groaned and bucked a bit, trying to force that symbol of her identity between my deliciously glossed lips, but I bobbed and weaved in sync, staying just close enough that she could feel my breath but far enough away to drive her mad.

"What are you waiting for, you twisted hussy? Do what your daddy says or I'll have to force you."

Another idea that would normally get my thighs rubbing together, but not tonight. That's when I knew I had her. She would tease me, thinking I was playing bad and wanted her to shove my face into her cock. This bought me the little bit of time I needed to craft my plan. I still had no idea what I was going to do, only that I would get her to reignite the fire between my legs somehow.

"Ooh, Daddy..." I purred, "it's not that I don't hunger to suck your delicious daddy dick..."

I flicked the dimple at the base of her cock head, making it bounce a bit, and then, after moistening the tip of my index finger with a little spit, rubbed it against the urethral opening hinted at by the dildo's designer with a tiny indent.

"Especially when I think how delicious your precome would taste in my mouth..."

I licked my finger seductively, my eyes rolling into the back of my head from the imagined taste of her longing.

"But your little girl wants you to do something for her if she's gonna let you use her every orifice as you please." I pouted cutely. The glint in Amanda's eye was enough to get me moist. Oh, yeah. She was into it. Although she had no idea what "it" was.

She smirked cockily. "You know your daddy always does whatever he can to please you, you insatiable slut." She leaned down, grabbed the back of my hair, and melted her tongue between my lips, dissolving the world around us and almost doing the same to my resolve. The thought of her fucking me 18 different ways, licking me until I passed out, fisting me, and then giving me my good night spanking, though predictable, was once again predictably enticing.

She yanked me back and looked cruelly into my eyes. "But if my little girl isn't satisfied by what her daddy has to offer…"

She fell back against the counter. The shock sent her cock vibrating. After letting me watch and salivate for long enough to make me gulp, she calmly stuffed it back into her pants, zipped them up, and then stood straight over me, looked me in the eyes…and spat on me.

"…then she's a thankless bitch."

She walked over me, lifting one leg over my head and around my body to get out of the kitchen. She went straight to the couch, got out a stroke mag and her vibrator, and pulled her cock out again, this time for her own amusement.

I don't know where to begin explaining how many ways this made me feel. I knew how I was *supposed* to react— Amanda knew the thing I hated most was for her to jack off without me. She knew my jealousy would drive me wild with rage and desire; that I would (normally) come begging for forgiveness and a fuck, promising her whatever she could imagine, let alone want, on God's green earth if she would just please, please pound me into submission and blissful ignorance (of the pile of dishes in the sink, my presentation tomorrow morning, the neighbors' need for sleep).

And it's not like we hadn't played hard before. She had slapped me in the face, made me lick clean the boots with which she was about to kick my ass. Hell, once she even started to pee on me before we both cracked up laughing, showered, and giggled ourselves to sleep. She was my daddy, but she was also my baby, and I trusted her love for me above anything.

Didn't I? Well, yes, yes, I did, but that didn't change the fact that I was fucking furious. Spitting on me was a level of degradation I associated with rape, queer bashing—hatred. Flat-out hatred. Everything else she had done while topping me had been acts associated with power, and were thus sexy as hell. But this shit? Spitting? I felt the wet spot on my scalp and ignited, not with desire, but rage. *Oh, no, baby*, I thought. *You just changed the rules of the game. You've got to learn some goddamn manners.* I got off my knees, scrubbed out the spit with a paper towel, stomped into the bathroom, and slammed the door.

"It's time to teach this punk how to behave like a gentleman."

I had a plan of action now. Gone was the sexy femme submissive she'd come to know and desire, and here came her worst nightmare. Amanda had incredibly specific tastes: She forced me to redefine high femme, pushing me to my limit with her insatiable appetite for push-up bras, stilettos, and corsets. Right now, I had on one of my many bland work suits, but underneath that was a custom-made supple fawn suede posture-corrective corset—it choked me each time I began to slouch. I suffered a near-brush with autononerotic asphyxiation during the removal of this device of death (I'd only ever been able to do so with Amanda's help), but finally managed to get it off and breathe for the first time all day.

Breathing more easily just made me angrier. I turned on the sink and brutally scratched and tore at my makeup, trying to remove it with hand soap, the only thing we had in the guest bathroom. I was wearing waterproof eyeliner and mascara, the goddamn eye-makeup remover was on the bedroom dresser, sitting right next to my Clinique cleanser, and there was no way I was walking through the living room to get it. It wasn't until the third washing attempt, looking at my blotchy face and raccoon eyes in the mirror, that the tears started to flow. They ironically did a great job of removing my eye makeup. And my will to go on.

"She doesn't love me anymore," I blubbered to myself. "It's all over. How can I even look at her, let alone have sex with her, after she did that to me?" And then, "Wait, hold on, calm down. She was playing a game. A game *you* got her into. You can't blame her, you created her."

My head fell into my arms against the sink and I openly sobbed. "I created a fucking monster!"

My sobbing was cut off by the sound of knocking. She was knocking on the door. I looked in the mirror to see myself the doppelgänger of the Pillsbury Dough Boy, my mouth a wide O. I realized I wasn't breathing when I heard her speak.

"Baby?"

I gasped.

"Baby? Are you crying? Come on, game over. Can I come in? Did I hurt you? I'm so sorry."

My relief thrust me into the door with a flood of screaming, streaming tears. I pushed it open and stumbled into her arms, graying her new black button-down with my snot and then falling into its open folds and soaking her wife-beater as I nuzzled her breasts—her beautiful, comforting, overflowing breasts—and wept the safe, thoroughly satisfying tears of gratitude and joy that come from remembering that you are loved.

After I blew my nose on her wife-beater (her idea), she pulled me up and kissed my face from top to bottom, recentering at my mouth and pushing her soul through my lips.

"I love you," she said.

She pulled back to assess the extent of my remaining hurt. I sulked and looked at my feet, finally feeling safe enough to say the words that stung my synapses.

"You *spat* on me."

She crumpled. Now it was her turn to look at her feet. "I know. I can't believe I did it. I honestly thought… It doesn't matter. I didn't mean to hurt you, but I did."

With that, she began to undo her pants and fiddle with the straps of her harness. With a few awkward yanks, her dick was hanging limp in her hand.

"Here," she said, plopping the entire package into my hand. "I don't deserve this anymore." She paused. "Not until I learn how to use it."

I almost dropped it, I was taken so aback. "I… I… What do you mean by that?"

"Well, like, you know how doms aren't allowed to dom until they're subbed, right? So they have compassion for the person being whipped and stuff?"

Though her point was crudely stated, I immediately realized that it mirrored the idea I had been so geared up to enact before my weepfest.

"Yeah…" I sniffled, trying to act slightly confused.

"Well, I want you to teach me how to be your daddy." She gulped and stood up straight. "I mean… I want you to teach me how to be a man. A gentleman."

I couldn't believe she said the *word*! I had known we were slightly psychic, but this was ridiculous. And wonderful. And frightening.

"How?" I asked, continuing the charade of ignorance. Though a smile was, rather obviously, pulling my lips out toward my ears.

"Well, like the sub teaches the dom by domming her, I want you to teach me by... Well, I mean, you know..."

I had to save her. I smiled innocently.

"By switching roles with you?" This was the most neutral way I could think to put it.

"Yes." Amanda beamed. "You understand." As she said this, the tension melted from her shoulders and she looked at me as though she was falling in love with me all over again, all gooey and sweet and warm. She grabbed my hand and suddenly looked as though she was about to propose. "Will you do it?"

I paused a little too long before answering. She grabbed my face in her hands and shot lasers into my eyes. "I fucked up too bad this time. I can't hurt you like that again," she said. "It would kill me."

"OK," I replied. "But I think you'll have to start by teaching *me*." I held up the dildo delicately between my fingers. "How do you put this thing on?"

Once she had lovingly undressed me and strapped me in, she left me to craft my new image, choosing the manly garb of my choice from her massive wardrobe. Though she was a butch, she was more like a fag than a straight man in her tastes. She'd never be caught dead in jeans and a T-shirt—unless the jeans were crisply pressed dark denim Dolce & Gabbana and the T-shirt was silk Club Monaco. I, on the other hand, wanted to feel like a heterosexual man. But I wasn't a man, by any means. I caught a glimpse of my lithe dancer's figure in the mirror and realized I had the figure of a 16-year old boy...or maybe an 18-year old boy?

"Amanda!" I barked through the door as I swiped my way through her rack of suits to the garment bags in the back.

"Yeah, baby, what is it?"

*Yes.* I'd found my prize. I lifted what felt like a garment bag full of bricks from the closet and hung it on the back of the bedroom door.

"Do you still have your prom dress?"

I unzipped the bag and marveled at the masculine beauty of its contents. The contrast. The history. The romance.

Amanda's reply broke through the haze of fantasy only slightly. "Yes...?"

"Good." I sharply asserted. I could already feel my cock swelling. "Put it on."

I slid my hands across the vintage satin lapel, the wool vest, the Egyptian cotton shirt. I shuddered at their sensuality. Their perfection. I remembered shuddering like this once before, the one time Amanda wore them for me, the most romantic night of my life. She was my Bogie, I her Bacall. We danced all night on the deck of that yacht on the Bay, the lights from the Golden Gate Bridge sparkling in our eyes, every other couple jealous of our obviously perfect chemistry. Tonight I was to be her—not Bogie. Not Gable. Not Valentino. I was to be her—Jimmy Stewart. The perfect gentleman. Masculine and dashing and gentle and kind. I dressed silently until I got to the final step, the bow tie, at which point I cursed quietly while reversing my perspective on a common ritual in our lives. Once I'd tied it to my satis-faction and put on Amanda's black alligator Oxfords, I straightened my tails and walked out to pick up my date for the prom.

I only regretted not having a corsage.

When Amanda saw me her eyes softened and widened as she took in the metamorphosis. Only after she had soaked me in did she remember her own evolution and blush. I had never before seen my lover sheepish.

Her hair was still Matt LeBlanc short, but she had soft-ened the gel with a brush and put in one of my barrettes. She had on the slightest hint of rosy eye shadow and mascara and the most beautiful burgundy lipstick emphasizing her Clara Bow bowlike lips. I'd only ever noticed the beauty of their shape when she was sleeping—the rest of the time, she kept them tight or sneering to hide their feminine curves. Her neck was bare, her chest and shoulders soft and exposed, begging to be kissed, and her breasts were milky orbs, burst-ing from the perfectly shaped cups of the strapless, corseted (now I saw where that fetish came from) wine-colored dress she was wearing. Her hands were clasped behind her back and she was barefoot, leaving her shorter than me for once.

I had planned to do a mini-prom, just the two of us, can-dles, romantic music, and some fun verbal role play/fore-play. But the quivering of her lips, the softness in her eyes, and the shallowness of her breath told me she only needed one thing from me. She needed from me what I had earlier needed from her. I realized that by giving it to her I'd be giving it to myself. As a gentleman, it was my duty to love her as tenderly as I could.

I strode across the room, my passion increasing with each step. As I neared, her eyes finally dared to implore from mine "Am I beautiful?" "Yes." I said out loud. "The most beauti-ful thing I've ever seen." I grabbed her tight around her waist and kissed her the way she had been kissing me since the first time, finally letting her relax into the heaven of being wanted, needed, loved, and held. She wrapped her arms around my neck and let her weight fall back, trusting my grip, made solid by the intoxicating power of responsibility. I moved one arm down below her bottom, crouched to center my weight, and scooped her up into my arms. I then carried her across the threshold of our bedroom (fantasizing about wedding days and romance novels the whole way) and to the bed, where I lay her gently, spreading her dress then stroking her cheek as I spoke, my voice lowered to mimic that of an 18-year-old boy.

"You're the most beautiful girl I've ever seen. You know I've been totally in love with you since you came to our school in fourth grade, and it was the greatest day of my life when you said you'd go out with me sophomore year. Well, that was two years ago, and I haven't even thought about another girl since."

To my incredible surprise, Amanda's eyes began to fill with tears. I continued, "I didn't even want to bring it up until I thought I was ready, 'cause I didn't want to be a dumb jerk and I didn't want to pressure you. But…" I started to hyperventilate. This felt more real than any game we'd ever played. "I was wondering if…" I kissed up her arm, across her breasts, and up her neck, finally whispering into her ear, "…you'd let me make love to you."

I was shaking. If she said no I was going to collapse. I had always wished Amanda and I had taken each other's virginity, and, as far as I was concerned, this was our chance to rewrite history.

"I'm scared," she said. I braced myself for rejection. "But I love you."

I raised my eyebrows. "So…?"

She studied my face for any bad intentions as I had hers so many times before, and, finding nothing but love and more than a little fear, glowed with a warm, soft smile.

"Yes," she nearly whispered.

I filled with ecstatic pride. Who cares that I'd never done this before? She knew I was a butch virgin and she wanted me anyway. She trusted me to love her, to teach her how to love me, trusted me so much she had reached 10 years back in time to find her inner femme, something none of my other butch girlfriends had ever been willing—or had even ever thought—to do.

I wasted no time in turning her over, unlacing her corset top, and slowly easing it off her body as I kissed my way down to her waist and then back up from her feet, up each leg, before pulling the dress out from under her completely. She had gone from panting nervously to giggling to moaning as I kissed my way across the entire voluptuous, smooth, and remarkably feminine landscape of her body. I realized I had never done this; had never been able to soak in her body this way. I was so grateful. *I only want to genderfuck,* I thought, *if, and only if, at the end of the day, I get to be grateful we're both women without feeling ashamed.*

As I looked lovingly at her near-nakedness I remembered how frighteningly naked I felt when the other person was fully clothed. Now it was her turn to enjoy being the agent of her own gaze and not merely the object of mine. I stripped slowly, sensually, and confidently, all the way down. I had decided against binding my breasts. I wanted to be a man inside and thought the discomfort might frustrate me, rendering me irritable. My focus was to be on Amanda's body tonight, not my own. By the time I had finished, and was standing naked before her, Amanda was visibly squirming, her PC muscles contracting like crazy and her scent filling my nose. I leaned in and kissed her warm moist lips through her underwear. I gripped the inner edges of her panty elastic with my thumbs, resting my fingers on her hips. The electricity between us was immediate, but I asked permission anyway, to be a gentleman. "May I?"

"Yes," Amanda growled, and she pulled her pelvis upward so as to pull the panties off for me. By the time I'd gotten them down around her knees, she started to kick them off. Her desire for me to make love to her ignited the fire between my legs, for sure, but this time it wasn't just in my cootchie, it was in my cock. I was committed to getting her as wet as humanly possible to facilitate the most sensual deflowering in history.

I now had full view of her vagina for the first time ever (the times she had let me go down on her it had been lights-off-clitoris-only) and could see that her hymen was perfectly intact. Pink and pearly and smooth and... Oh, God, I understood how men felt about the whole thing, now. It was so fucking hot to think of it being mine.

I buried my face in her already-copious juices and sucked and drank and probed until I was grabbed by the hair and dragged back out.

"Now. I want you inside of me *now*," she moaned.

The fierceness in her eyes mirrored what I'd felt whenever she'd gone down on me too long. Like I had so many times before, she hungered for cock.

She pulled my face up to hers and kissed and licked my mouth, chin, cheeks, and neck, drunk off the taste of her own come. Then she started to shiver as she remembered what we were about to do. I grabbed her to me and squeezed her tight. "I love you. We'll only do what you want to do," I told her.

"I know. It's OK. I'm ready." Her gaze was calm and steady. She seemed less scared than I was.

At that, I spread her legs wider with one hand while positioning my cock with the other. For all of my mocking of the contraptions involved, there was no denying at that moment that it was my cock. My real cock. And I was about to feel it inside of the woman I loved. I pushed it through Amanda's outer labia.

"Jesus!" Nothing had prepared me for that. The second I felt the pressure of being surrounded by her folds, pressing against her inner labia, the very tip touching her hymen, I came. Not like I'd ever come before, though. This was more like an electric shock. I started shaking wildly and uncontrollably against poor Amanda's body and couldn't stop until it was over. I was horribly embarrassed; I couldn't believe I'd prematurely ejaculated. But she kissed me and reassured me, said, "It's OK." I silently thanked God my cock was silicone, pulled myself together, and continued pushing gently and firmly into her. Her eyes widened as more and more of my head stretched her hymen and she began to feel pain.

"Should I stop?" I asked.

"*No*," she groaned, and pulled me into her, letting out a horror-movie shriek as I ripped through her and all the way up to her cervix. I yelled in unison with her and went stiff all the way through my body, electricity tingling my every nerve, my senses too stimulated to react. So she began moving me, using my hips as handles and forcing me back and forth into her, slowly at first and then faster, coming and screaming so hard I thought we might die together. I hardly remember the next few minutes—I only know we didn't speak, just lay there, my body on top of hers, our eyes wide and our breath shallow, each in shock from the most terrifyingly intense orgasm of our lives.

At some point she rolled me over and straddled me while I lay there, stunned, and rocked herself to a second orgasm that was so incredibly beautiful I cried. When she was thoroughly satisfied and exhausted, she fell onto me and let me lick the sweat from her face while stroking her hair. I was pulled from the depths of my post-orgasmic hair-stroking trance by her voice, childlike and quivering. "My pussy hurts," she said. She pulled her legs tight together and tucked them to her body as I pulled away to give her space. "I just noticed, but it hurts bad."

I ran to make a cold compress with a washcloth and a tub of ice water. Her face, pinched tight, relaxed in relief when I pressed the icy fabric against her. I could feel her blood pounding against my hand, as if her heart had migrated down south for the winter, and the compress went warm in seconds, starting a healing ritual back and forth between cooling her soreness and bloodying the tub of water.

"You're being so tender."

I looked up from my ministrations to see Amanda crying again. I'd never before seen her cry, and now it had been twice in one day. I didn't know what to say. It seemed so obvious to me, so natural. Yet I had never given her aftercare like this. Amanda never wanted me to. She'd always been too tough.

"Well, it's about time you let me," I replied, after a long pause. It hurt to think of all the times I'd wanted this, all the times I had suppressed my self to fit her fantasy. I swallowed, but my mouth was dry. I turned my face away and blinked back the tears beginning to sting my eyes. "I…I don't even know what to say, I'm so tired." Amanda held me close to her and waited. My eyes darted over to catch a glimpse of her rather neutral response, then I continued, emboldened in equal parts by postorgasmic vulnerability and anger. "I'm sick of fucking. I want—"

"—to make love," we said in unison. Amanda grabbed my hand and looked me deep in the eyes, smiling. "I understand. Me, too. Me, too."

# First Date

## M. Damian

Five months after my girlfriend dumped me, I figured I was sufficiently past the pain and anger stages to start dating again. I had deliberately, albeit very impatiently, waited before venturing out because I didn't want to do the rebound thing, knowing it wouldn't be fair to whomever I went out with. But after five months I was pretty much over the grief and resentment and even had a tentative friendship going with my ex. (Why is it that lesbians simply have to have their exes in their lives?) Anyway, I wanted to start having fun again. I'd been down in the doldrums long enough and it was time, as that tired old cliché recommends, to get on with my life. Availing myself of technology, I hopped onto the Internet and got busy browsing through the personals on PlanetOut.

There were plenty of ads to choose from; the trick was to find someone who was compatible with me and my likes and dislikes. Personal ads always intimidate me—all the listed "prerequisites" always make me feel so inadequate, so...boring. I mean, *I* think I'm funny, personable, and intelligent, but who's to say someone else would? And as for looks? *I* think I'm cute, but isn't one's self-assessment totally biased? As you can see, I'm my own worst enemy. But I wouldn't allow myself to become daunted. Dating in this new millennium has become literally as easy as letting your fingers do the walking; I wouldn't even have to disturb myself to go out hunting in the bars. I could just sit at my keyboard and let the candidates come to me.

I responded to several ads before I found Lauren's. None of the others had panned out, but I wasn't discouraged. I'd met nice women, made some new friends, and was having fun along the way, so it had been a good experience so far. Anyway, I wasn't desperately looking. If something clicked with someone, great. If not, then no harm, no foul. I remember I was sitting at work, scrolling through the latest offerings on PlanetOut when her profile flashed up on the screen. I'm of the butch persuasion and she was a femme, so I was immediately attracted to her description, but it was this funky little quiz she had that really got my attention: Whoever could agree with all eight of her 12 "requirements," she'd answer; anyone who got less, she suggested they move on to someone else. I'm not competitive or aggressive, but the challenge Lauren presented with this compatibility quiz was something I couldn't pass up. In my response to her posted ad, I crowed that not only did I match her in all her points, but I aced her eligibility test by scoring a 12. Pure butch conceit!

I didn't expect to hear anything, if indeed she even responded at all, until the next day. Not everyone has a job like mine, where I can play on the Internet whenever I want. But lo and behold, a scant hour after I sent my reply, there she was, sending me an instant message. Would I accept? Hell, yeah!

We stayed online most of the day. About 20 minutes into our conversation, she volunteered to send me some pictures of her. Of course I quickly accepted, wanting to know what she looked like. She sent me two snapshots that showed she was a petite, cute woman with blond hair and a great smile.

I was enchanted; I knew I wanted to get to know her better. At the end of our marathon I.M. session, she asked me if I'd like her number. I was surprised to be offered it so fast because during our instant messaging she had told me she had certain rule, one of which was that she didn't immediately give out her phone number. When I asked how I'd rated such a special favor, she said she had a good feeling about me. It looked as if we were off to a great start.

I had a tough time waiting until 8 o'clock to call her; impatiently I kept glancing at the clock, willing the minutes to pass. In case I haven't mentioned it, I'm very impatient where something I want is concerned, and I knew by this time I wanted Lauren. When the little hand finally landed on the 8, I quickly dialed her number. Busy. Damn it! My first thought was that she had told someone else to call her. I know femmes are at a premium, and I didn't delude myself into thinking I was the only butch interested in her, although I wanted it to be that way. I kept trying, and after about the zillionth try she finally answered. My qualms about there being someone else on the phone were immediately laid to rest when she breathlessly informed me she was talking to her sister, the one who never shut up.

We chatted for four hours that night, with me mostly asking questions and then listening intently to the answers. I wanted to know everything I could about this woman because I had a very good feeling about her. She had these quirky little ways she used to measure how well it was going between us. She'd say, "Yeah, we're really clicking on that one," or "I'm so glad we agree on that." I was happy we were getting along so well. We joked about her little quiz; she told me she had never placed an ad before and that she'd written the quiz as a joke, never realizing it would be included in the actual ad. She also had rules she wanted women who responded to her ad to follow: (1) the first date is a "meet" only, lasting no longer than an hour; (2) don't ask for a second date while out on the first; and last, but most definitely not least, no sex for three months. Her third rule posed no problem for me. My last two relationships had begun with sex and then had mellowed into love. I figured that jumping into the sack was the surest way of ruining any beginning relationship, at least for me. That was one pattern I did not want to repeat again.

Ensuing days would find Lauren "popping" in on me when I was on the computer at work. I was always pleasantly surprised when she did; I was so looking forward to learning more about her. Each chat session let me learn something new about her and her life; each phone call added to my store of information. She had an erratic work schedule, so phone calls could come at any time of the day or, more especially, night. It was hard for her to plan too far in advance, but after a couple of weeks she suggested we meet. I was thrilled— positively, absolutely thrilled! So you can imagine my vast disappointment when she called at the last minute to cancel. The holidays were coming up. She came from a big family, so the chances of seeing her anytime in the near future were practically nonexistent. She had so much to do! What could I do? What could I say? My hands were tied.

"I didn't say I wasn't going to see you, silly," she said when I told her how bummed I was that we couldn't meet. It took a few seconds for me to decipher that; when I did, I couldn't believe my luck. "Are you busy the day after Thanksgiving?" If I had been, I would have canceled any other plans immediately. "Then why don't we make a day of it, just you and me?"

I was floored! "What about your rules?" I asked. "No more than an hour."

"Mmm, you're right," she replied, "but I seem to be breaking rules all over the place for you."

I was walking on air for the next week. A whole day with Lauren! Man-oh-man, how did I get to be so lucky?

The days until I was to finally meet her in person passed slowly, but eventually "Black Friday" dawned: brilliant sunshine and warm temps. We had made plans to meet at 9. I was about an hour away and out of the house a good hour before I needed to leave—so anxious was I to get the date started. Not surprisingly, I got to Lauren's house beforehand and then just drove around, knowing better than to arrive too early. She had told me many times about doing the "femme" thing—putting on makeup, being particular about getting dressed, etc.—and I didn't want to rush her or get there before she was finished. When I eventually drove up, Lauren came out of her apartment to meet me, limping slightly. She had broken her foot about a month before and still needed to walk with crutches.

She was adorable—and so effervescent. When I walked up to her, she grabbed my chin, squealing, "You're so cute! You're so cute! Can I give you a hug?" Usually, first meetings between people who meet on the Internet aren't so free. I felt kind of awkward as she put her arms around me, but reveled in her greeting. She certainly was a friendly little thing!

When we got on the road—sun streaming through the windows, a CD playing softly—we chatted amicably, without strain. It was so easy with her, as if I'd known her more than a scant few weeks. We touched on many different topics, including the music we were listening to. Lauren had brought along some CDs. One of her favorite artists, Enya, I had never heard before. Not a regular listener of New Age music, I found that I indeed liked her music. When I mentioned this to Lauren, she responded enthusiastically, "We're clickin', baby, we're *clickin'*!"

Seventy-degree temperatures are abnormal for November where I live. Because of the mildness of the day, a lot of people were out shopping, much more than the day after Thanksgiving warranted. We were waiting in a long queue of cars snaking into the parking lot of the shopping outlet Lauren had chosen. I sat there, looking ahead, keeping an eye on the slow-moving line in front of me, when Lauren leaned behind my bucket seat, looking for something in her bag that was behind me. When she found what she was looking for, she eased back into her seat, and then suddenly she leaned toward me and kissed me on the lips. Once. Twice. I felt my cheeks flame hot! I was totally and completely unprepared for this. Unfortunately, she took my stunned silence the wrong way. "I just wanted to see how it would feel," she mumbled, staring hard out her window. "I'm sorry."

I was speechless for several seconds, until finally I stammered out, "No, don't be! I liked it. I was just surprised. You know, your rules…"

Lauren turned from the window and gave me a mischievous smile. "I seem to be breaking *all* my rules for you." My heart hammered in my chest as a little voice inside sang, *She likes me! She really likes me!*

Emboldened by this first move, when I finally parked the car, I leaned across the console and asked, "Can we break the rules a little more?"

She glanced around at the people milling about in the parking lot. "With all these people here?" she asked shyly.

"Ah, the beauty of tinted windows," I smirked. "I guarantee no one can see in." Taking control, I leaned in and kissed her on the mouth, as she had done to me. Her sweet, soft lips kept me happily kissing her, closemouthed, for some 10 minutes until she breathlessly pulled away.

"I think that's enough for now," she said, blushing prettily, "or I might not have any rules left to break."

With a happy smile on my face, I eased her out of the car, handed her the crutches she needed for support, and helped her across the street. She was pretty good on the sticks, but people are people—even when they saw her struggling, they still didn't step out of the way. I made sure I walked behind her with my hand occasionally on her back, helping her thread her way through the shoppers. Mindful of her condition, I was making sure no one stupidly bumped into her and maybe knocked her off her feet. I didn't want her to think, however, that I was taking liberties with her, so I leaned over and said in her ear, "I don't mean to keep touching you, but I don't want you to fall."

She glanced at me over her shoulder and murmured with what could only be construed as a come-hither look, "Stay close. I think I might need more hands-on help."

We browsed as best we could, fighting with the hordes of pre-holiday shoppers. When we tried to find a restaurant for lunch, we found they all had outrageous waiting times. We finally settled for a cup of mint chocolate ice cream for her, a soda for me, and a bench. I would've been happy with water, just to have her near me. She settled her ankle over my legs and we talked. She fed me ice cream, and I felt so fortunate that I had met her. People walking by gave us stares, but it was as if we were in our own little world; neither of us cared what people thought. When we finished our "lunch," we started walking again. Lauren was looking for one particular outlet. We found a map of the entire complex, delineating store locations, and she sat down because her ankle was beginning to throb with all the walking she'd been doing. As she sat, I stood over her, both of us looking at the map. When she told me where she wanted to go—an intimate apparel store—I said, "I think the sight of you in lingerie will give me a heart attack." I was delighted when she leaned forward and kissed me lightly on the cheek.

On the ride back I had my arm around her. She leaned in close to the console and let me gently stroke her back. It might sound goofy, but after all her talk of rules, I had expected to have a pretty reserved day. I was giddy about how unrestricted it had been. When I pulled up in front of her house, I got her CDs from the player in the trunk and helped her with her crutches, and we went into her apartment. I sat on the couch while she put her CDs away, all the while thinking of how I could get her to kiss me again. I sat gazing at her, at how cute she was and remembering how her lips had felt against mine, until finally, plucking up my nerve, I moved in for the kill, knowing I probably wouldn't get a better chance. She responded with alacrity, moving in close to me until we were really lip-locked. We kissed for a while, until she abruptly stood up. "Whew!" she said, fanning her hand in front of her face. "That was hot."

Loathe to leave, I stood also. When I moved close to her, she knew my intent and didn't try to stop me. I knew my time with her was short. She had dinner plans, so I had to make the most of it. I kissed her eyelids and traveled down to her neck, planting warm, tantalizing kisses on her soft skin. After a few minutes I noticed she kept shifting her feet. I knew her foot must be bothering her, so I gently moved her back and stood her against the wall. "Better?" I murmured breathlessly into her ear. When her shoulders shuddered delicately, I knew my hot, tickling breath was having an effect on her. Sure enough, after 20 minutes of intense making out, I felt her lips give way under mine. I leaned back, feigning surprise, and cocked my left eyebrow questioningly. She gazed up at me, grabbed my head in her hands, and silently pulled my mouth onto hers.

The sensation of her tongue sliding into my mouth made my knees weak. I put my hands on the wall over her head and dipped my face down. It was a classic pose, one that fueled both of our feelings of desire. She liked my dominance; I loved her femininity. Our kissing became more passionate, more heated. I was leaning my body into hers, and got hot when I felt her mold herself onto me. One of my legs was between hers, and I moved my thigh up to where her legs formed her body's delicious *V*.

At first she demurred. "My rules," she murmured helplessly, but when I bent my head to kiss her neck again, she gave in, parting her legs slightly. I rubbed my thigh against her mound, feeling her pussy's warmth on my denim-clad leg. My excitement was evident by my stiffening clit, but I knew better than to be overly aggressive. We stayed like that for a long time, kissing deeply, my leg between hers, her body molded hotly against mine.

Finally, I said huskily, "Don't you think you should take some pressure off that ankle? It's not good for you to stand so long on it. I don't want it to get swollen."

"It's not my ankle I'm worried about getting swollen," she answered in a similarly husky voice.

Elation surged through me, but again I didn't let it show, not wanting to scare her off. I solicitously led her to the couch and then knelt between her legs, bowing low at her feet. "Here, let me massage it for you," I volunteered, letting the double entendre stand. I removed her shoe, then eased her sock off. Her ankle really did look a little swollen. "I think you need to elevate this," I said. "Why don't you lie on the couch and I'll massage it?" I took her other shoe off, and she lay down. I wanted to pounce on her then and there but figured that would scare the hell out of her, so instead I knelt back down and gently took her foot in my hand, tenderly massaging her ankle. A few minutes after I started, little moans of pleasure started wafting down to me. She loved what I was doing to her! "Would you like a massage?" I asked impetuously. I wasn't expecting much—just sort of threw the question out there and was euphoric when she nodded, her eyes closed. "OK. Turn over." She didn't move; she just lay there. "You need to turn over, hon, if you want it."

"No, I don't," she murmured.

I might be a little slow on the uptake, but when her message registered, it really registered! Our eyes locked; smoldering passion devoured me. "What about your three-month rule?" I asked bluntly, not wanting to get involved and then have my advances shut down.

"I've broken every other one for you," she responded, green eyes shining. "I guess that one's going too."

"What about your plans for tonight?"

"They weren't important."

"And this is?" I questioned.

"Yesss. This is important. *You're* important."

I wasted no more time with words. I'd been handed a gift, and I wasn't going to waste any more time unwrapping it. I explored her body with my hands, running them over her legs, up and down her arms. I knew I was heating her up by the convulsive little shudders that twitched throughout her body. I opened my hand wide and slid it up her left leg, my thumb just grazing her mound. She gave a moan then, short and low. Continuing my explorations, I kept my hand open wide, the palm slowly skidding over her left breast. When I slid my hand down the right side of her body, I could feel her erect nipple under the light sweater she was wearing. I looked into her eyes and gave her a lazy smile. Oh, yeah, this was going to be fun.

When my roaming hand reached the bottom of her sweater, I wriggled my fingers up underneath it. Her skin was warm and smooth to my touch. My breathing came faster as I inched up her body to be stopped by her bra. Deliberately holding Lauren's eyes with my own, I slithered my fingers under the bra and let my hand rest in the valley between her breasts. Her eyes never wavered from mine as my fingers crept over to her right breast, bumping over the hard tip of her nipple. I licked my lips for added effect and got rewarded with Lauren's body slightly shivering in anticipation. "Why don't we take your sweater off?" I asked. "Here," I said, not waiting for an answer, "lean forward."

Silently, she bent forward enough so I could pull the sweater over her head. Her bra was white lace, its intricate design showing alternate patches of skin. Her two points stuck out sharply. "My," I teased, "someone's excited." She got embarrassed, crossing her arms over her chest. "No, no, none of that, babe," I chided, gently pulling her hands away. "No need to be shy."

"I can't believe I'm doing this," she wailed. "I can't believe I dropped all my rules for you."

"Hey," I said, lightening the mood so she wouldn't change her mind, "I'm special, remember? I'm the butch who aced your test." She smiled then, a demure smile. Everything would be fine.

"Lie back down, sweetheart." When she did, I pushed her bra up under her chin, exposing her breasts to my hungry sight. I let a throaty moan escape. "Man-oh-man, they are beautiful." And they were. For a petite woman, Lauren's nipples were made for sucking and tugging. They stood out juicily, like nice, big pink erasers. Flashing her a mischievous grin, I lowered my head and put my lips on the nipple nearest to me, stretching it out between my pursed lips, gently biting it with the barest pressure, and sucking hungrily on it. My hand instinctively went to the other breast, fondling its erect tip. Lauren was breathing rapidly, ruffling my hair with short gasps as I played with her. *Well*, I thought, *your breathing is going to get a lot more labored before I'm done with you, missy.*

Now that I knew her rules were kaput, I was the butch in charge, which is who she wanted me to be. Our little talks had let me learn a lot about Lauren. I knew that being an emotionally strong woman, and one who took charge during sex, was a plus in her book. I had played it slow in the beginning because I didn't want to spook her, but knowing she was OK with me taking the lead let me guide her to where I wanted her to be—namely, the bedroom. But that would come in time—as would she.

I heaved out a breath. "It's getting hot in here," I said, leaning away from her and pulling off the shell I was wearing. "There, that's better." I breathed a sighed of relief as I felt a snatch of coolness hit. "Now, where was I?"

She took my hand and placed it on her breast. "Right there," she said breathlessly.

My clit responded to both her gesture and tone. It pushed

up against the seam in my pants, spurring me on. I reached for the button on her jeans and opened it. Grabbed the tab on the zipper and slid it all the way down. I got a glimpse of white lace before turning my head to kiss her again. My heart was thumping wildly in my chest while my tongue tangled with hers, fingers crawling into her panties. I knew the exact second when my digits hit her clit: Her eyes opened wide, and her tongue lashed mine furiously. She was hot and wet, her pubic hair a damp tangle. Not taking my mouth from hers, I slid my finger down her soaking gash and without any preamble, entered her. She broke the kiss and gasped.

"Too much?" I asked fearfully, quickly pulling out.

"Oh, you feel *so* good," she moaned.

I gave her a lopsided grin. "My thoughts exactly," I said playfully. I slid my middle finger back in as far as it could go. Slid it in and out, enjoying the slipperiness of her pussy. Suddenly, urgent lust replaced my playfulness. Snatching my hand out of her snatch, I grabbed the waistband of her jeans and started tugging them and her panties down her legs. Lauren helped by lifting her hips off the cushion. In a rush, I threw the clothes on the rug and then sat back on my haunches, appreciating the view. Bashfully, she placed her hands over the light-brown triangle between her legs. When I looked at her face, her lower lip was caught between her teeth. That turned me on even more. "We'll have none of that, darlin'," I drawled, lifting her hands away. "I want to admire your lovely assets." I pushed her legs slightly apart, got a whiff of her musk, then stroked her mound, the hair soft under my fingertips. My own body was screaming, my clit torturing me—the way it was swollen and pushing up against my seam. I wanted her so badly.

I decided to go for it. Lifting myself up on my knees, I

went into a sidewise sixty-nine position, but I guess with just one of us doing it, it was more of a "six" position. I opened her legs wide, putting her right foot on the floor. Then I took my fingers and opened up the slippery lips of her cunt. My heart was beating wildly in my throat as I dipped my head and gave her a fast swipe of my tongue. She jerked away as if a hot poker had skimmed her cunt. I laughed inwardly. I like women who have strong reactions to my eating them. Very lightly, barely a skim, I traced her outer lips with my tongue, feeling her shudder slightly. Her smell was getting stronger now, pungent, inviting. Burrowing my head way down, I slid my tongue inside her wet hole, exploring. When Lauren felt it thrusting in and out, she started arching her hips to meet it, a moan beginning to break out of her. I had my hands on either leg, forcibly splaying her open as my head went in and out. I felt the blood rush to my head, just as I knew it was rushing to her clit, making it hot and stiff for me.

She moaned my name when I pulled my tongue out of her cunt. "Marie…"

"Don't worry, honey. I'm really gonna give you something to moan about." My words were muffled by her pussy as I dragged my eager mouth up to her clit. Pulling her lips apart again, I used my index finger to pull the hood back, exposing her jewel to my gaze. It was a nice-sized nub, berry-red and swollen. Without any further ado, I put my mouth on it and sucked hard. Lauren jumped at the unexpected assault. I was at fever-pitch with wanting to eat her. My clit was painfully throbbing, my nipples tingling with desire. I kept her open while my tongue beat against her bud. As I alternated between sucking and licking, Lauren started trembling. I didn't know any sexual details about her, but I knew when a woman seems to be on the verge of coming. I kept my head moving up and down while the tip of my tongue put pressure on her clit.

Her head was in my lap as I sat on the couch about 15 minutes after her orgasm. I sat playing with her hair when I asked, "Think you can walk, babe?"

"Barely," she replied. "Why?"

Her nakedness, enhanced by her shirt and bra pushed up under her chin, was arousing me again. I wanted another go at her on my knees, but I wanted a different venue. "I thought we'd go into the bedroom." She opened her eyes and looked into my face, searching it. She lifted herself up and kissed me long and deep. I matched her intensity until we were both caught up in a burst of unbridled passion. Instead of letting her walk, I picked her up and carried her into the bedroom, setting her down on the edge of her mattress. My throat was thick with desire as, wordlessly, I parted her legs until her cunt came into view. My breathing was fast, almost panting. "Lay back, babe." Obediently, she did; I put my hands under the smooth cheeks of her ass, lifting her up off the mattress. My face was bare inches from the treasure trove between her legs. "Open up for me, babe. Show me you want me."

Putting the heels of her feet on the frame of the bed, she opened her legs wide. Her lips split open, revealing the fleshy inside of her drooling pussy. She was wet again, anticipating having my mouth on her. I gladly obliged, tipping her up to my mouth. I burrowed my face between her creamy thighs, her pubes tickling my nose. I tugged lightly on them with my teeth, sending a little prickle of pleasure up into her cunt. With my nose, I pushed her outer lips apart and then ran its tip up and down her wet slash, savoring her smell, making sure she heard my groans of pure appreciation. In my experience, nothing excites a woman so much as knowing her lover is enjoying what she's doing. And I really, really, really *do* enjoy cunnilingus.

Sometimes, I like to play with my "food" a lot before eating. I kept my face between Lauren's legs—licking, kissing, sucking, flicking her clit with my tongue—holding her ass up off the bed and jamming my tongue as far up her hole as it could go. I gently sucked her inner lips into my mouth, first one, then the other, all the time monitoring her body's reactions to what I was doing to her. I heard her breathing become more and more rapid, felt the tremor in her legs as her orgasm built. I deliberately took my time, slowly coaxing her to an orgasm I'm sure she had never had before. I took my hands out from under her ass, moved them up and tugged on her hot, hard nipples. She was moaning almost nonstop by this point. I enjoyed watching her belly go up and down with her ragged breaths.

My angle was perfect for exerting pressure on her clit. Once again I lifted the hood from her burning ember and gave it a couple of fast flicks with my tongue. A groan from deep inside her burst from her lips. I knew her clit was on the cusp of a pleasurably painful, bursting feeling. Any time I touched it would bring her exquisite pain. My own breath was coming faster as I finally got down to business. With my thumbs holding the hood up, I attacked her clit, alternating between sucking on it and then flagellating it back and forth with my tongue. The sensations she was feeling were driving her absolutely crazy. Her hands buried themselves in my hair, and she made sure my head didn't move, which was fine with me. I get hot when a woman does that while I'm feasting on her pussy. Fastening my lips around her clit,

I went in for the kill, my tongue moving faster than a hummingbird's wings. Her hips started bucking, but I kept my mouth glued to her twat. She was chanting now, "Yes-yes-yes-yes-yes-*yes*," her voice picking up in volume. She let go of my hair and hastily clamped a pillow over her face. I knew she was losing control and didn't want anyone to hear her scream when she came. I kept my mouth's tempo tuned to her body's rhythm: she was pushing her cunt up against my mouth. Our moves and countermoves were in perfect sync until her legs started jerking spasmodically and she arched herself up high, lingering like that for several seconds, and then fell back down onto the bed.

I felt a glow of pure butch satisfaction as I got up from my knees and tenderly hoisted her legs over onto the mattress. She offered no resistance, just let me move her and then lay down next to her. I gathered her up in my arms, kissing the top of her head. "That was wonderful," she murmured sleepily into my chest. "I've never come like that before."

"Shh, shh, go to sleep, sweetheart. Plenty more where that came from after you've rested." I knew she needed a break. She was going to need it. I could fuck her all night.

Which is exactly what I did. Lauren took a little power nap. When she woke up (or rather, when I woke her up by nuzzling between her legs), we went at it again. I had a very swollen hard-on, but I was intent on satisfying her. She asked if I was solely a "pitcher" and smiled when I exclaimed, "Hell, no! I'm not stupid!"

But when I told her that my clit was stiff but didn't want my sexual needs taken care of, she gave me a special smile and said, "You know, that's making me horny." I would never tell her that I knew it would. All the women I've been with got extremely turned on when I let them know that I was thinking of their needs and desires above my own. Their reciprocity showed no bounds when it was my turn.

Her sweater and bra had been thrown off during the night. Having her completely naked while I was almost fully dressed added to the eroticism. I lay on the bed and watched her ride my leg, rubbing herself back and forth on my thigh, a huge wet mark on my jeans from her juicy cunt. When she was almost climaxing, I had her stop and finished her off myself. Another short rest, and this time she stood by the side of the bed while I fucked her from behind, pumping my fingers in and out of her hungry hole while she writhed beneath them. When we got hungry in the middle of the night, we went into the kitchen. I not only ate a sandwich at the kitchen table, but I had her *on* the kitchen table as well. When the sun finally came up, we were both bleary-eyed from fucking. My lips were sore, and her clit was bright red from all the licking and touching. When I commented that I hoped I hadn't hurt her, she replied that she'd never had so much wonderful sex in such a short amount of time, so any pain she had to suffer was most definitely worth it!

Our first date was over. She stood at the door of her apartment, her body wrapped in a short silk robe while we said goodbye, a goodbye that lasted through many deep kisses and groping hands, both hers and mine. "So, is it OK to ask if I'll be seeing you again?" I quipped, referring to rule number 2: no asking for a second date while out on the first. She smiled bashfully, catching her lip charmingly between her teeth as she shyly nodded yes. In parting I gave her a melting stare with my baby blues and left. Two seconds later, before she had time to close the door, I was back in her arms, kissing her again and again while she molded herself against my body. It was as if we would never be satisfied.

Summoning up a deep reservoir of willpower, I pried myself away from her and left her staring after me as I got into my car and drove home, thinking, *Well, that went well.*

Our all-nighter didn't propel us into a relationship, as I had hoped it would. When all was said and done, it turned out to be a simple fuckfest. That all-night cunnilingus festival was the first and last time I ever saw Lauren. But things happen for a reason. Six weeks after I had that one night with Lauren, my ex broke up with the woman she had left me for. Once the thrill of the chase was over, her new girlfriend started acting like the asshole she really was. Chris gladly came running back after finding out the grass isn't always necessarily greener on the other side of the lesbian fence. We're happy now, happier than we were the first time around, because this time we both know it'll be for keeps.

I hope Lauren is just as lucky.

# Caged

STEFKA

With a final spritz of hairspray, I tossed my brush on the bathroom counter and patted my short spiky hair. I clicked off the light before heading to the bedroom, where my girl-friend, Rachel, was putting her own finishing touches on her face and hair. It was fetish night, the third Sunday of the month, and we were heading out to the local lesbian and gay club to enjoy its darkly erotic atmosphere, as we'd been doing for the past four months.

I leaned on the doorjamb and shoved my hands in the pockets of my vinyl pants, half-hearing the unique sound they made (like wet plastic sticking together), as I watched her tie her high-heeled shoes. The smile I usually wore whenever I looked at her grew as I stared. She was in rare form tonight, having chosen to wear a Catholic schoolgirl uni-form, with a few alterations.

At first glance it actually looked authentic, until I caught a glimpse of the black leather corset that encased her bounti-ful breasts and tummy under the pristine white blouse. Her red checked skirt was about two inches shorter than the norm. To finish off the outfit, she wore high white stockings with little bows on the back. I swallowed hard as she uncon-sciously flicked her long, curly auburn hair over her shoulder as she stood up and smoothed her skirt in place. My body was already heating up as she slowly turned and caught sight of me, her blue eyes widening as her own smile broadened.

I cleared my throat and straightened before heading to the chair to pick up my leather jacket. It completed my own outfit of vinyl pants, white T-shirt, and leather vest with biker boots. I shrugged it on, enjoying the pleasant heaviness of it as Rachel retrieved her small purse and jacket. Looking at her, I nearly grabbed her to toss her on the rumpled bed, fetish night be damned, but her smile of anticipation squashed that idea. Instead, I flicked off the light before grabbing her hand and tugging her along. She giggled like the schoolgirl she was dressed as and I smiled.

Thirty minutes later we entered a world most people I knew didn't even dream about. The pulsating music blared, and I felt its magic working on both of us. We waited in line for our drinks, Rachel clinging to my arm in the possessive manner she usually had when we came here, as she smiled charmingly at the bartender. It was all I could to hold in my laughter as I paid for the drinks and headed for the room where all the action was.

The crowd was fairly thin, but I knew within an hour or two it would be packed with the usual crowd, some dressed in leather or full vinyl, some with barely anything on, while others, usually those who had no clue what they'd walked into, were dressed in normal nightclub attire. Rachel and I, completely at ease in this atmosphere, quickly found a table near the stage where a few of our friends were seated and sat down.

Rachel was an expert in slipping into whatever role she desired, and she didn't disappoint me this time. She became the prim and proper Catholic schoolgirl as she carefully positioned herself on the stool, her legs carefully crossed and her lace-gloved hands draped across her while she looked around the bar.

Sasha, the woman who ran fetish night, saw us and headed

over. She was dressed in a full black bodysuit, showing off her full curves, her face painted like a cat but still giving off the presence of the dom she was. She hugged us both, immediately commenting on Rachel's choice of costume, nodding her approval to me. We chatted for a few minutes before she disappeared to prepare for whatever she had planned. She usually came up with some really quirky games to entertain everyone, and I was looking forward to participating in them.

Rachel and I soaked up the attention we got as we danced to the pounding music, swaying erotically with our eyes locked on each other. Our relationship was new, and we had eyes for only each other. Being in a place like this, on a night like this, we acted freely. Our hands tormented the other as our eyes spoke of the delights that awaited us when we returned home later. My heart thudded and my body was beginning to overheat as she tortured me with her wide-eyed gaze. It promised many decadent things, none of which a schoolgirl should be thinking. I loved it.

As the song slipped into another pulse-pounding beat, we were headed for our table once more when Sasha came over again.

"You know, you two need to be in the cage upstairs," she said.

I smirked as I lit a cigarette, blowing the smoke away from them while tucking my Zippo into my vest pocket.

"Why?" I asked as I caressed Rachel's hand.

Sasha grinned, flashing her surprisingly real-looking fangs at us as she leaned in closer.

"To entertain us. I think it would be cool."

I looked at Rachel, who was grinning like a Cheshire cat, and I nodded. I wasn't surprised that she wanted to do it—she had been a stripper and was always game for entertaining others. I, on the other hand, had never been in a cage, let alone danced in one for the sake of entertaining anyone, so I was pretty nervous as we headed up the stairs to it.

My heart was hammering hard and I began to sweat in earnest when we were let in, jolting as the door closed ominously behind us. I wanted to turn back around and get out when I saw the people down on the floor, some staring up at us while others remained oblivious. I really couldn't dance worth a damn and I wasn't into public humiliation, but one look at Rachel's glittering eyes and wicked smile and I knew I was going to stay and endure it.

Sighing, I shrugged out of my vest and shirt and hung them up on the chain-link fence before looking at her, not knowing what to do next. The bright lights on the floor nearby were already heating us up, and I could feel sweat dripping down my back as Rachel began to sway to the music that had started to play. Watching her move, her hips swaying seductively as her gaze melted into a come-hither look, I began to move as well. I really couldn't help it with Rachel around. She had a knack for drawing me into her moods with just a look, and this night was no exception.

Being up here, alone with her, I soon forgot others were staring up at us. I felt as if we were the only two around, and I began to seduce her with my eyes and my body, swaying with her as the music guided me. She responded in kind and soon we were dancing as if we were having sex. Each leg movement, caress, or pump emulated what we did in bed, and it charged me, creating the familiar heat I felt whenever I was with Rachel. It was pounding at me like a raging river, and she could tell. Her hands and lips touched me as her eyes spoke to me. No words were needed as we swayed and gyrated to the beat that surrounded us.

I don't know where the flogger came from, but one minute

she was rubbing against me as I turned around to grab a pole, and the next she was holding it, a decadently nasty grin on her pretty face. Already in a sexual frame of mind, I grinned back as I hastily shucked off my wet tank top and stood before her in my sports bra. With a shake of her head, she motioned for me to remove it as well, and I quickly did her bidding, my nipples already hard.

Usually, Sasha flogged me while Rachel watched, reserving her strength for when we were alone, but this time I could see she really wanted to do it herself. For an instant I remembered we weren't alone, that we were in a bar with a bunch of other people who had twisted ideas just like us. They were all watching from down below, but one rake from her nails on my back quickly pushed the thought of me calling it to a halt far from my mind. I held on tightly to the chain-link fence, bracing my feet apart in anticipation as I waited for her to begin.

The music switched yet again to a darker beat, and my hips began to sway to it as the first whack of the heavy flogger hit my sweat-coated back. Immediately, I undulated against the fence as I moaned, shuddering from the sting. I flung my head back and closed my eyes as she hit me again, my mouth opening in a sigh as a fire began its slow burn across my back.

Music continued to drive my hips as I swayed with each stroke of the flogger, my mind already slipping into the familiar place where pleasure and pain collide with the end results. A soul-shattering release, I knew, was to follow. Rachel slowly increased her power and strength with each swing of the flogger, and my back began to get hotter as the sting grew in potency. I gyrated and swayed with each blow while my moans and sighs blended with the music, creating a symphony reserved for those individuals like myself who loved what a good beating could give them. I was in heaven.

Rachel knew how to push me by pausing every so often to rake her nails down my welt-covered back, eliciting a deeper moan from me before she continued with the flogging. Unlike when Sasha flogged me, with Rachel it was more emotional and intense. When Rachel positioned me so I was gripping two thin poles spread as far apart as I could handle, facing the crowd, I shuddered in need. I didn't care about all the eyes on me, staring at my naked breasts with the black electrical tape covering my rock-hard nipples; all I cared about was Rachel, and the next stinging kiss of the flogger she was wielding so expertly on my exposed and throbbing back.

I gripped the poles as my arms strained with the length they were stretched to. Sweat coated me all over now, my vinyl pants sticking to my legs as they bent and swayed with the music and the blows. I danced for my pleasure, I danced for my pain, I danced for those watching, but mostly I danced for her. I wanted to show her I could endure, I wanted to show her I loved what she was doing, and I wanted to show her I was ready.

Each swish of the flogger rattled my cage. It bit into my overly sensitive skin, sending me closer and closer to the edge. I shuddered and swayed, moaning her name over and over, even though I knew she couldn't hear me. I moved where she positioned me, my back screaming as my skin tugged at the welts that covered it with each movement. I found myself facing the wall, my hands high above it as I was arched once more, waiting for the next sweet tormenting kiss of the flog. Her blessed nails tortured me as they raked down my aching back and I shivered uncontrollably. I was ready, so fucking ready for the release that was just around the corner.

In my head I was chanting *Please...please...please* as she

stopped to move closer to me, her hot breath on my back. Her tongue licked the salty sweat on my back. I sucked in my breath sharply as her tongue caressed one of the welts. I moaned in ecstasy as one of her hands trailed down my quivering belly to toy with the snap on my pants. I tried to stand still as she unsnapped it and received a sharp blow of the flogger on my fiery back when I didn't. Her teeth nipped at my moist neck as her hand slipped inside and began to torment my hard clit. My poor body didn't know what to make of the sensations it was receiving, but my head was screaming in total abandonment. I shuddered with restraint as I stood there with my legs apart, my arms above me clenched in fists while I lay my forehead on the pale blue wall.

She continued to use her talented fingers, urging my body into a shuddering mass. She continued to torture my back with the flogger until I was in the world where reality and dreams blend together and nothing else can penetrate. I felt myself slip further and further into that world until the familiar electricity began coursing through me. My body, once tense and needy, shuddered with a powerful release and I moaned just as the music shifted again. Weakly, I straightened and looked over my shoulder, trying to smile as aftershocks rocked my body.

Rachel was standing next to me, her eyes dark and glittery as she placed a light kiss on my wet shoulder. Her own hair was wet with her exertion as she smoothed mine, and her cheeks were flushed. Her smile was gentle before she suddenly rubbed her face, giving me a look I was quite familiar with. I chuckled softly.

"Frustrated?" I asked as I reached for my bra. My back protested, but I ignored it as I slipped the suddenly too-tight bra back on.

"What do you think?" She replied indignantly as she handed me my tank top and shirt. Out of pure playful meanness, she raked her nails down my back once more before she moved off. Even when my knees threatened to buckle from the incredible wave of pain and pleasure received from her wicked nails, I chuckled. I had my answer as I quickly got dressed, my back burning pleasantly.

As we walked down the stairs, the DJ gave us a large grin and my face flamed. I suddenly remembered there had been others watching us. When we reached the landing of the main floor, everyone was clapping. She was basking in it, attention whore that she was. I just wanted to run. She clutched at my arm, preventing my escape, as she grinned at our friends. I got back at her by burying my hand in her hair and tugging, just the way she liked it. She was suddenly reminded of the state she was in. I smiled smugly before lighting a much-needed smoke and winked at her. From her impatient pout, I knew she wanted to go home, but the night was still young, and I just love anticipation. Especially hers.

# You Swallowed My Hand, I Followed You Home

### S.W. BORTHWICK

My first gift to her was a purple gift box filled with syringes from the West Side needle exchange. I gave it to her as a quid pro quo for her gift to me, a box of nail polish and bath soap. It was like the door prize for my first sleepover; she could be generous with objects that way.

I had been to the apartment once before. That night she'd been wearing a latex mini-dress and 5-inch heels, hitting the pavement twice while trying to walk in them. After an evening of sticking needles into her at a play party, I thought it polite to see her home. I think of myself as courteous like that.

The apartment was a luxury building in the financial district, directly across the street from the administration offices for the Board of Education. Their windows were never fully dark, and in the late-night hours you could see in and watch the cleaning crews doing their thing. She left the shades open. Did it feed her exhibitionist streak to give some janitor a thrill?

In the living room sat a futon folded up to mimic a couch. It seemed like the last surviving remnant of her college days, and about as comfortable. She looked me up and down and commented on my jacket and tie. "So, this is your butch look."

I smiled and gave her the purple gift box. She opened it with almost giddy excitement. Laid out inside were hypodermic needles of various lengths, like a chocolate sampler.

I'd taken a little of everything available at the needle exchange. Several junkies chatted with me while I waited on line. I was surprised how un-junkie-like they appeared. Inevitably, the conversation went to injection strategies. I confessed that I had a different use for them. One woman, who looked like she was stopping off on the way home from her job at Merrill Lynch, commented, "That's sick."

But Astrid, the recipient of the spiky assortment, had a better response. "They're gorgeous." She sat down on the sofa to look at the various colors, each denoting a different thickness. For a moment, she drifted into reverie over the orange ones we'd used the weekend before. Snapping back to the present, she placed the box on the coffee table and said, "I'll save these for another time."

I sat down next to her on the sofa-futon. She looked me up and down as if assessing property for development. "Have you ever been topped?" she asked.

I swallowed hard. "No."

"Let's start with that," she said and stood up.

She turned to face me and without comment grabbed the lapels of my jacket and pulled them down over my shoulders, pinning my arms in place. My tie served as the leash she used to pull me forward and down to my knees. She placed her bare foot in the center of my chest and forced me backward until I lost balance and flopped on my back. From the floor, she towered above me like the 50-foot woman.

"Off with everything," she said.

She undid my jacket and shirt. Even though my arms were now free, I felt more helpless than before. She yanked my sports bra off over my head, then straddled me. I tried to cover my exposed chest, sensing danger. She pushed my arms aside and raked her nails across my pecs.

"Ouch!"

"Sorry," she smirked.

She brought her hand up and I shut my eyes, thinking she was going to slap my face. Instead, she whacked the top of my breast. I tried to roll to safety. "Sit still," she said, and whacked the other one. I put my hands up to block the next blow. "Covering up, are we?" She pushed my hands aside. I winced. "Not much of a bottom, are we? You can dish it out, but you can't take it." I offered no response. "What's the matter, top got your tongue?" She got off me and stood up. "Come on, useless, get up."

I thought we were done, but as soon as I got to my feet she sank her nails into the soft flesh just under my armpit and marched me to the bedroom. The bedroom was alight with the soft glow of bodega Jesus candles. It felt odd to have several bearded Christs staring back at me. She unzipped her dress and stepped out of it. "Hang that up for me," she said.

"Do you have a wire hanger, Ms. Crawford?"

"Not funny," she said.

She stretched out on the bed. I'd seen her naked before, but under the light of the Jesus candles she took on an angelic glow. "You know what to do," she said, looking up at me.

I fumbled with the buttons on my jeans.

"No," she said. "This isn't about you."

I had five fingers into her before my hand started to cramp. She'd plateaued just short of climax. "Make it happen!" she shouted.

I gripped my wrist with my other hand for extra leverage. Even that wasn't enough.

She reached under her pillow and brought out what looked like a small baseball bat with a large knob on it the size of a tennis ball. Its chord ran under the pillow and plugged right into the wall. She turned it on. The buzz filled the room. I'd used power drills with less torque. She placed the whirring knob just above where my hand disappeared into her. "Oh, fucking Jesus, God." I looked over at the candles for a response; they had none. I felt the first drops of a kind of rain. I turned back in time to see the jet of water shoot out from her and hit me square in the chest. In the future, I would learn to put my hand up to block the spray. This time, however, I got soaked; so did the mattress and the sheets. A stain expanded between her legs larger than Kansas. Her body shook. Her eyes rolled back in her head and she went limp as if in a coma. I sat there, mouth open, drenched. Minutes later she came to, got up, and went to the bathroom on wobbly legs.

While she was gone, I eyed the vibrator, wondered what that felt like; I picked it up and turned it on and the buzz shot up my arm into my shoulder. Wow! I put it near my crotch.

"What do you think you're doing?" boomed the voice behind me.

"Nothing."

"No, you are most definitely doing something. And you don't have permission to do it."

She stepped closer, put her hand on my chest right where she'd juiced me with her water cannon. A sharp push and I was on my back. "OK, now you'll get yours."

She unzipped my jeans and pulled them down. I tried to wriggle out of my underwear, but she smacked my hand away. "I'm in charge here. You're my bitch."

She grabbed the tool and nudged the switch to high. "What if we try putting this...?"

I couldn't open my mouth wide enough to let out the groan. The entire lower half of my body convulsed. I flopped around like a fish on a deck. My throat felt raw like sandpaper from shrieking. My hands flailed around as if I were falling through space. I latched onto the curtains, pulling them down around us. Still she kept the tool buried in my crotch. My last convulsion sent me off the bed onto the floor. I lay crumpled in a heap near her feet.

"Who's in charge?"

"You are."

"Never forget that."

# Coming Soon
## to a Theater Near Me

BREE COVEN

My boyfriend is a lesbian porn star. He used to be a lesbian. Sometimes he still is. I met him on butch-femme.com. I know. But having plowed through most of the butches in New York like a dyke dervish on a quest for the holy clit, I needed something new. So I imported. Answered an ad specifically on the West Coast. A sex ad. "Transgender butch boi seeks slippery submissive femme for surreptitious sex and/or spankings." Alliteration makes me wet. So do spankings. I fired off an immediate response, safe in the knowledge that since Mr. Tranny Butch Boi was so far away, nothing was likely to come of it. So I wasn't intimidated. It was easy to be utterly honest. And bold. He said he was always packing, so I asked if he traveled. "If you're ever in New York," I taunted, "let me know, and I'll meet you in a nice dark alley somewhere."

When I first saw his picture, I recognized him immediately. There was no mistaking the cool blue gaze, shoulders too broad to be a girl's, lips too lush to belong to a boy. The gentle slope of nose a stark, breathtaking contrast to the strong, angular jaw. The sexy blond wave of hair screaming "stroke me." I knew his face well, though we'd never met. I'd been watching him for years, had jerked off to him furtively all through college.

"Um, forgive me," my e-mail began politely. "I don't mean to be impudent, but you look really familiar. Is it possible, by any chance, have you, um, starred in any lesbian porn? I'm thinking *San Francisco Lesbians 4, 5,* and *6*—my personal favorite series—the scene where the pregnant femme is picnicking with her girlfriend and out of nowhere this big butch stud comes in with a toolbox, fucks her sweetly up the ass, and then leaves?" I'd said too much. Or just enough.

I stared at the screen barely blinking until the reply came. Checking and rechecking. Five full minutes, then finally it appeared. Subject header: "Yes." I clicked on the message, holding my breath.

"Yes, that's me."

My wet dream come true.

We talked on the phone that night for the first time. I immediately confessed to blowing off my college graduation party to cram into a crowded dorm room with four femme friends, one of whom had secretly borrowed the video from an older cousin, to watch and rewind and watch that scene over and over again. We'd convinced the only girl on campus with a VCR to let us take over her room. She was a religion major. When we popped in the movie, she murmured, "Oh, my God."

I knew that whole scene by heart, and the other ones, too—the threesome, the shaving scene. I used my graduation money to buy my own VCR and order my own copy. I proudly displayed the glossy cardboard box in my room as a centerpiece and catalyst for countless conversations. The cover featured the blond beefcake butch towering above his costars, staring straight ahead with that cocky gaze a silent, relentless dare. A ripped men's work shirt hung open, revealing the impossibly smooth expanse of skin beneath.

Tight abs and completely flat chest—he looked like a boy even then. For years I continued to watch my favorite blond porn star over my girlfriend's shoulder as she fucked me, my eyes intent on my pet porn stud's ass, perfectly framed by the leather harness, thrusting over and over again. I fantasized about being on the receiving end of that equation. I dreamed about my own private audition for *San Francisco Lesbians,* of starring opposite this butch, becoming the Fred Astaire and Ginger Rogers of the S.F. lezzie porn set.

And now, eight years later, here he is, chatting me up and asking if I have a hot date for Valentine's Day. *Well,* I thought, *I do now.* His porn career largely behind him, he told me he'd moved on to work as a male model in magazine fashion shoots with titles like "The New Gender Euphorics." Gender documentaries chronicled his patient, thoughtful, continuing transition from lesbian to boy and from female toward male. I've always been drawn to masculine women and feminine men. When you have to ask "Is that a boy or a girl?" is about when I get interested. The answer is less important than the question. So what could be hotter than having my genderfuck porn star fantasy come to New York on Valentine's Day to fuck me with his cock as hard as Cupid's arrow—the strap-on kind *and* the one he's growing himself.

He sent another enticing photo of himself modeling the detachable version—a primed, jutting, huge dick complete with balls in a smooth, inky, rich jet-black that matched his harness. My own dyke daddy Dirk Diggler. He called it the Big Black Nemesis. Simultaneously thrilled and terrified, I immediately did a Google search for "big black nemesis," hoping to learn its exact dimensions to see what I was getting myself into. I'd been out 12 years and knew my way around a dildo, even had the courage and audacity in moments to refer to myself as a size queen, but this was quite frankly the largest dick I'd ever seen, and it was more than a little daunting. It seemed enormous even against his 6-foot frame. Here was my dream date offering himself to me, and I was scared I couldn't handle it. What if he was too big? What if I blew it?

Despite searching all the sex toy stores and bravely asking for it by name, I was unsuccessful in locating the exact measurements of the Big Black Nemesis, so I started training with my girly gold glitter dick, hoping I could work up to the nemesis before its arrival. I popped in the video. That's the cool thing about dating a porn star—how many girls get to preview their lover before they actually meet? I'd never met him, yet I already knew his voice, the sharp sure thrusts of his hips, the sound of the smack of his hand on bare ass, how he looked fucking a girl, how he'd look fucking me. What I couldn't imagine was how it would feel. I hoped that in real life he'd growl, "Yeah, that's a good girl" if I sucked his dick just right like in the movie. I hoped he'd really pull his wife-beater up and back around his neck when he got all sweaty and started getting close, just like I'd watched him do countless times in series 4. I hoped he'd let me fuck him back, like he never allowed any of the girls in the videos to do.

In the 16 days preceding his arrival, I came hard for him every night, bucking furiously against my own hand, his name rolling on my tongue. My fantasy went like this: I'm waiting for him at the airport gate. I'm wearing my slutty black mini-dress, low cut, push-up bra edging my breasts out of the top. Short skirt. I want him to see my legs immediately. I want him to know how they'll be wrapped around his waist soon. Very soon. Not soon enough. I stand by the gate, nervous and excited, tucking my hair behind my ears. In a blast, with no warning, the doors open and he's the first out—the doors seem to echo behind him and I hear my own breath in my ears. I'm wet for him already. His strides are long as he walks right toward me without looking around. Those eyes bore into me, so intense, that same stern, still blue from the picture.

He walks right up to me, his hands landing on my ass, and lifts me up to him. Before we say hello, before I hear his voice, before I can ask how the flight was or even confirm that it's me, his mouth is on me, devouring my tongue, probing my lips. He places me down gently and takes my hand without a word, leading me through twists, turns, and corners, like this airport is his home. He guides me to a dimly lit blue passageway and before we turn right, he leans down—he's so tall, I feel miniature beside him—and whispers his first words in my ear: "I can't wait." My ear is damp from the heat of his breath.

All at once, my back is against a brick wall and his hand is under my skirt. It's so fast, but I don't say no. I want it, too. He's horny, like a boy, biting my neck, pushing his tongue in and out between my lips, fucking my mouth and pinning me to the wall with an unmistakable hardness I know he chose for me. He grinds into me, chafing my thighs with his jeans. I wrap my legs around his waist. He pulls me up, positioning me over his cock, which has already found its way out of his briefs.

His hand is quick—the condom glides on and he nudges against me, butting up against my clit, which pulses dramatically. He kisses me gently, with tenderness, before biting my lip, not too hard, just enough to keep me on my toes. His fingers graze my lips. I catch his thumb and lick it slowly, sucking it into my mouth, pushing my pelvis against him and willing his cock to slip inside me on its own. His hand caresses my face, my chin, my neck, my hair so gently—then he slaps me. I lose my breath, then find it, and then his hand is between my legs, stroking me gently, then pushing in hard. He rips the fishnets I bought for this occasion, right up the crotch, just as I was hoping he might.

I turn myself over to his care, my breasts his to beat and bruise and bathe with his tongue, my velvety bare pussy his to invade, consume, and display. He sears into me and my head, heart, cunt open to him, welcoming, buckling, giving way. His mouth clamps down on my neck as he moves inside me, the contrast of his impossibly soft skin enveloping solid muscle mirrored in his fucking: the hard, soft, rough, mean, gentle, sweet, vicious, tender, savage, voracious ravaging of my body just past breaking point.

His cock pushes sounds from deep in my throat. I grunt and wail—and he shuts me up, smothering my mouth with his. His broad hands hold me still as his narrow hips thrust over and over. He fucks me fast and hard and eager, like he's got to get off and I'm the only one that can do this for him. His cock claims its place inside me, burrowed deep, and I cry out, flooding us both with an orgasmic display that rivals the professionals. His name is spelled inside me in his come, my sweat and tears. I did not know what need was. I have only wanted. As I come, I come to, in the safe, spent, warm release with this relative stranger who somehow already knows my body as well as I ever have.

He holds me to him for a moment, our sweaty skin melding, then, hands tangled in my hair, he is pushing me down where I belong, hovering over me. My mouth aches for him—needy, insistent, I suck at the empty air, searching with every breath for his cock. He tears off the harness and tosses it aside. I part him and discover the biggest boy-clit

I've ever seen. I steady myself, holding onto his furry ass, and take his perfect mouthful of cock between my lips, sucking it against the roof of my mouth. He shudders and leans back against the wall, letting it support him while he pumps his little dick into my mouth. It lengthens and stiffens against the flat of my tongue. I circle the tip of his cockhead and it gives a little jump. He stops being gentle and slams against my face, furiously shoving as much of himself as he can into me. I twist and suck with a ferocious thirst to feed on him. I slowly pull off him, then my mouth finds him again, devouring, fiercely working his cocklet as the tension in his thighs builds and he clamps down, his legs squeezing the sides of my head. Only when he's done, only when he's heaved into me, leaning his full weight against me, does he finally relax, take my hand in his, still sticky with me, and we walk out, flushed and calm, impervious, untouchable.

I fuck myself to this scenario 29 times in 16 days, coaxing orgasm after salty orgasm from my sopping, aching cunt, and by the time he arrives, I am no longer scared of his Big Black Nemesis, I am hungry for it. I only hope both will live up to my fantasy. When they arrive, I am waiting by the gate in my little black dress, having traipsed undeterred through six inches of snow in 4-inch-heels to greet him. I am rewarded at once. He is exactly as I have imagined—a pulsing, vibrant version of the freeze-frame fantasy in my VCR. He leans into me, the length of our bodies not yet touching, and his mouth melts my ear with his whispered first words: "I can't wait." My ear is damp from the heat of his breath.

The fantasy continues daily without interruption. As he likes to say, it's not about the destination. It's the trip. We don't miss a stop on the subversive sexuality spectrum, stretching and expanding to fill the vast landscape of erotic possibility in the space between boy and girl, fantasy and reality. This lesbian porn star becomes my first boyfriend, and I find our inconsistency irresistible. I revel in the dissonance, relish the in-between. Maybe that's what draws me to him. He's full of contradictions. He uses the men's room with a driver's license that reads "female" tucked in his pocket. He's a guy with ovaries. A dyke with a dick. A sweet, sensitive sadist. The quintessential queer. The boi next door. The labels fall away as easily as our clothes, as gracefully as my fears. All that's left is this throat-parching desire. Be my boyfriend, my girlfriend, my porn star, my lover, my fantasy, my special occasion, my everyday, my habit, my ritual, my heat, my heart. Just be mine. And let me be yours. Your little angel baby girl, booty call princess, girlfriend lover, slut whore bitch. For more than male or female, boy or girl, he's a top. You can call him he or she, but I call him Daddy as I beg him to please, please, please fuck me, just like those girls in his movies. And he does.

# Made to Order

RACHEL KRAMER BUSSEL

"Touch yourself for me. Make yourself come." She barked it out in her haughty British accent, with nary a thought as to what my reaction would be. She said it with total assurance and coolness—no "I want you to" or "Please" to preface it, the way I would have. This tone suited her, though, and I should've expected it after picking her up at a sex party, all decked out in slick, shiny black rubber and spike-heeled boots. She looked like a dominatrix, partly because of the clothes, but even more so because of her posture and the sneering look on her face. The way she sat and surveyed the room, and then me, told me she was the kind of girl who could get anything she wanted, and usually did.

She was my type, though; I liked feisty women who could throw me off guard, titillate me into confusion. I didn't want someone meek like me; the pair of us would probably never get past holding hands. Though I was drawn to her, I was a little afraid of her, or maybe I just wanted to be afraid of her. Either way, I wanted to please her.

There was something in her tone—the way she commanded me like she knew without a doubt that I'd obey—that made me *want* to obey. Her request made me reconsider masturbation as a one-woman show. Sure, other lovers had asked that I do the same, but they'd always followed up their request with a girlish set of giggles, letting me know that it was as amusing to them as it sounded to me. They seemed to say it just to hear the words echo in the air, presuming they'd set off a sudden erotic chain reaction. But she succeeded, turning me on with the idea that my pussy was enough to get both of us off.

I did as she requested, lying back, closing my eyes in an attempt to be slightly less aware of her direct gaze, which spared me nothing in its appraisal. I wouldn't have chosen this form of sex, would've preferred something a bit more mutual, more sensual. I was worried I wouldn't be able to come, that it wouldn't be the same with her watching. Maybe I could fake it? No, that wouldn't do either; I was too on edge.

My index and middle fingers worked my clit, parting the hood and rubbing, rubbing, gently, then faster and faster. I tried up and down, then a circle, rocking against my fingers to increase the pressure. I tried to relax, to let my whole body sink into the bed, to focus all my energy on my clit. My breath starting coming out in quick pants, almost getting stuck in my throat. I didn't have energy to waste on breathing, only on my restless, relentless fingers.

I resisted the urge to move closer to her, to rub myself against her, to cuddle in the warmth of her skin. There'd be plenty of time for that later. I shut my eyes harder and shoved my fingers inside my pussy, then pulled them out and returned to my clit.

"Do it the way you do when you're alone, at home." I almost laughed at that, because at home I rely on my handy vibrator to do this work for me, and all my hand has to do is make sure the toy doesn't fall. I'd stopped using my hand the moment I found my first vibrator, and hadn't returned. So this was a bit of a reacquaintance for my hand and my cunt. I tried to go back to the pre-vibrator times, when my fingers and imagination had been my sole guides.

She kept me pinned with her eyes, with her spoken request that I not get up before I came. She didn't try to come herself, didn't appear visibly moved by my actions, but I could sense that her pleasure lay in her power to command me to come, to make me make myself get off, to fall apart and resurrect myself while she calmly looked on.

"That's it, now come for me. I need to watch you, to see your face when you reach that magic moment. Come!" She was close to screaming the last word; she sounded like she needed it more than I did. Her voice carried such force, like she was the Queen of the Universe, or at least, of my bedroom. She spoke like she was made to order me around, to command me to come. In turn, I was there to obey, to fulfill her every wish.

I rubbed my clit even more frantically, calling out as I reached the point where I couldn't stop even if I'd wanted to. My fingers moved almost of their own accord, in a race with my clit to push me over the edge, into the fiery chill of orgasm, when my body barely knows what direction it's going and I could be anywhere on earth. My eyes closed and small teardrops formed at the edge of my eyes, mimicking the liquid that began to build inside me, teasing and threatening to release. As I teetered, she must have been staring closely enough to judge my arousal. All of a sudden she yanked sharply on my hair, sending a wave of heat and pain and pleasure from my scalp shooting down to my cunt. As she pulled, I came, the liquid evidence pouring out of me.

I quivered and shook, loving the way my orgasm led itself throughout my body, leaving me tender and aroused. She kissed my pussy, gently, like a pat on the head for a job well done. I wrapped my legs around her meaty thigh, burrowed into her neck, and went to sleep.

# Dream a Little Dream

STACY M. BIAS

I had a dream last night. It was a fuck dream. There was nothing sensual or sweet about it. It was one of those legs spread wide, slick with wet, finger in the corner of your mouth with your pink tongue swirling type of dreams. I woke up parched and swollen.

Our sex, it's vanilla for the most part. Now and then we speak in hushed tones of fantasies that seem possible in those frenetic precome moments, but which disappear as quickly as our climaxes. "Dirty" words for "dirty" deeds we both want but never give ourselves. This dream is something I would tell you about in one of those sweaty moments. Instead I'm telling you now.

You were dressing in the late hours, pulling your jeans off (the ones that make your ass look so adorable) and rummaging through the hamper for your flannels. I was lying in bed, waiting and watching, loving the curve of your leg as it rose to meet your youngish cotton panties. The woman meets the girl. Such an apropos analogy that is your body to your mind. Half sexy as hell, half innocent as the day you were born. It's a big part of why I love you.

You lifted your feet one at a time to slide them into your pj's and pulled the fabric slowly up to your thighs, wiggling a bit as you pulled it over your ass. Crossing your arms, you grabbed each side of your T-shirt and pulled it over your head, shoulder muscles rippling. I love the way you look in a pair of pants and your sports bra. Such a little jock. My karate girl; sensual, magical, and determined. As you removed your bra, leaving your firm breasts in clear view while you picked up your nightshirt, you smiled sweetly. I didn't; too intent on watching you, memorizing you, wanting you—to mask my intentions.

Expressionless, I reached over and tugged your nightshirt out of your fingers. You wrinkled your brow in confusion and grabbed at it, but I dangled it away from you, shaking my head. I haven't been a bold lover with you. When we started dating I recognized your inherent need for control in sexual situations and I toned down my aggressions accordingly, but sometimes a girl needs what a girl needs—and right then, I needed you down. Bent. Under. Open. Wide.

You reached out once more for your nightshirt, still confused and a little irritated. I yanked the shirt back and caught your wrist, pulling you toward me. You lost your balance and fell gracelessly onto the bed, facedown. "What the...?!" came your muffled exclamation as I slid off the bed, took that wrist of yours, and wrangled it up above you, all the while fishing for your other arm to pull it up likewise, and finally gave you the shirt back, but in a way you hadn't quite intended.

Pulling the cotton tight around your wrists, I bound your hands together above your head. You struggled and mumbled beneath me, and bending slowly at the waist I placed my lips against your ear and breathed "You can get out of it if you want to, but you'll miss out on one hell of a fuck."

Your body stilled and I grinned as I watched you silently weigh your options. When it was clear you were making no moves to free yourself, I leaned in a little closer and bit playfully at your earlobe. "Good choice," I whispered, watching the gooseflesh ripple down your forearms.

Standing up, I reached for the waistband of your pj's and slowly slid them down to the floor. As you stepped out I rolled you over onto your back, urging you further up onto the bed. There was a wonderful mix of curiosity and confusion on your face, a wry smile with a "Just what do you think you're up to?" arch to your eyebrow.

Determined to keep you guessing, I only stood above you, letting my eyes roam your flesh unfettered. I took in your long neck, your delicate collarbone, the smooth rise of your flesh as it darkened at its peaks into diminutive nipples, then sloped down into the concave of your stomach, into the convex of your hips and the soft down of your sex. Your body flushed with the intensity of my attentions and you began to curl your body in, trying to cover yourself. I bent down instead and kissed you, softer than I wanted to but harder than you were used to.

My hands began to trace the paths that my eyes had burned into your skin—rougher than I'd been before, taking liberties with you that I hadn't dared to previously. You responded, pushing against me, pushing more of yourself into my palms, between my splayed fingers. My teeth found the curve of your neck as my fingertips kneaded your erect nipples and you moaned, called out, raised your hips. I stopped long enough to strip down and then placed my knee between your thighs. You wasted no time in grinding yourself against my leg, and I could feel that you were already dripping.

I stood up then, leaving my knee between your legs, and towered above you—I spread your lips and slid my thumb into your pussy, finding your clit and gliding over it, just a few times—just enough to make you jump, just enough to make you arch your back. Mmm, nope. Not that easy. Not that quick.

Pulling away from you, I rolled you over onto your stomach and told you to get up—to get up and spread your thighs. I wanted you on your hands and knees in front of me, laid out, splayed out, and wide open. I ran my hands up the small of your back, across your shoulder blades, slid them up around your neck and then back down to rest on your shoulders. I gripped you and pulled you back against my bare stomach, your sex wet, hot, and prickly against my skin. With you close against me, I reached into the bedside drawer and pulled out our lube. I held it high above your ass and squeezed, hearing the wet smack and your sharp intake of breath as the cold liquid hit your cheeks, and then your soft moan as I guided the flow down between your folds, pooling in my waiting palm and then pressed into your already dripping cunt.

I dropped the lube on the bed beside us and slid my free hand up underneath you, up and down your thighs, across your stomach and up to your aching nipples. You told me to pinch you and I did, all the while slowly sliding first one, then two, then three, then four fingers in and out of your pussy. Soon you were throwing yourself backward against me—wanting me in further, deeper, harder, faster. Fighting to keep my balance, I wrestled you onto your back, all the while keeping my fingers deep inside you.

It was fucking beautiful—you spread wide, arms bound above you, tits heaving, hips grinding, mouth gaping, eyes squeezed shut, begging me to make you come. I dropped to my knees in front of the bed and spread your lips wider, breathing in that scent that fucking kills me every time, gives me butterflies, makes me lightheaded. I couldn't stand it anymore and I spread you out as wide as you could go, buried my fingers in your cunt, and set to work devouring your clit.

It took only seconds before my tongue sent you screaming into climax. You came loud. You came HARD. Clamping your thighs around my head, you wailed and writhed and bucked and spasmed until finally the wave passed over you, leaving you spent and limp against the sheets.

Sliding my fingers gently out of you, I brought them up to my lips, and then, climbing next to you on the bed, to your lips—to our lips, mingling tongues, fingers, and teeth in a kiss that went on for ages.

When I woke, you lay next to me—the hem of your white cotton T-shirt askew across your stomach. I rolled, buried my face into your neck, and silently memorized my dream for its retelling.

# If SpongeBob Could Talk
GROVER

I had the itch. You might know it. The I've-been-in-the-same-underwear-for-three-days get-me-the-fuck-off-this-tour-bus itch. I was calling this tour my "celibacy tour," politely returning the "I wonder if I can fuck the roadie" glances with a polite smile, having no desire to break my sacred commitment to bachelor freedom and angsty poetry. We rolled into Delaware, an hour late as usual. I pulled the pile of clothes from next to my driver's seat out and threw on the leather suspenders over the Spice Girls' shirt. A quick stop in the bathroom to spike the Mohawk, and we were off.

It was the time in the band's set when they played that one heart-wrenching song—you know, the one that makes you think about your ex and your mom and the state of foreign policy all at once—when just like a Disney movie, she rolled in the door. Her roll was actually more like a flutter, because she was a ball of pink sparkly energy, and being the magic fairy princess she was, she landed right in my arms. I met her in a faraway city in a restaurant across the street from an ex lover's where Fairy Princess was a waitress. I'd been hitting on her every time I was in the city, making a stop at least once on each trip just to smile at her and giggle like the 10-year-olds we really were at heart. We giggled at each other for the rest of the show, then I struck the venue fast as a flash, grabbed some shit from the RV, and as a final thought asked my kid if I could borrow some safer-sex supplies and hightailed it out of live-where-you-sleep-where-you-eat-where-you-work land.

On my friends' couch that night we were making conversation intermingled with hand-holding and kissing and cuddling. As everyone began to make their sleeping arrangements, it was pretty apparent no private bed was being arranged for us, so I asked her to go on a walk. Having a brief morality attack, I decided bringing my backpack was tacky and assuming and bent down to grab one glove to shove into my pocket on our way out.

I suddenly realized I didn't know anything about her at all. Our conversation during our meander through the empty city streets consisted of "What's your favorite color?" and "How many brothers and sisters do you have?" Our walking led us to our empty tour bus. My boss's one set rule rang true in my head: "NO SEX IN THE RV." Damn it. We headed toward the railroad tracks behind the venue, walked down them a few feet, and settled ourselves against a wall. An elementary school stood directly across the tracks. With one hand in her hair and the other in a hole in the crotch of her jeans, I was no longer feeling like a shy 10-year-old. Maybe a seventh or eighth grader, I'd say, but not an innocent 10-year-old.

She reminded me of a time in her restaurant when I'd given her her tip on my knees in proper leather-boy position, with the money in my teeth, and how hot and overwhelming it had been for her. Right then I dropped to my knees in the gravel and started undoing her button-fly jeans with my teeth. Exposing the thong underneath, I closed my eyes and shook my head. It had been a long time since this faggot had been with a girl, and how very, very sweet it was.

Running my hands under her shirt and standing back up, I whispered into her ear, "If I could make you feel one thing, what would it be?"

"Safe," she answered. I pulled back, looking into her piercing eyes at the genuine soul that is so rare in this world lurking inside.

After what seemed like 60 seconds of silence to remember the bad sex and broken hearts that passed in the beginning of this conversation, she asked me the same question, to which I answered, "Chivalrous."

I kissed down the side of her rosy face, down her neck, and stuck my hand on top of that little patch that covers the goods on a thong. Putting pressure on her clit by balling up my hand, I asked if that was OK. She nodded yes and promised to tell me if I crossed any boundaries. I asked her not to touch my clit, and other than that, I'd let her know, too. She asked if I had safer-sex supplies, to which I proudly whipped out the one glove I'd snatched before we walked out the door. She did one of those moves I swear only femmes know, pulling me tight to her by my shoulders, pushing my fist into her clit harder, and asking me sweetly and politely to touch her with the glove. Accustomed to demands and instructions, I stopped for a minute, a little shocked, and slipped the glove over my right hand. I reentered through the hole in her button-fly jeans and ran my index finger along the seam of her thong until I made direct contact with her already soaked pussy. Running my finger up, I returned my pressure to her clit and slipped my hand up her shirt to feel the soft skin on her back. I lightly dragged my nails up and down her back as the pressure on her clit grew harder and faster. She started breathing shallowly, and as I dug my nails deeper, she produced a little whimper.

I asked if I could enter her. She nodded, and I slowly slipped one, then two fingers inside her cunt. Her breath quickened. I held her tight to me with the nails digging into her back, staring intensely into her eyes. With every whimper and breath, she escaped warm air onto my lips. I moved my two fingers circularly inside her tight cunt, leaving then returning to my favorite little G-spot. I kissed her as the intensity increased and she bit hard on my lip, sending heat to my crotch.

When she released my lip I felt the butch dick that lives through my hand about to let loose, so I lifted her onto the waist-high wall running parallel to the tracks. Yanking her pants to her knees, I slipped my left arm out of the cut-off blue button-up shirt with little boys skateboarding on it, ran it down my right arm still safely inside her cunt, and put it underneath her sweet ass so it wouldn't get cold against the concrete wall. She smiled while biting the left side of her lip, holding up her end of the deal, making me feel chivalrous as a prince. My index fingers again massaged her swollen G-spot; my thumb stimulated her clit. My left hand ventured to her breasts, discovering a steel piercing through her nipple. I pinched and worked the metal pierced through her flesh. She whimpered once again, her eyes closing halfway when suddenly they shot open and one hand came to the back of my newly clipped head and yanked the back of my Mohawk hard, sending my head back and my hips forward to connect with the side of her body.

Her hand ripped that cock ring right off, and as my arm pumped furiously into her fiery cunt through a hole in her Levi's and the side of red thong undies, I heard a train off in the distance. I felt the explosion rip through my fingertips like a superhero about to scale a wall as she pulled my hair hard and lifted her hips off the ground. She let out a scream seconds before the blue engine blew its whistle, and as brown boxcars sped past five feet away, Ms. G-spot herself ripped open a fire hydrant and started a riot on her 3-inch street, sending her juices all over our clothes.

I rested my lips on her tummy as the shaking and twitching slowed and lifted my head to kiss her sweet lips softly. The thumping in our fingers and cunts was echoed by the late-night train racing off in the distance. I glanced around, suddenly aware of our semipublic position, and saw SpongeBob SquarePants admiring us from the window of the elementary school. Giggling again, I climbed on top of her on the wall as we giggled and gazed at SpongeBob, the only witness to our explosive encounter.

As the morning turned soggy and chilly, the sun was beginning to peak over the roof of the school. We packed up our one glove and my soggy shirt, and as I bent her over the concrete wall one last time, I told her how next time I wouldn't be a dufus and would bring my dick and fuck her ass so hard she'd be able to suck SpongeBob's dick from across the tracks. I lifted the back of her shirt to deliver a kiss and was greeted with one stiletto boot, then another. My eyes grew wide as I lifted the shirt over the expanse of her back to see a leather girl with fairy wings, bound at the wrist, wearing a tight skirt and tall stiletto boots, gazing with tempting eyes. The Daddy hiding in my dick, waiting until I grow up more to burst out, shot a load right then and there in my Superman undies at this girl who was hiding on the wall all the time. She giggled and said, "I see you've met my girl." I stared in shock, making incomprehensive babble, and then this little boy started jumping up and down screaming "OH MY GOD THAT WAS SO COOL!"

Sometime between hugging her and doing boy band dances the little boy who was hiding inside butch chivalry, thinking it was high time he grow up, found his little leather girl playmate. The little leather girl and leather boy, gentleman butch and fairy princess femme, skipped hand and hand down the train tracks into the sunrise, suddenly aware of what SpongeBob knew all along.

# What I Remember

HEIDI COWGIRL

I hopped onto the 3 P.M. Amtrak train from Albany, Oregon, to San Francisco carrying a small black suitcase. My bleach-blond hair was in a crew cut, and I wore chunky red jelly sandals with my white eyelet dress. I may or may not have been wearing panties, and you could have seen my bra through the thin fabric of my dress. It was the middle of July in the middle of one of my sluttiest summers ever. I was flying and taking the train all over the country with the goal of getting laid in as many different states, with as many different girls, as possible—oh, yeah, and organizing against the right wing. This particular trip was to a queer youth conference in San Francisco.

Soon after sliding my suitcase into the rack above my coach seat, I settled into the tacky booth of the café car and sipped a margarita-from-a can. I savored the then-rare pleasure of underage drinking, as well as the luxurious "I don't have anything to do but lay back and enjoy this feeling" caused by drinking a margarita, even a margarita from a can, on a sultry summer afternoon.

I slipped my finger under the edge of the envelope I knew would hold a completely pornographic letter from one of my newest lovers. She'd always write me fabulous smut that would leave me trembling and blushing when I read her letters in public places.

I hadn't finished reading the first paragraph when a

shadow fell across my page. I looked up and there stood a uniformed Amtrak attendant. She was a California soft butch with long, sun-streaked hair, and I could tell she was tan and muscular under all that polyester. She smiled and launched into a silly pickup story. I didn't care that the story was silly. All I cared about was that I was being picked up, and I liked it. She finished the story and offered me a tour of the train. I knew what that meant and immediately accepted.

The tour was short and to the point. I learned that she was in charge of a sleeper car and she had a spare room. Would I like an upgrade? Of course. I'd never had a sleeper car before. What's more, I'd never done it on a train before. We moved my black bag up from coach and settled me into the small space, conveniently across the hall from hers.

We flirted and drank free champagne all afternoon. The train sped through Oregon and into the Russian River Valley. The afternoon sun sparkled through the leaves and on the water, then set during our late dinner. The sky turned dark blue with what seemed like a million stars. The full moon kept the view out the train window half-lit in a luscious indigo velvet. I relaxed in my car, admiring the views and sipping champagne, while she helped her other passengers turn their sleeper-car seats into beds. She saved me for last.

She slipped through the dark curtains of my room and slid the door shut behind her. She flipped the center table up and into its slot but left the two seats facing each other. She sat across from me and we began making out heavily. She kissed me softly, then harder, then softly again. I ran my hands up her neck and into her hair. She felt good. She tasted good. Still kissing, she ran her fingers down the front of my dress, slowly undoing the small pearl buttons until my lace bra was completely accessible. I began working her T-shirt out from under her waistband. No panties. Good girl. I ran my hands up inside her shirt and found small firm breasts. Yum. I worked her belt out of her pants and began to unzip. I got on my knees in the car and took a deep breath in anticipation of her taste.

"No," she said, "I want to lie down." So, together, we turned the seats into a bed, and I helped her off with the rest of her clothes, me still with my dress around my waist. She was tan and gorgeous, with a long, lean runner's body. Small nipples, almost like a boy's—my favorite. Her stomach was smooth and tan, and her cunt hair formed a sweet little bush. I knelt down. One of the most perfect cunts I have ever seen. I tried to get between her legs, and again she said no. "I like to be able to squeeze my legs together," she explained. "It increases the tension." Having slept with a lot of college girls, I wasn't used to a woman telling me what she liked, but I was starting to like it.

I knelt by the side of the bed and teased her outer labia with my tongue, just a little bit below her clit. When her cunt opened slightly I moved my tongue up to the root of her clit and then, slowly, to her clit itself, every so often talking little dips down into what cunt juice I could get to with her legs squeezed closed. As she got more and more turned on, these side trips into the cunt juice had to end, and I was left wrapping my arms around her thighs for dear life as her sweet clit jumped into my mouth over and over and over. When I saw a slight opening in her legs, I slipped my first and middle fingers into her and began slowly but intensely stroking her G-spot. I sucked her clit into my mouth, licking her and fucking her until she spasmed violently and let out a series of husky moans.

"Oh, girly, you eat pussy like an angel," she said. I swear, it's true.

I eased off the bottom half of my dress, and she gasped at my freshly shaved cunt and at the scars from my recent cutting. I told her the cutting was nothing to worry about, really. I was quite stoic at that age. To tell the truth, I still am.

She helped me onto the bed, kissing me. She moved down, easing my breasts out of my bra. The combination of the sex and the alcohol and the constant motion of the train had made me woozy—in a very aware way. I closed my eyes and felt as if I were weightless. I floated there in my mind as her mouth moved down my breasts, onto my stomach—even the cutting—and onto my smooth pussy. I lay back as if I were Cleopatra on the Nile being fed peeled grapes, and spread my legs so she could see the glint of my cunt juice in the moonlight. I opened my eyes and saw her head bent over my pussy. She looked so beautiful in that way that soft butches can. I leaned forward and kissed her hard on the mouth, so I could taste all of her. I laid back and saw the moon against the dark sky, the dark blue clouds, the trees rushing by. I closed my eyes and smiled as I felt her tongue lick me slowly, then harder as she discovered how wet I truly was. I somehow reached into my black bag and found some gloves and some lube. She looked at me as if I were crazy.

"Trust me." I smiled. I helped her ease the glove onto her small right hand. Her tongue returned to my clit, and she began licking me insistently while adding fingers to my pussy. When she reached four without much effort, she looked up at me with a look of slight surprise. I smiled.

"See what I mean?" I said as I drizzled some lube into the palm of her glove.

"Yeah. Wow."

She added her thumb and slid her fist into me easily. My cunt instantly tightened around her. Now she knelt between my legs and ran her left hand over my breasts and stomach, coming to rest on the top of my shaved pussy. She began strumming my clit with her thumb at the same tempo she was fisting me. I spread my legs wider, lifting them onto her shoulders, and left my eyes closed, still floating. My mind didn't know exactly what my pussy was doing, only that it felt good and I didn't want it to stop. In this way, getting my brains fucked out while in a state of total clarity and disorientation, I struggled between coming and not coming until I came hard, my pussy clamping down on her hand until she was afraid I would break it.

What happened after that I don't know exactly. But I can tell you this: We fucked like that for the rest of the night, and she brought me breakfast before I had to get off the train in the morning. While I was in San Francisco, I bought a gigantic black dick and harness, and on a later trip she strapped it on over her uniform, lifted up my dress, and fucked me for two hours while the train was stopped for no apparent reason. And she *is* the woman who taught me how to fuck. I can definitely tell you that.

# Contributors

**L. Elise Bland** is an Alabama native living in Texas. She writes nonfiction and fiction inspired by her bisexual adventures in the BDSM scene and in the world of professional perversion. Her work has appeared in *Scarlet Letters, Faster Pussycats,* and *Shameless.* She also has a story forthcoming in *Back to Basics: A Butch/Femme Erotic Journey.* In her free time she practices the art of Middle Eastern dance and indulges in European cheeses.

**S. W. Borthwick** lives in New York. Her essays and reviews have appeared in several monthly and weekly publications. She has been twice anthologized as a poet. This is her first work of published fiction. Currently she is finishing a collection of linked short stories.

**Diana Cage** has detailed her sexual exploits in many publications, but most frequently in *On Our Backs* magazine, of which she's the editor. She also the editor of *On Our Backs Guide to Lesbian Sex* (Alyson Books, 2004) and a regular contributor to *Girlfriends* magazine and *Kitchen Sink* magazine. She thinks a lot about sex.

**Khadijah Caturani** is a writer, filmmaker, smut peddler, and rabble-rouser. "Ungentlemanly Behavior" is her first published piece of erotic fiction (though certainly not her last! Do you people know how fun this is?). Her short film, *Femme Fatale,* is currently on the road playing at festivals and screenings, and her three screenplays are ready and waiting to be produced. Don't even get her started about her novel! E-mail her at khadijah@nakedfilmsinternational.com or visit her Web site at www.nakedfilmsinternational.com.

**Charlotte Cooper** is from London, England, and will never stop loving The Stooges (the band, silly). She also wrote a novel called *Cherry* and has been published all over the place. Find out more at www.CharlotteCooper.net.

**Bree Coven** originated the baby-dyke column "Hey, Baby!" for *Deneuve* (now *Curve*) magazine, where she was a regular columnist and contributor for three years. Her writing has also been published in the anthologies *Best of the Best Lesbian Erotica*, *Generation Q*, *The Femme Mystique*, *Best Lesbian Erotica 1997*, *Pillow Talk II*, *Cast Out: Queer Lives in the Theatre*, and the forthcoming *No Such Thing* as well as *Harrington Lesbian Fiction Quarterly*, *Pucker Up* magazine, and *Masquerade Journal*. Recently, Bree was a reviewer for *Erotic New York: A Guide to the Best Sex in the City*. *Publishers Weekly* named her "one to watch."

**Heidi Cowgirl** is now old enough to drink. She lives in Brooklyn and practices law in New York City while trying not to be too much of a grownup yet.

**M. Damian** lives on Staten Island, N.Y., with the love of her life, her eight-month-old Yorkie puppy, Peg o' My Heart. Two of her erotica stories will be published next year in an upcoming anthology by Alyson Books.

**Alison Dubois** is a Dutch-American writer, author of the book *Voices from the White Noise* and the forthcoming *She Kissed Me*, a pictorial anthology of lesbians kissing.

She is also ghosting a separate project scheduled for release next year and living in the beautiful Pacific Northwest with her domestic partner of three years and her German Shepherd.

**Mary Dumars** lives in her hometown in Louisiana with her partner and their middle-aged feline companion. After 10 years of studying in New Orleans, beach-hopping in Florida, and shoveling snow in New Hampshire, the prodigal daughter returned to her beloved South. She values time spent with family and friends, and planning spontaneous gatherings. She spends her days working hard and looks forward to frequent weekend road trips with her best girl and copilot at her side, a luxury hotel in mind, and camping gear always handy in the trunk, just in case.

**Amie M. Evans** is a white-girl, confirmed femme-bottom who lives life like a spontaneously choreographed performance. She is the founder of The Princesses of Porn With the Dukes of Dykedom, PussyWhipped Productions, and *Philogyny: Girls Who Kiss and Tell*. Her works have appeared in *Lip Service, Best Lesbian Erotica, Best S/M Erotica, Set in Stone, Harrington Lesbian Fiction Quarterly*, and *On Our Backs*. She firmly believes queer liberation cannot happen through mainstreaming that demands the fringe elements of our community be isolated and marginalized, and that sacrificing our queer sexuality in order to achieve a false sense of equality is not a valid option.

**Reggie Granwalter**, as her partner always told her, is a Renaissance woman. She enjoys sewing and crafts, gardening, building, and computers—often combining them in various projects. She is studying metaphysics, karate, writing, Web design, and anything else that piques her interest at the moment. During her "free time" she has a job in computer security.

**Anne Grip** lives in New Haven, Conn., with her girlfriend. She would like to thank the contributing cast for making this story possible, most especially her princess. This is her first published piece of fiction.

**Grover** is a trannie butch dyke kid living in Brooklyn, N.Y. S/he is a cornfield-bred working-class writer, performance artist, spoken word poet, political drag king, activist, dildo hocker, and bike rider extraordinaire. S/he's a huge leather fag and femme worshiper and likes to sing and dance his butch boy ass off in women's drum circles. Grover can be contacted at boygrover@yahoo.com.

**Rosalind Christine Lloyd**'s work has appeared in many anthologies, including *Best American Erotica 2001, Hot & Bothered II* and *III, Pillow Talk II*, and *Faster Pussycats* as well as on Kuma and Amoret, erotic Web sites for literature. Currently obsessing over her first novel, this native New Yorker and Harlem resident lives with her pet feline Nile while contemplating the platitudes of monogamy.

**Rachel Medlock** spends her days teaching P.E. in an elementary school (she told you she was a butch stereotype, didn't she?). When she's not hanging out with her favorite 7-year-olds, she writes, studies karate, builds Web pages, and hangs out at the Buddhist center. Rachel's work also appears in the book *Radical Spirit: Spiritual Writing From the Voices of Tomorrow*.

**LA Mooney** is a radical, fat, kinky, sex-positive femme dyke poet and smut storyteller living in Seattle with an enormous wig collection and her cat, Lady Annabell. Her work appears onstage in fabulously queer cabarets and in various local zines and online magazines, including Scarlet Letters. You can e-mail her at leatherandvelvet@angelfire.com.

**Jean Roberta** teaches English at a Canadian prairie university and embarrasses her friends and relatives with her erotic writing. Her stories have appeared on Web sites, in print journals, in the *Best Lesbian Erotica* series (2000 and 2001), and in *Ripe Fruit,* an erotic anthology about women over age 50. Her erotic novel, *Prairie Gothic,* is in the catalog of Amatory Ink (www.amatory-ink.co.uk).

**Julie Levin Russo** plans to get a Ph.D., but in the meantime she's living a life of adventure in New York City. Office sex is only the tip of the iceberg, and you may spot her doing something naughty if you keep your eyes peeled. Her work has appeared in *Best Lesbian Erotica 2003.*

**Stephanie Schroeder** is a writer living in Brooklyn with her partner of two years and their two crazy pooches. She deals with asthma, Tourette's syndrome, and bipolar disorder on a daily basis. She is incredibly grateful be a Brooklyn gal after 12 years in "the City." She has been published on the Web site Technodyke.com, in the lesbian sex magazine *Bad Attitude,* in the lesbian erotic anthology *Hot & Bothered 3: Short, Short Fiction on Lesbian Desire,* and as a reviewer in the tasty guidebook *Erotic New York: The Best Sex in the City.*

261

**Micky Small** is a femme lesbian writer/performer and S/M model. She is working on her first novel, an erotic vampire thriller. She lives in NYC with her partner in crime, Chris, and looks forward to writing more about her favorite topic: sex!

**Stefka** has been published in *Bad Attitude* and has completed two novels. Currently she's in a relationship with a wonderful woman named Rebekah. She also has a fondness for vampires and dragons, and has six cats.

**Therese Szymanski**'s first three books (the Brett Higgins Mysteries *When the Dancing Stops, When the Dead Speak,* and *When Some Body Disappears*) are available from Naiad Press, while her latest book, *When Evil Changes Face,* which was a 2001 Lambda Literary Award finalist for best lesbian mystery, was published by Bella Books. Her short stories have appeared in numerous anthologies, and she has also written literary reviews, humor columns, political essays, and other items for various publications. An award-winning playwright residing in D.C., she believes in erotic freedom and maximizing the erotic content of life. She plans someday on taking another woman to a certain Saugatuck bar, especially since she's heard other dykes have had some fun there as well.

**Tristan Taormino** is the author of *Pucker Up: A Hands-on Guide to Ecstatic Sex, The Ultimate Guide to Anal Sex for Women,* and *True Lust: Adventures in Sex, Porn, and Perversion.* She is editor of the series *Best Lesbian Erotica,* for which she has edited nine volumes. She is a columnist for *The Village Voice, Taboo,* and *On Our Backs.* She has been featured in more than 300 publications and has appeared on *The Howard Stern Show, Loveline, The Other Half, Ricki*

*Lake*, and the Discovery Channel. She also teaches sex workshops around the country. Visit www.puckerup.com.

**Stephanie Taylor** lives in London with her partner. She has been writing for 10 years as a hobby, although this is her first published story. She has enjoyed many wonderful times in the BDSM scene but says she is open to all experiences. She takes an interest in women's studies and gender sociology and participates in many sports, soccer being her favorite.

**Alison Tyler**'s novels include *Learning to Love It, Strictly Confidential, Sweet Thing*, and *Sticky Fingers*. Her stories have appeared in many anthologies, including *Sweet Life I & II, Erotic Travel Tales I & II, Best Women's Erotica 2002, 2003*, and *Best Fetish Erotica* (all published by Cleis Press), and in *Wicked Words 4, 5*, and *6* (Black Lace). She is the editorial director of Pretty Things Press (www.prettythingspress.com). Ms. Tyler lives in the San Francisco Bay Area with her partner of seven years—but she misses L.A.

**Zonna** is old enough to be Britney Spears's mother (and the less said about that, the better). You may have seen her short stories in anthologies from Alyson Books, Arsenal Pulp Press, Seal Press, Odd Girls Press, or Black Books. When she isn't writing, she's usually changing her cat's litter box.

# About the Editors

**Rachel Kramer Bussel** writes about sex and popular culture in New York City. She revised Wendy Caster's *The Lesbian Sex Book*, coauthored *The Erotic Writer's Market Guide*, and coedited *The Burning Bush: Jewish Women Write About Sexuality*. She is also a contributing editor at Cleansheets.com. Her fiction and nonfiction have been published in *AVN*, *Bust*, *Curve*, *Diva*, *Girlfriends*, *On Our Backs*, *Rockgrl*, *The San Francisco Chronicle*, *Velvet Park*, and in more than 20 erotic anthologies, including *Best Lesbian Erotica 2001* and *2004*, *Best American Erotica 2004*, *Starf\*cker*, *Faster Pussycats*, *Hot & Bothered 3*, and *Tough Girls*. Find out more at www.rachelkramerbussel.com.

**Stacy M. Bias** is the owner and editrix of TechnoDyke.com, the Internet's second leading online publication and community for queer women. Her myriad additional projects include Pussy Pucker Pots vegan lip balm, DykeTees.com, and FatGirl Speaks, an annual event in Portland, Oregon, celebrating women of size. Her writing has been published in *Bust* magazine and in anthologies published by Alyson Books. Her combined projects have been mentioned in *Girlfriends*, *Curve*, *On Our Backs*, *Bust*, *Venus*, *Velvet Park*, *Nervy Girl*, *Guava*, *Diva UK*, *OUT*, *Playtime*, *Playboy*, *Swank*, *AVN*, the *Village Voice*, and on Salon.com. Visit Stacy at www.technodyke.com